PSYCHIC
HANGOVER

Other titles by Elizabeth Maxim

Non-fiction

Riding the Waves: Diagnosing, Treating and Living with EMF Sensitivity

After Here: The Celestial Plane and What Happens When We Die

PSYCHIC HANGOVER

A Novel By

Elizabeth Maxim

Published by Elizabeth Maxim

ISBN-13: 978-0-9831020-1-4
ISBN-10: 0-9831020-1-5

elizabethmaxim.com

*Touchstone [**tuhch**-stohn]: A measure by which the validity or merit of a concept can be tested; a reference point against which other things can be evaluated.*

May all who are as fortunate as I, also have one...

PSYCHIC

HANGOVER

CHAPTER ONE

"Hey, doc."

Absorbed in her work, Kaila Ross was oblivious to the graduate student standing nearby. Music blared from her iPod as she knelt in the dirt, brushing gently at shards of clay.

"*Doc*," Hal repeated. Even two feet away, he could make out the words to Alice Cooper's *Poison*. Shaking his head, he reached out and tapped a canteen against her shoulder, hoping she wouldn't be too startled.

Jerking away from the touch, Kaila sent a look that was half annoyance, half curiosity over her left shoulder. Recognition ending in a smile, she pushed the Bose headphones from her ears, strands of wavy blonde hair flying out in all directions, and accepted the offered water.

"Thanks."

He jerked a thumb behind him.

"There's some guy just showed up, said he needs to talk to you."

Taking a deep swallow from the canteen, she angled her head to get a look at the visitor. Standing, she handed over the canteen and a little wheeled brush.

"Take over here."

With a sigh, she began walking toward where the man, looking decidedly uncomfortable and definitely out of place in a suit, shifted from foot to foot. She rubbed her hands on her shorts, knowing the effort was in vain. The ground where they were digging was mineral rich and had stained her skin. She stopped an appropriate distance away and thrust out her hand.

"I'm Kaila Ross, what can I do for you?"

"Senora Ross, my name is Fernando Juarez. I'm afraid I have some bad news for you. Agent Hernandez has been reassigned and will no longer be able to provide security for you and your team. As a result," he continued after a momentary, yet meaningful pause, but she held up a hand.

"We will no longer be able to remain since the Chilean government cannot be responsible for our safety," she finished, her voice filled with resignation. When Juan hadn't shown up for the past two days and her calls to him went unreturned, she'd guessed that something had happened. *Well, hell.*

"I am sorry to be the one to deliver such unpleasant tidings, Senora Ross."

"Hey, don't shoot the messenger, right?"

"I'm sorry?"

"Never mind."

He looked past her, sweeping the area in unconcealed interest.

"How long do we have?"

"It would appear you have a benefactor, Senora Ross. Usually, under such circumstances, you would be required to leave the country within twenty-four hours, as your visas would have been terminated. However, you have been given three days to remain and search for a suitable replacement."

"That's very generous," she replied, absently pushing at blonde strands that had come loose from the braid she often wore while working.

He continued to stare at her expectantly, openly curious as to who had granted such largess. Of course she knew who it was, but she was unwilling to share that information with a perfect stranger. Her relationship with government officials was strictly need to know as far as she was concerned.

"We're just about finished for the day, anyway," she said dismissively. "Who do I contact if I am able to get a suitable replacement?"

"Leave a message with Agent Hernandez and he will contact the appropriate authorities."

"Thank you," she replied, thrusting out her hand.

"I wish you luck, Senora Ross," he said, grasping it warmly.

She waited until he got into his car before turning back to the dig.

To the untrained eye it would appear as chaos, she supposed, looking, as it did, like a demolition team had been through, but to her it was heaven. Digging up history was more than work; it was a place of refuge. And now she was about to be evicted, damn it to hell.

The three archeology students with whom she had been toiling for the last three weeks were walking in her direction. She pasted what she hoped was a look of confidence on her face.

"So, we're out, eh?" Theresa, a first year grad student from Minneapolis, surmised.

"Our security has been reassigned. Unless we can find a suitable replacement within three days, we're out."

"Define suitable," Hal replied, even as the third student, Derek, theorized that it shouldn't be too difficult to find a replacement.

"No," she said, grimacing, "Hal has it right. Suitable is the key here. If we don't find someone suitable to the Chilean government, we have to leave." She sighed. "So, that means we have three days to find someone who either isn't already assigned or who won't expect to be paid exorbitant amounts of money."

"And who isn't on the take," Hal added, referring to officials paid to look the other way while precious South American artifacts were smuggled out to be sold on the black market.

"Right," she confirmed.

"So," Theresa asked, smiling, "what do we do?"

"We call it a day and I put my thinking cap on," Kaila replied, working to keep her tone from betraying her concerns.

"Do you think the site is safe?" Derek asked, his hazel eyes roaming over artifacts in various states of exposure.

"Unless that guy is on the take," she replied, thrusting her chin toward where Juarez sat in his vehicle speaking into a cell phone, "I'd say he is our replacement for three days."

"He's looking this way," Derek pointed out.

She didn't care if the man knew they were talking about him. She wanted him to know she'd be watching him as much as he'd be watching her.

"*Him?*" Hal asked, incredulously. "He couldn't look any more out of place were he a pig at a prom."

"Where on earth do you get these phrases?" Kaila shook her head. "Never mind. Let's wrap up for the day and meet for breakfast tomorrow at six. Hopefully, I'll have some good news."

Without another word, she set about securing the site for the night, glancing once again at the man sitting in the car. He was watching her intently so she sent a brief smile in his direction before turning back to her work. She tried not to let dejection overwhelm her.

The phone in her trailer began to ring.

"We can finish up here," Derek called from where he was kneeling and gathering up tools. "Why don't you go on in and answer that."

"Thanks, see you in the morning."

Once inside the trailer, she let her shoulders fall and fisted her hands in frustration. So close. They were so damn close to finishing this dig. Her cell began to ring again.

"Hola," she said automatically, assuming it was someone local.

"Still playing with the dead?"

"Kian? I didn't expect to hear from you. Are you still in Hawaii?"

"We're heading back tomorrow. I was wondering when we'd be seeing your face back in the states again. That is, unless you've decided to make permanent plans in Chile."

"If you mean Juan, I told you, it isn't like that. It never was. We're just friends."

Laughter came through quite clearly in spite of the miles between them and for a moment, Kaila felt homesick. That was silly. As Vice President of a software startup in Palo Alto, her big sister would have plenty to keep her busy in the weeks and months ahead and would certainly have no time for family gatherings.

"I like him."

"I like him, too, which is why we're friends," she answered, hoping her sister would take the hint.

"Is he there?"

She sighed. Kian never was one for subtle.

"No, he has been reassigned; and as a result, unless I can find a suitable replacement within three days, we're out."

"Oh, Kaila, I'm sorry. Hell. Isn't there someone he can recommend?"

"I haven't seen or heard from him in over two days."

"Maybe you could call Tim Brightman?" her sister suggested, referring to someone they knew at the US Embassy in Santiago.

"I could but I won't. I don't like tapping people for favors unless it's important."

"This isn't important? Being kicked out of a country and off a dig?"

"It was an impromptu thing to begin with, one of those fortune meets opportunity meets timing kind of things? It isn't the end of the world."

"Might your students feel differently?"

"They knew this was a lark going in. When the Mammoth Lakes project was canceled, they were more than happy to milk it for the time they could. Experience is everything in this field and now they have something to add to their resumes. They're grown-ups, they'll get over it."

For several seconds there was silence on the line.

"Hmm, cold tone of voice. Very telling."

"What are you talking about?" she snapped impatiently.

"Nothing, except that whenever you are truly upset, you go cold."

"What?"

"Your voice goes flat, you become distant. If I didn't know you so well, which, being your sister, I do, I'd think you were heartless because it's at the times when things are upsetting you the most that you turn into an ice queen, like nothing in the world can penetrate your exterior."

"Kian, I have three students out there counting on me to find a way out of this. If I let my personal feelings about it get in the way I can't think, and we'll never find a replacement that way."

"So, you do want to stay?"

"Of course I do, but that doesn't mean I'm going to lose it and become depressed if I'm unable to find a replacement. And before you go saying anything about the students again, if they want to be in this line of work, then they'd better get used to disappointments like this. I can't count the number of times a grant didn't come through, someone else got credit for work I did, or artifacts from a dig were stolen and sold on the black market into someone's private collection. The hours are long, the days are hot, a lot of the times you're working in a geography that is completely unstable, if not unsafe."

"So, then why'd you go into it?"

Reflexively, Kaila's hand went to the pendant that hung around her neck.

"Listen, I've gotta run. Thanks for the call. Say hi to Sean for me," and before her sister could argue, she hung up.

Sighing, she opened her fridge and pulled out a diet Coke. Three days. She had three days to find a suitable replacement. Well, she'd better get on it, she decided, and dialed a familiar number. It went straight to voicemail, as she'd anticipated. She waited for the beep, then spoke, forcing herself to sound more cheerful than she felt.

"Juan, it's Kaila. Listen, I got the message that something's up and you had to move on. If you have any ideas on who we can hire as a replacement, can you give me a shout? In the meantime, good luck and hasta la vista."

She set the phone on the counter and got out the fixings for a sandwich. Slicing the bread diagonally, she sighed. When was the last time she'd eaten a hot meal? Well, she had no one to blame but herself. After all, the trailer she was renting had a full kitchen. Besides, she reflected, it wasn't like she would enjoy a hot meal any more than the cold sandwich. Eating alone was eating alone. In reality, she ought not to complain. After all, it wasn't as if she was on vacation. She was working. Roughing it was par for the course.

She stared around her trailer and smiled. It was luxurious to the verge of decadence; about as far from roughing it as one could get outside a hotel.

Normally, she wouldn't have spent the money, especially since it was more than she could really afford, but after everything she'd been through recently, she'd made the decision to treat herself. She sank into a comfy sofa that doubled as a bed, picked up a magazine, and sighed, glad she'd splurged.

She stared at the glossy pages but her mind was elsewhere. What were they going to do? Kian was too perceptive by far. This dig indeed meant a great deal to her, but not for the reasons her sister thought. She just had to hope Juan would have an idea.

She closed the magazine, tossed it aside and thought about the phone call. She'd dodged a bullet that time. Her reasons for pursuing archeology were something she refused to discuss in-depth, knowing that no one could possibly understand them. Sighing, she fingered the necklace and took another swig of soda. No, Kaila Ross knew she would never be able to make anyone understand the dark secret she kept; it wasn't even worth trying.

CHAPTER TWO

"A toast."

The room went quiet and all eyes turned to the head table. A man in Air Force dress blues covered in medals held a glass toward the guest of honor, a warm smile in his eyes.

"To Major Dan Foster. May he find civilian life every bit as exciting and successful as he found life in the service."

"Here, here," numerous voices concurred.

Thirty-seven year old Dan Foster raised a glass to his former commander, Colonel Brad Thomas, and followed with a sweeping motion in the general direction of the hundred or so men and women seated around the room, his eyes landing briefly on colleagues he knew he'd be in touch with for years to come.

Sipping from his champagne and wishing desperately it was beer, he found himself looking into the laughing eyes of his best friend, former Air Force Captain, Sean Andrews. Damn if he didn't look as if he was enjoying his friend's discomfiture.

There were few things in life Dan hated more than being the center of attention. He hadn't wanted the going away party in the first place. When he'd thought about his last hurrah, he'd pictured meeting at a local bar, a few of his closest comrades along for the ride; a manly gathering. He looked at the men and women in formal attire, dozens of round tables covered in white cloth, china and crystal, and sighed, drinking deeply of the champagne. Nothing manly about this at all. *Hell.*

Someone tapped him on the shoulder and handed him a slip of paper. He unfolded it, scanned the words, and worked to keep from grinning. A quick glance showed that no one was the wiser, so he slipped the paper into his pocket and nodded imperceptibly to a woman sitting next to his friend at a nearby table, Kian Ross.

As he spread foie gras on a cracker, Dan let his gaze fall to his watch. Just thirty minutes more. Surely, a man who'd endured the hell to be found in the Middle Eastern desert could handle thirty more minutes in a tuxedo. He fought the urge to try and loosen his collar.

"Got any immediate plans?" Brad asked from where he sat beside him.

"No, sir, nothing immediate."

A brunette with big breasts set a salad plate in front of him and smiled in a way that let him know she was his for the evening if he so desired. Stuffing the cracker in his mouth, he bit down and glanced meaningfully at Kian. It had the intended effect. Shrugging good-naturedly, she moved to place a salad in front of the Colonel.

"Are you thinking of remaining in the islands?"

"No, sir. I'm a mainland boy, born and raised. I won't say I've had the opportunity to get island fever, but I think my future lies on other shores."

"We're going to miss you, Major."

Not so much that you were willing to green stamp my promotion, you cold-hearted bastard.

Although Dan's promotion to major had come through, the colonel had not been supportive, going so far as to go on record saying that Dan's history of questioning authority and periodically sidestepping orders cast doubt on his qualifications for leadership.

Smiling dutifully, he replied, "Thank you, sir. I'm sure the days ahead will find me wondering what the hell I'm going to do with myself. Fortunately," he said, nodding toward his friend, "I have someone who can assist me with the transition."

"Ah, yes, Captain Andrews." It was said with all the sincerity of a man saying *I do* at a shotgun wedding. "Well,

I'm certain Sean can help you as he has many times in the past."

Still pissed about the Hindu Kush, eh? Good.

"He's actually offered me a position in his company," Dan replied, giving as good as he got. He let out a sigh. "Though I appreciated the gesture, I'm not interested in corporate life. Too starched, too confining."

It was well known that Brad Thomas, born and raised in the heartland, had champagne taste to go with his Boone's Farm mathematics, making him one of those people who salivated after other people's success. Although neither man would call the other a nemesis, neither would they turn their back on the other.

"I want to thank you for the send off, Colonel."

Which you knew I'd hate more than a root canal.

"Not at all, not at all. It was only fitting for a man with your years of service. The least we could do," he said, smiling with the eyes of a tiger about to attack its prey.

The brunette, her ample breasts pressing against the buttons of her crisp white shirt had returned, setting down a plate of beef Wellington and sending him a smile that made it clear she was his forever if he wished and Kian Ross be damned. Women, he thought, never picked up subtlety.

"Thank you," he said simply, and winked in Kian's direction. The woman shrugged, smiled, and moved off to serve the next contestant.

"So, when do you plan to leave Honolulu?"

That's more like it, you bastard. Let your true feelings for me come through. You know you can't wait to get me off this paradise.

"Sunday night, sir. A brief stop in California, as Sean thinks he can persuade me to join the firm if I but see the perks to be had in Silicon Valley. From there, I'm not exactly sure."

"Well, I wish you success and happiness," he said finally, sounding surprisingly sincere.

Dan glanced down at his watch.

"Sir? I'm sorry but I have a previous engagement."

"I understand. I wish you well, Major Foster. May God go with you."

"And you, sir," he said, and hastened toward the door, unwilling to spare any empathy for the hateful old man.

Outside the Officer's Club, Dan gulped of the night air. Free. He was free. He had no idea what that meant yet, only that it was true. For this moment this was his place on earth. He would figure out the rest later. With that in mind, he jogged toward where a chauffeur was opening the door to a stretch limo.

"Good evening, Major Foster."

"Not anymore," he replied with an easy smile, "just Mister." He slid gratefully across the leather seat. "Opening the door to the mini bar, he perused the contents. Pulling out a Primo and grabbing a bottle opener, he called to the driver.

"Where we headed?"

"The Shack, Mr. Foster. By the way, Ms. Ross felt you'd be more comfortable if you were able to change. You'll find more appropriate clothing in the back, I believe."

For the first time he noticed a gym bag on an adjacent seat. God bless Kian Ross. He unzipped the bag and withdrew a pair of jeans, a New England Patriots t-shirt, and his tennis shoes.

He changed quickly, sat back and savored the bitter flavor of the brew, the lights out the window passing into a blur as they headed for the sports bar. Grabbing the slip of paper, he reread the words.

The real party awaits your pleasure. Transportation outside. See you at 10pm. KR

Sean was one lucky man, he reflected, thinking of the petite blonde he'd met six months ago. What a meeting it had been, too. Sean, along with Kian, her sister, and Agent Juan Hernandez of the US Embassy in Santiago, Chile, had been kidnapped while on a business trip in South America by a fairly amateur international crime syndicate.

As his close friend had been one of the victims, Dan had been only too happy to lead his Special Forces team alongside undercover agents in the rescue. Taking a long swallow, he smiled. It was that final mission that had sealed the deal on his promotion. His success had earned him the gratitude of some rather prestigious individuals with the local government in Santiago, not to mention the US embassies in both Panama and Chile, effectively removing any leverage Colonel Thomas may have had in swaying the review board against him.

"We're here," the driver called, bringing his focus back to the present. The driver opened the door and offered him a smile.

"Enjoy your party, sir. You can leave your things on the seat. I'll be waiting when you're ready to go home."

"Thank you." Breathing deeply of the night air, he walked to where the real party awaited his pleasure.

The bar was standing room only. Members of his unit had been notified in advance and had been leaving the more formal dinner at staggered times, all managing to arrive before he had.

"Kian, I can't thank you enough," he said an hour later, planting a noisy kiss on her cheek.

"It was Sean's doing, really," she answered, blushing prettily beneath his attention.

Yep, Sean was one lucky bastard.

"He told me how much you hate the formality and attention and then launched into a rather lengthy diatribe of his own experience. He lamented how much better it would have been to just have his close buddies get together for a drink or two or ten."

"Or a hundred," Sean put in, his cheeks a rosy glow.

Feeling no pain there, Dan thought, and clicked his mug against that of his friend.

"So, talk to your sister lately?" Dan asked, hoping his tone was casual enough.

"As a matter of fact, I talked to her this afternoon. Bad news. Juan was reassigned, so she has three days to find a security replacement or her archeology dig is kaput. She and the students working with her will have to leave the country."

"Agent Hernandez? What does he have to do with her archeology dig?"

Dan frowned at his mug. How many of those had he had? Too many, he decided, if Sean's expression was any indication. Turning his eyes back to Kian, he pointedly ignored the look his friend was sending his way. Damn beautiful women, anyway.

"As I understand it," she answered neutrally, "he had been providing security, ensuring that the artifacts recovered didn't wind up on the black market. It wasn't a big deal since he was between assignments. Well, that changed and now they are without any security, something the Chilean government won't tolerate."

"Why doesn't she call Tim Brightman?" Sean asked, still eyeing his friend speculatively.

"She said she didn't want to abuse the favor. That's Kaila, though, all pride and stubbornness. It's really a shame. This dig meant a lot to her, although she won't admit it."

"Are you sure?" Dan asked, ignoring the eyes burning into him from across the table. "If she isn't upset about it then maybe it doesn't bother her as much as you think."

Kian shook her head. "This was her first post-doctoral assignment, not to mention it's the first time she was leading a team on her own. That's a big deal in her profession. The fact that it was international would have brought more visibility as well."

"Why don't you go down there?" Sean asked, suddenly.

The effect was the same as if Colonel Thomas had snuck up behind him and yelled *attention*!

"*Me?*"

"Yeah, you. You'd be perfect. Besides, what else have you got on your calendar?"

"I'm supposed to be going to Palo Alto with you, remember?"

"Come on, Dan, we both know you have no interest in corporate life. You were just coming along to kill some time while you figure out what the hell you want to do next. So, do that down in Chile instead of in California."

"I don't know, Sean," Kian spoke up. "Kaila mentioned that whoever was hired had to be approved by the local authorities. Dan's an American citizen. I don't think -."

"He will pass the bar," Sean answered. "I'd bet on it. In fact -." He pulled out his cell phone and punched in a number. "Hey, man, still running at 4am?"

"Who's he talking to?" Dan hissed at Kian.

"Tim Brightman would be my guess."

"He called Santiago? What time is it there?"

"It's all set," Sean said, placing the phone back in his pocket.

"The hell it's all set," Dan argued, "I haven't agreed to this."

"Dan," Kian spoke up, "you know, Sean might have it right. This could be just the thing to help you transition from the military. Besides, you'd get to work in a beautiful exotic locale -."

"Talk about beautiful exotic locale," he fired back, making a sweeping motion toward the other islands that made up the Hawaiian chain.

"It would mean a lot to Kaila," she said quietly.

Dan stared at his beer.

"Please don't judge my sister based on what happened down in Talca."

He grimaced at the memory. Thinking him to be one of the captors, Kian's younger sister had proceeded to sneak up on him and nearly kick his ass. Pride dictated that he remind himself he had been taken by surprise and had been so busy working to avoid hurting her that he'd had no time to explain who he was, let alone stop the beating he was taking. It had only gone downhill from there.

"Listen," Sean said, setting down his empty mug and signaling for a refill, "if it's between you and getting kicked out of the country, I think she'll be happy enough to see you."

The image of Kaila Ross swam before him. Standing five foot six, she had wavy blonde hair that hung to her waist, and vivid green eyes that turned up in the corners, making him think of a leprechaun. Or a woodland fairy. Again he eyed his mug suspiciously and tried to push the image away.

"Hell," he muttered.

"Thank you," Kaila whispered, kissing him on the cheek. "I don't think you'll regret it."

No, but she may.

CHAPTER THREE

Kaila Ross stood frowning at her cell phone, unaware of the beautiful late October sky. Shades of violet and indigo collided with vivid reds and oranges as the sun crept over the Andes Mountains in the early morning.

"Uh-oh, must be bad if you're still in your jams," Theresa said, walking up and sliding a thermos full of strong black coffee into her line of vision.

"Thanks," she replied absently, taking the thermos but making no move to open it.

"Want to get it off your chest? You might feel better."

"What?" She lifted her head and looked around. "Oh, good morning Theresa."

"Listen, I was talking with the guys and we're really all right with what happened, okay? We know this isn't what you planned. I mean, shit happens, right? Don't be so hard on yourself."

"Huh?" She blinked as if seeing the young woman with red hair and soft blue eyes for the first time. "Oh, no. That was Tim Brightman's office."

"The guy at the embassy?"

"Yeah. We don't have to leave."

"Really? They found a replacement for us?"

"Apparently so; I guess he's on his way."

"Then we don't have to deal with frumps anymore," Derek said, walking up and munching on a stale donut. "Cool. That guy was a total dweeb."

"Who is it?" Hal asked, "another US Embassy agent?"

Kaila continued to frown. "No, they said it was some private security agent, from the states, no less. I guess he came highly recommended."

"By who?" Hal asked, suspicious.

"I have no idea," she answered, sighing. "Maybe Juan, I don't know. What I do know is we are to expect him by the end of the day and if he doesn't show, I'm to call Tim back right away."

"Does that mean we can go back to work?" Theresa asked, uncertainly.

"Um, yeah, I guess," she said absently.

"Hey, doc? Why don't you have something to eat first," Derek suggested, "and have a gulp or two of that coffee. You look as if you're still asleep."

Self-consciously she pushed at her hair, suddenly aware that she was standing in her pajamas, her feet bare. Today had been D-Day and she hadn't been able to find the energy to comb her hair, let alone shower or put on clean clothes. The cell phone had rung just as she was preparing to tell her team that unless a miracle happened, they were out of luck and to start packing.

"Yeah, okay. I'll be out in about a half hour."

Stepping under the warm shower spray, Kaila puzzled over the pending arrival. Had Juan pulled in a favor and located someone?

What worried her about whoever was coming was that they were private security. More often than not, that meant someone a little too gung ho; an ex-cop, perhaps, or worse, ex-military. She shook her head, sighed. Maybe she shouldn't look a gift horse in the mouth. Maybe Mr. Testosterone wouldn't be the one to show up. *A sensitive security guard?* She laughed at the absurdity and finished rinsing her long blonde hair.

Dressing quickly, she pulled her hair into a pony tail, grabbed a diet Coke, and popped a bagel in the toaster. She pursed her lips, staring into space. Hopefully, he was suited for the job, she thought grimly, and gulped down her caffeine source of choice. She yanked the bagel out of the toaster before it burned and liberally spread peanut butter across the browned surface.

What if he was the prude sort? He'd be sharing the other trailer with her students, two of whom were living together out of wedlock. She shrugged. For the short amount of time it would take to finish the dig she could put up with Godzilla. Feeling more optimistic than she had in days, she quickly cleaned up and went to join the students. Behind her, the cell phone began to ring. Grabbing it absently, she opened the door to step out, hit the answer button, and froze.

"You have *got* to be kidding me," she gasped.

"Does that mean you've met your new security guard?" Her sister's voice was full of mirth.

"Kian? *You did this?*"

Thirty feet away, Dan Foster stood next to her students, his expression unreadable behind aviator sunglasses.

"Listen, -."

If her sister had been providing an explanation, Kaila never heard it; she'd hung up. Setting the cell phone on a table, she pulled the door shut behind her and walked over to the new arrival.

Dan remained completely still as she approached and she noticed, with some amusement, that the closer she got, the clearer her reflection in his sunglasses became. Finally, they stood practically toe to toe. For several seconds, neither said a word.

"This is a bit of a surprise," she managed, finally.

"I can see that. Kian didn't call you?"

"That was her on the phone. I hung up."

"Listen, if this is going to be a problem -."

Her students were wearing various expressions, all of them saying they thought she'd lost her mind.

"No, no, not at all," she stammered, trying to recover. "I just wasn't expecting to see you here. I thought you were stationed in Hawaii?"

"Retired," he said, his tone completely neutral, "just got out."

"I see," she said, though clearly, she didn't.

"Like I said; if this is going to be a problem."

"It isn't," she rushed. They had to finish this dig. Don't look a gift horse in the mouth, right? "I'm just surprised. You caught me off guard."

"Well then," he drawled, a smile slowly making its way over infuriatingly handsome features, "I guess that puts us in the way of being even, doesn't it?"

"I didn't realize you were keeping score, Captain," she answered coolly, not missing the reference to when she had mistaken him for one of several men responsible for kidnapping. He had been more than surprised to find out that the woman who had attacked him was not Kian, a competitive kick boxer, but her younger sister. Things had gone downhill from there.

"Actually, it was major, but the key word in that phrase is *was*," he replied, just as coolly. "So, it's just Dan, from now on."

"Okay, just Dan. I see you've met the crew."

"That I have."

Oh, she could see this was going to be a lot of fun. Five minutes and they'd already run through their repertoire of small talk.

"Did they show you around or haven't you been here long enough?"

"Actually, they suggested I wait and let you do it."

"Have you had anything to eat, Captain?" She caught the change in his expression. "Sorry, Dan."

"I had breakfast, thank you."

"Okay, then. Derek, why don't you show Dan where he'll be staying while I go over and talk with Senor Juarez. Hal? Theresa? Get to work. Dan, when I'm through talking with him," she nodded toward where the other man stood stiffly by his car, "I'll show you around."

"You have my congratulations, Senora Ross," the Chilean offered as she approached. He was obviously uncomfortable, but equally as obvious was his effort to hide that fact. He gave her a weak smile.

"Thank you, Senor Juarez. Thank you for all your help these last days. As you can see, we were fortunate to find a replacement suitable in the eyes of your superiors. If there is nothing else, I think we can take it from here."

"No, no, nothing else. My *superiors* wanted me to make sure that your replacement had arrived safely."

"Oh? Then you brought Captain Foster?" Major, she mentally corrected.

"No, Senor Foster managed his own transportation."

For the first time, Kaila noticed the silver Jeep Cherokee parked next to the black sedan Senor Juarez had been camped out in while he acted as their quasi-security agent.

"I wish you Buenos Dias, Senora Ross."

"And a good day to you, Senor Juarez."

She watched the dust settle back to the earth as the sedan disappeared from view, and sighed. *Time to face the music.* Turning back to the site, she paused. Standing next to her trailer, Dan Foster was staring in her direction, his sunglasses obscuring his eyes, though she had no doubt they were pinned to her face.

The man was too good looking, damn it. Standing in jeans and a white t-shirt stretched tightly over an obviously very fit body, she was reminded of Mickey Rourke in *9 ½ Weeks*. Yep, too good looking. Letting out a breath, she began walking in his direction. She knew that she had to make an effort to ease the tension between them; it was in everyone's best interest. The better she made this situation, the more likely things would go smoothly during the remainder of the project.

"I really do appreciate your coming to our rescue, Dan," she spoke as she reached his side.

"Did you get everything settled then?" he asked.

"What?"

He thrust his chin toward where the sedan had been.

"Oh, Juarez? Yes, I think he's satisfied that everything's in order."

"I wouldn't be so sure about that," he answered, dubiously.

"Oh?" She waited; one heartbeat, two. "What makes you think there's a problem?"

"He didn't seem too pleased that I was here."

"How do you know that? Did you talk to him?"

"We had a few words."

"You argued with him?"

"No, that's not what I meant."

It infuriated her that she couldn't read his expression.

"Would you mind taking off your sunglasses, please?" she snapped, then mentally chastised herself. That tone certainly wouldn't ease tensions. Still, it had worked; she found herself staring into piercing blue eyes.

"I didn't argue with him but during the few minutes we did converse, I got the distinct impression he wasn't too thrilled about my being here."

"Maybe he doesn't like that you aren't a Chilean citizen," she theorized, glancing back to where Dan's Jeep was parked like a sentry guarding their dig.

"I think it's more than that," he replied, "but for now why don't we move on? Would you like to show me around?"

Turning back, she met his gaze. *Never seen eyes so blue*? She blinked. Damned musicians.

"Yeah, okay. So, Derek showed you where you'll be sleeping?"

"Actually, I'm not going to stay in there with them. It's cramped enough with the three of them. They don't need my intrusion."

If he thought he would be sharing her trailer, he had another thing coming. She was prepared to explain that when he spoke.

"Provided the weather holds," he said easily, "I'll be sleeping under the stars."

"Out here?"

"Makes sense, doesn't it? How can I keep an eye on the site if I'm snug inside a trailer?"

He had a point. She had given Juan the sofa inside her trailer, but he'd had sound equipment and a perimeter alarm he'd brought from home, wherever that was. She brushed the thought away as quickly as it surfaced. She had no right to be annoyed just because she felt he had been a little too aloof. After all, they were just friends.

"You okay?" he asked.

She shook herself, nodded. "I'm just a little tired. I didn't get much sleep last night. I thought we'd be packing it in today. Thanks again for helping us out."

"No problem."

"How did you end up here?"

"I happened to be with Kian and Sean in Honolulu and they mentioned your situation. I'm in between assignments at the moment so -." He stopped, letting her fill in the blank.

"Well, that was luck, wasn't it? So, we keep it pretty lean around here," she said, walking toward where her students were busy with the various chores that took place during a dig. "One of us goes into town every few days and picks up whatever supplies we need." She stopped, looked at him.

"Did you bring something to do?"

"What?"

"A book or something?"

"I thought I'd be guarding things here."

"True, but it's relatively safe. I mean, we haven't had any problems to speak of. So, you'll probably spend a lot of time just sitting around watching the horizon."

"What did Agent Hernandez do to keep occupied?"

CHAPTER FOUR

Kaila tried to determine if there was anything in Dan's tone to suggest the question was other than what it appeared on the surface. His expression inscrutable, he stood watching her.

"Honestly? I don't have any idea. I didn't pay too much attention to him."

That was a lie. She had always been very aware of Juan's presence, though it certainly hadn't been reciprocated. In point of fact, he had rarely pulled his nose up from where it had been pointed into the middle of a laptop. She'd asked him only once what he was working on and he'd smiled and explained that it was classified.

Dan cleared his throat, bringing her attention back to the present.

"As a matter of fact, I do have a few books I brought along. I've a bit of experience with this sort of thing so I came as prepared as I could."

"You've been a security guard before?"

"Let's just say there can be plenty of downtime in the military," he replied, venturing nothing further.

"Hey, doc? I've finished cataloguing what we've got here. Would you like me and Theresa to start on the next grid?"

"Yeah, thanks, Hal. By the way, how many times have I've told you guys? It's Kaila."

"Right-o," he replied, waving and walking toward the next square in the layout, his tool belt slapping against his thigh.

She turned to finish going over things with her new security guard but he was nowhere to be found.

"If you're looking for Dan, he's over at his Jeep," Derek said from where he was kneeling not far away, gently cleaning a clay shard. He looked up at her. "I'm glad he's able to help out," he said quietly.

"So am I." Knowing she was an easy read, she turned her gaze toward where he was pulling several bags from the back of his Jeep. "What the -?" She hurried over to him.

"What is all that?"

"I wasn't sure how long it had been since you'd gotten into town for supplies, so I brought a few things," he answered, setting another grocery bag next to the Jeep.

"Wow, I don't know what to say," she replied, genuinely grateful. "Thank you. It was incredibly generous of you. Here," she said, leaning forward and snatching up a bag from his arms, "let me help you carry these back. We'll store them in my trailer."

"This is nice," he said, looking around the interior of the Royals International.

Nice didn't begin to describe it. In point of fact, it was luxurious, plain and simple. A full kitchen with honey maple cabinets and granite countertops was only the beginning. The bedroom offered a comfortable queen sized bed and a double sink vanity.

Taking in the almost decadent surroundings, she could imagine how it might appear to him. She cleared her throat. Damned if she didn't feel self-conscious about the largess, but she'd be more damned if she'd let him know that. It was none of his business.

"I'm glad you decided to treat yourself."

She studied him intently, attempting to gauge if he was sincere.

"I mean it," he answered, apparently reading her mind. "After what you went through recently, why shouldn't you?"

She smiled. Maybe the next few weeks wouldn't be so difficult after all. She let out a sigh.

"Yeah, that's kind of what I was thinking when I decided to get this. We don't actually spend that much time in the trailers, though, unless it's raining. Then I usually invite everyone in here. Except for sleeping," she added meaningfully.

"Listen," he said, suddenly. "Why don't you go ahead and unpack everything in here and I'll take a walk around outside, get a feel for the area. I'm also going to check in with Tim and Sean, let them know we've hooked up. See ya later."

For several seconds she stared at his retreating form. When she caught her gaze lingering just a little too long on his behind, she jerked her head and turned to unpack the bags.

She was impressed. He certainly understood their situation; being away from most conveniences. There were foil packages of nuts, dried fruits, and even tuna. She pulled out boxes of protein bars, all varieties and flavors, and lots of bottled water.

The next bag showed he had gone over the top. It was filled with everyday items considered absolute luxuries when you were out on a dig. He'd bought Band-aids, peroxide, aspirin, toilet paper, shampoo, soap, tooth paste, even a few tooth brushes. Reaching into the bag again, she frowned in concentration as her hand brushed up against a cardboard box. Pulling it out, she smiled, then laughed. It was an unusual man, if not a brave one, she thought wryly, who would have remembered that women have unique needs. Then she remembered; he'd been married. Her smile faded; maybe not so unusual after all.

"I just thought -."

She turned to see him leaning in the door, his eyes on her hand on the box.

"Thanks, on behalf of both Theresa and myself. It was very thoughtful of you."

He cleared his throat, shifted. "Derek said he needs you right away."

"Then why the hell didn't he just yell?" she snapped, annoyed. "You aren't his messenger boy."

"No big deal; I was coming this way anyhow. I'd like to take a closer look around in here if you don't mind; as part of my security evaluation."

"Have at it," she said, breezing past him.

When she returned she found the space empty, of Dan and everything else. He'd put away all the supplies. Since it was time for lunch, she pulled bread, meat and cheese from the fridge, laying it all out buffet style. Usually they took their meals separately, forgoing schedules and eating whenever they got hungry, but she thought it a good idea to make an exception this time. It would give them a chance to get to know one another a little better and hopefully, get comfortable with each other. After all, they would be living together in relatively close quarters for the next couple of weeks while they finished up the dig.

Frowning at the plates stacked on the counter, she wondered if she'd ever be able to get comfortable around her new security guard. It wasn't just that they'd started out on the wrong foot all those months ago, it was who he was, what he did for a living.

She wasn't sure what annoyed her more, the fact that he was ex-military or that she was holding it against him, perhaps unfairly. After all, what did she really know about the man? He had been a pilot in the US Air Force and part of a Special Forces team. He'd been married only a short time when his wife died, of what she had no idea. Kian said it was the only thing Sean went completely tight-lipped about. She shrugged. It was none of her business and she didn't plan on getting to know him well enough to go there.

She walked to the door ready to call in the troops, but paused. Halfway between her trailer and his Jeep, Dan was setting up what she assumed would be his quarters. In spite of herself, she smiled. It reminded her of the campsites she'd prepared when she'd been earning her Girl Scout camping badge. She glanced up at the sky, noting with interest that there were very few clouds. What would she do if a downpour opened in the middle of the night? Would she open her door to him or force him into the already cramped quarters of her students? Her smile widening as she played over alternating scenarios, she opened her mouth to call everyone to lunch, but clamped it shut again. The man had stopped what he was doing and was staring at her, his expression impassive. She swallowed, attempting to recover, and looked over to see Derek staring at her, one side of his mouth turned up. He wiggled his eyebrows.

"Lunch is ready," she called, grateful her voice held steady.

"We don't normally eat like this," she said when they were all seated. "I thought it might be a nice way to get better acquainted."

Dan nodded but did not reply.

"When did you retire?" Hal spoke up and Kaila wasn't the least bit surprised. A master at small talk, the grad student was at ease in any situation.

"Three days ago," Dan replied, taking a deep drink of water.

"I had no idea," Kaila responded, her tone so soft even she had trouble hearing it. She cleared her throat, took a drink of diet Coke.

"How long were you in the service?" Theresa picked up the thread.

"Twenty years."

"Wow, that's a long time. You must have really enjoyed it," Hal responded.

"Some of it was amazing and some of it was just plain awful."

"I take it you did time in one of the big three," Kaila asked.

Dan's body jerked and his eyes snapped to hers. "You get that from Sean?"

"No," she replied calmly. "I can honestly say that I've never discussed your military career with Sean outside of the fact that you were in Special Forces. I didn't even know about your promotion to major. Congratulations, by the way." She knew that being promoted before he left the service meant better retirement pay.

"I spent some time in the Middle East," he said, finally.

"Do you prefer Dan or Daniel?" Theresa asked, gracefully changing the subject.

"Actually," he said, smiling the first genuine smile since he'd arrived, "I prefer Foster. I've been going by that name for as long as I can remember."

"You want us to call you Foster?" Kaila asked dubiously.

"I'll answer however you wish." He looked back at Theresa. "Though I would prefer something other than Daniel. I haven't been called that since I was a kid."

"Mom?" the student guessed, smiling easily.

"Nope, not even my mom called me that. My Aunt Noreen was the only one who ever called me Daniel."

"Well then, we'll make sure Aunt Noreen's entitlement is safe."

"Foster," Hal said, then smiled. "I like it, it's got character."

For the love of god, Kaila thought sourly. This wasn't going well at all. She wanted to get comfortable with the man and he wanted her to call him Foster? She let out a breath. It was going to be a long few weeks.

Thanks to her students, the rest of the meal went relatively smoothly. They were enthusiastic about sharing their academic pursuits with the former major and he seemed almost eager to find out more about them.

"Listen," Kaila said, standing and starting to clear the table, "we need to get back at it. We narrowly missed losing this gig." She glanced at Dan, then back to her students. "Let's not waste the opportunity fortune has given us."

The students filed out but Dan remained, helping her clean up.

"I take it you're no stranger to Special Forces."

His casual tone didn't fool her for a minute. He wanted to know just how much she knew.

"Let's just say I'm not a stranger to the military and leave it at that."

"The big three is a very special tag, Kaila. I'm curious how you came to know about it, if it wasn't Sean."

"It's amazing how you can make a simple question sound like an interrogation," she said by way of an answer. "I guess you can take the man out of Special Forces -."

"Is there a reason not to answer?" he asked, tension vibrating the air around him as he fought to keep his frustration in check. "It's a simple enough question."

She shrugged impatiently. "I dated a guy at Moffett Field."

"Moffett hasn't been in the hands of the military in quite awhile," he responded, his tone accusatory.

"I suggest you check your facts, Dan. NASA? You think NASA doesn't rub elbows with the military?"

"Why do we always seem to be arguing?" he asked, tiredly.

"I would venture it's because we're both used to being right," she replied, throwing the towel she'd been using into the sink. She walked silently past him, down the steps, and toward her students.

CHAPTER FIVE

"We have a bit of a situation here, Bob."

Bob Murphy, General in the Air Force Special Ops, sat on the other side of a small round table in his office and stared benignly at the security liaison, his pale blue eyes reflecting none of what he was truly feeling. "Tell me."

"The package was never delivered."

The General leaned back, inhaled and let it out slowly, saying nothing for several seconds. "I see."

"I don't think you do."

"Actually," he said, one side of his mouth going up, "I see quite clearly. Your organization fucked up and now you want my guys not only to bail you out but to save your ass while we're at it."

"Bob -."

"No."

"But -."

"No," he repeated, forcefully. "I still don't have the president off my ass after that crap with the nuclear security and that wasn't anywhere near my gate of control. I'm not letting my guys hang in the press so you can make good come appropriations time. I have plenty of Senate contacts myself, Jack, and I'm tired of -."

"I will personally guarantee your organization won't appear anywhere. The Air Force will not take a hit for this."

"And how the hell are you going to pull that off if my guys fix this?"

"Because if we use your organization; they were never involved."

"I don't know how you plan to manage that, Jack, but I'm listening."

Jack Porter, longtime friend and White House security liaison to the military, smiled.

"You already have a man on the inside that can help."

"What the hell are you talking about? None of my -."

"He doesn't know it yet."

"Jack, I have a meeting in twenty minutes and I don't want to go in there ready to kick someone's ass because I'm mad at you. Get to it already."

In spite of his irritation, the General's voice never rose beyond what was considered polite.

"By a twist of fate we've been handed a perfect opportunity to salvage this without anyone the wiser."

"How?"

"The less you know the better."

"If it involves one of my men -."

"He's slated for retirement."

The officer sat straighter, his gaze piercing. "Foster?"

The security liaison nodded. "More than opportunistic, wouldn't you say?"

"If he's retired then how do you propose having him involved?"

"As it so happens, he's already unwittingly inserted himself smack into the middle of it."

"Jack, in about one minute I'm going to haul your ass across this table and make you sorry you interrupted my coffee break. Spit it out, in clear detail, and in English, not that pseudo-spy lingo you like to throw around."

The security liaison began to pace. "Okay. I really didn't want to have to do this -."

"It's code?" the General interrupted, his tone deceptively calm.

"Afraid so." Jack shook his head, sighed. "We have a pretty good idea where the chain lost the link but it's too soon to start throwing out names."

"Go on." The Air Force officer was leaning forward, an indication that the news had rattled him.

"We originally believed that the package was still in the Bay Area, maybe even in Monterey. We were completely prepared to throw local resources on it and call it a day."

The General waited patiently, his heart thumping double time.

"New intelligence suggests that the package may have found its way into Venezuela."

"*Damn.*"

"Yeah."

"Are the Russians involved?"

"Russians, Iranians, hell, at this point we could point the finger at several suspects, including a few of our own allies."

"And Dan Foster is somehow in the middle of this? I find that hard to believe."

The General thought of the young officer. The major may have had a bit of rebellion in him but he wouldn't involve himself in something like this. But Jack had said unwittingly, hadn't he? The General looked up to see his friend quietly studying him.

"Major Foster is currently down in South America."

"What the hell is he doing in Venezuela?" he snapped.

"I said South America, not Venezuela. Actually, he's down in Chile."

"What the hell is he doing in Chile?" the General roared, his last thread of patience stretched to the limit.

"He's acting as a security guard to an archeologist and her team."

The senior officer let that sink in. "How did you find this out?"

"Let's just say if I didn't believe in a supreme being before now, this has convinced me. Would you believe that the archeologist is an operative?"

"Active?"

"On sabbatical," he replied, using the term that described those who had *retired* from one of the national security organizations. In reality, no one ever retired, they were just considered on unpaid leave until and unless their country needed them.

"And this operative -?"

"We were about to send someone to make contact because we believe she can help us retrieve the package."

"I see. You said you were about to send someone. So, as of now, no one has been in touch with her? She isn't involved, officially, or otherwise?"

"No."

The General sat back, let out a sigh.

"What do you need me to do?" he said, resignedly.

"Stop the press."

"You want me to put a hold on Foster's retirement paperwork?"

The man nodded.

"Well, shit, Jack, you aren't asking for much, are you? Do you realize I'm not only going to have to call Washington, I'm going to have to call that jackass at Hickam?"

"And I'd start dialing, if I were you; his retirement party was last week."

"All right," he said after several seconds during which he studied the ceiling with great intensity. "What else?"

"That's it."

"What do you mean, that's it? What about a team? What about contact with Foster."

"We don't want him to be contacted; at least not at this point."

"I don't like the sound of this. It's beginning to sound like you're going to let one of my guys hang -."

"We will handle all contact, should it become necessary."

"Should it become necessary? What, are you some sort of psycho? Once that operative becomes involved, Dan's life will be in danger. *I think it's fair he be notified of that, don't you?*" he snarled.

"We will handle it. I assure you, we won't do anything to purposely endanger Major Foster's life."

"And you won't do anything to help him, either, you heartless bastard. I am not going sit here and do nothing while you -."

"Before you go any further, Bob; here. Read this." The liaison slid a folder across the table and stood patiently while his friend scanned the contents. He sighed. Sometimes he hated his job with a passion that went bone deep. There were days he avoided shaving so he never had to meet his own eyes in the mirror.

"I see," the General said after several minutes. The phone rang and he yanked it up. "Yeah? "Tell them I'm running late. I don't give a flying damn who is on the agenda, I said they can wait." He slammed the phone down and looked at the security man.

"I think you finally are beginning to see," Jack said, smiling. "Did the file on Ms. Ross help you find enlightenment?"

"I suppose you could say that. Promise me one thing."

"I'll try."

"Foster. He's one of our own. We take care of our own, Jack. If he gets anywhere near trouble, give me a head's up. My team will be at your disposal."

"Bob, I know you and the major are close. I know all about you overriding Thomas to approve his promotion. The thing of it is, your organization can't become involved any further than it already is. This, I can hide. Officially, he's retired. Only a select few will know otherwise. If your team becomes involved -."

"Cart blanche, Jack."

"I beg your pardon?"

"If the need is there, if I assign you a team from my organization, I release them to your authority, cart blanche."

For several seconds the liaison studied the General. "Very close, indeed. Okay, Bob, that's the least I can do." He put a hand to the doorknob. "I was never here. You'll be hearing from the right people if the need arises. In the meantime, I want to thank you for your cooperation and I meant what I said; your organization won't be anywhere on the radar. No one will know the Air Force was ever involved. Give my best to Kate and the kids." Donning his hat, he stepped through the door, pulling it closed behind him.

For several minutes, Bob Murphy drummed his fingers on a round table and stared off into space. Goddamn security organizations. A necessary evil but more often than not, not worth the trouble they caused. He yanked up the phone.

"Adelaide? Go tell Colonel Straight I won't be joining them. Because," he snarled into the receiver, "a goddamned emergency came up. And when you get back, bring me the file on Major Dan Foster."

He hung up and began dialing again.

"This is General Murphy, I need to speak to Colonel Thomas. It's urgent."

While he waited, he drummed his fingers. Normally an easygoing man, even for a General, there were few people he didn't get along with. Unfortunately, the man about to get on the other end of this conversation was one of them.

"Brad? It's Bob. Are you sitting down? Okay, I have a directive. Would you like to have it come from me or from the White House? All right, then; listen, and don't interrupt and when I'm through? I don't want even a hint of a debate, let alone an argument, you got that?" He took a deep breath and explained.

"Well, that went well," he said ten minutes later, letting out a sigh and pinching the bridge of his nose. "Only one out and out tantrum, and I only had to hold the phone away from my ear four times." He pulled open his top desk drawer and grabbed a key. He was about to unlock a cupboard behind which he stashed a bottle of Johnnie Walker Red, when there was a knock at the door.

"Oh, for the love of God, what now?" He yanked open the door.

"I have Major Foster's file and I thought you might find this useful?"

His secretary, a woman for whom he had a deep respect, entered, carrying a tray. She set it down on the table and handed him a folder. "Would you like for me to call Kate and tell her you'll be a little late?" She poured amber liquid over two ice cubes and handed him the glass.

"Thanks," he said, accepting the scotch, "I would appreciate that."

She turned to leave.

"Adelaide?"

She looked at him over her shoulder.

"I'm sorry I chewed you out. My beef certainly wasn't with you."

"I understand," she said with a small smile, a mischievous twinkle in her eye. "You're usually like this after Mr. Porter has been to visit. If you need anything else, let me know. I'll be staying late myself."

General Murphy shook his head and drank deeply of the whiskey, thinking what a lucky man he was to be surrounded by such competent people.

He set down the major's file and picked up the one for Kaila Ross. An hour later he closed the folder, locking it alongside Foster's in his private cabinet.

"Well, Dan," he said to the empty office as he prepared to leave, "I think you're in good hands this time. If you have someone covering your back, you could probably do worse than a gifted psychic working for the CIA." Turning off the light, he pulled the door closed and started for home.

CHAPTER SIX

Kaila bolted upright, confused. For several seconds she tried to understand what had brought her out of a dead sleep but couldn't. She hadn't been dreaming. She looked over to where a small clock on a nearby table glowed in the dark; four in the morning. With a sigh, she shoved herself out of bed and headed for the shower. The rest of the crew would start their day within an hour or so; there was no point lying in bed puzzling over what had brought her out of a deep slumber.

She stood in front of the bathroom mirror unbuttoning her pajamas. Her eyes fell to where the necklace lay between her breasts. It felt heavy around her neck which meant it was time to recharge it. Sighing, she reached around behind her and undid the lobster clasp she had upgraded to after nearly losing the white gold chain years before.

Standing in her pajama bottoms, she glanced down at the small crystal in her hand. She hated taking it off but once it felt heavy, she knew it had become saturated and that it would no longer function anyway. At that point, the longer she kept wearing it, the more likely she was to develop a headache. She walked across the trailer and hung the chain in a southeast facing window. She'd placed a little suction cup hook there knowing the direction the window faced would guarantee several hours of bright light each day.

The sunlight acted to not only recharge the crystal over a period of seventy-two hours; it would remove any residual negative energy remaining.

Kaila had been using the crystal to redirect and diffuse overwhelming energy bursts since she discovered its capability to do so when she was a teenager. She had received the necklace as a gift, one her mother had purchased at a kiosk at the local shopping mall. It was only after a few years of interesting coincidences that she realized the true gift she had received. Since then, she only removed the necklace when it became necessary, such as for recharging.

A knock at the door yanked her back to reality. She ran back and snatched her pajama top, hastily buttoning it as she went to answer.

"Is everything okay?"

She blinked. Dan Foster stood in jeans and a t-shirt, his face a mask of concern.

"Yes, fine, why?"

"When I saw the light on -." He shifted. "I wanted to make sure everything was okay." His gaze fell to where her hand bunched her shirt together. She hadn't finished buttoning the top and not wanting to freak out one of her students, she'd scrunched it closed. Now, her eyes on his, she dropped her hand. The shirt fell, the buttons done unevenly, but managing to accomplish a fair amount of modesty anyway.

"Thanks, but I'm fine. What about you? Why aren't you still sleeping?"

"I was walking around camp, checking on things."

She stared at him. "Do you always walk around in the dark in the middle of night?"

"You are paying me to protect your camp. Walking a perimeter is part of doing that," he replied, his voice flat.

"I don't expect you to go without sleep, Foster."

"I would have gone back to sleep eventually. It doesn't take much for me. I trained myself over the years to be able to do that."

Inwardly, she sighed. They had to get past this formality. They were not enemies, for god's sake, yet they couldn't seem to stop tippy-toeing around each other's temperaments. It was becoming a challenge to keep it up without lashing out in frustration. What was more, it was draining.

"Have you had breakfast yet?"

"No."

The lights in the other trailer were still out, but she knew her students would be waking shortly. She stepped back and pushed her door wide.

"Bagels and peanut butter okay with you?"

"Perfect, and thanks."

"Do you want coffee?" she asked, setting a diet Coke on the counter.

"Don't make it just for me," he replied, taking a seat. "Besides, Theresa makes a big pot every morning and she usually brings me a filled thermos."

"She's very thoughtful that way. They're a good group."

"How did you get together with them? Are they your students?"

She glanced over from where she was waiting next to the toaster.

"No, if you mean am I their professor. Yes, if you mean are they my responsibility at this stage in their career aspirations."

"How did you find them if they aren't in a class of yours?"

She spread peanut butter on bagels and piled them on a plate. Filling a glass with water, she brought everything to the table.

"Sláinte," she said, raising her soda can.

"Right," he replied, taking a sip of water.

"Well, first of all, I'm not on the faculty. I'm recently graduated and this was an opportunity. Part of the sponsorship requirement was that I have a team of students under my direction. Between Stanford and Berkeley, it's easy enough to find candidates. It's a small community and word gets out. Usually, by the time they are finishing their master's thesis, most students are actively seeking hands-on experience. If they're serious about their careers, that is."

"Sean said you had some definite ideas about what separated serious archeologists from the hobbyists."

"Oh, you mean how I took care of Juan after he was shot? That I had the medical expertise?"

It was an opening he'd been looking for. Munching down on a bagel, he nodded. "How have you been? I mean since the capture?"

She smiled. "I'm fine. Happy ending, right? No small thanks to you and your team."

"I wasn't fishing for compliments, Kaila; I want to know how you are doing after such an ordeal. That was pretty traumatic. You're kidnapped at gunpoint, locked in a shipping container for days with barely enough supplies to survive and no privacy whatsoever, not to mention you were in there with two men you'd never met before."

"Well, my sister knew Sean, so that helped, and Juan is an agent who works for the US embassy in Santiago. It's not as if they were a threat. As co-captives go, I think I did pretty well."

"So, no post traumatic stress? No nightmares?"

"Is that what you thought was wrong, why you came to the door this morning? You saw my light on and thought I'd had a nightmare?"

She'd sidestepped the answer but he let it go. "You're usually asleep until six. I wanted to make sure you weren't sick or anything like that."

She smiled. "Thank you for your concern, but as you can see, everything is just fine."

"So, why were you awake at four in the morning?"

Before she had to answer, someone was knocking at the door.

"I'll get it," he said, and stood before she could move. He reached through the door. "Oh, thank you, Theresa."

He went over to a cupboard and grabbed a cup. He held out the thermos. "Do you want some?"

"No, thanks. She makes a good cup, as coffee goes, but I don't really care for the stuff. It's too bitter."

"Listen, I'm going to let you get to it," he said, walking toward the door. "Thanks for breakfast. See you in awhile."

Cleaning up, she went back to the bathroom. A glance in the mirror had her laughing. Her pajama shirt looked as if a kindergartner had buttoned it. Oh well, she'd been covered up and that's what had been important. She undressed and stepped beneath the warm spray.

Although she hadn't gotten a chance to answer the former major, she didn't, in truth, suffer from nightmares or post traumatic stress. Years ago she had learned how to manage the normal everyday challenges that were a part of living, including the more traumatic events that peppered everyone's life from time to time. So far, the methodology had worked, knock on wood.

Her mind focused on their conversation. So, the man knew her routine well enough to know what time she got up? Being familiar with the routine of the camp was probably par for the course, but knowing that an attractive man knew what time she got up each day brought with it a certain feeling of contentment. And he had come to check on her, showing that underneath the stiff front he presented each day, he cared. That he'd inquired about how she was faring after the kidnapping let her know that he was interested in her for real, not just the polite *how are you* that people threw around these days. He really wanted to know.

So, if it wasn't a nightmare that had woken her, what had? She was normally a very sound sleeper. This morning she'd come out of a dead sleep with a sense of foreboding.

She sighed. Time to figure it out or she'd never have peace of mind. Still, she was reluctant to pursue that avenue without the protection of the crystal, not to mention while standing in the shower. The negative ion atmosphere created by water left her more vulnerable than she wanted to admit.

She blew air through her lips. *Time for a little ethereal investigating.* She closed her eyes, placed her hands over her solar plexus and began to reach out. She smiled and fought down a giggle. Every time she did this she was reminded of something one of her instructors had once said. *The same as what Obi Wan and Yoda taught.*

As corny as it sounded, she indeed followed in the footsteps of Luke Skywalker and stretched out with her feelings.

She started by psychically sweeping the energy of the camp, glad to be able to eliminate it as the source of the sinking feeling. Next, she projected herself to her family. Sensing nothing amiss, she psychically swept the families of her students, and then Dan's. Nothing. Sighing, she opened her eyes and turned into the spray. Well, that, at least, was good news.

Turning around again, she closed her eyes, let her hands fall to the sides, and mentally reached out, sweeping direction by direction until she felt it. There; a quiver, followed by a tightening in her gut; as if someone had slammed a fist into her stomach. Gritting her teeth against the pain, she continued pushing psychically against the energy, following it to its source, attempting to gauge the distance. It was north of where her camp was and north of the country they were in. For a moment her mind jumped to North America and the pain receded. She moved south to Mexico and the pain stayed at bay. She continued south until she felt the burning pain dramatically increase. Inhaling sharply, she fisted her hands and continued probing with her mind until she narrowed the field of energy to likely geographic candidates. Finally, she could stand the pain no longer.

Hugging herself, she made certain to cover her solar plexus and turned full into the shower spray. She grabbed the bottle of apple cider vinegar she kept in the shower and dumped its contents over her head, gasping as the icy liquid cascaded over her skin. She knew the smell would dissipate and the cold discomfort was a small price to pay for the psychic first aid it provided. She quickly finished rinsing and stepped out.

A disturbance in The Force? She smiled. Someday, she hoped to meet Mr. Lucas. She imagined he was a psychic himself and that his inspiration had come from personal experience, not just from some eastern religious ideology. It would certainly be a safe way of telling the world he was one of the many who walked this earth in touch with more than what the body's five basic senses fed in.

She sat down on the bed and did some deep breathing. God but that had hurt. Because she had been unable to diffuse the energy burst with the crystal, she'd suffered an onslaught of belligerent energy. It was as if she was being screamed at by someone standing less than three feet away. And worse, since she was a psychic sensitive, it didn't stop there. For her, the effects of being hit by such energy transmuted into painful physical sensations, as if her body was under attack. Which, she thought with a grimace, it was.

Feeling shaky, but better, she braided her hair and got dressed. Grabbing her book of maps from the kitchen cupboard, she sat down at the dining table and opened to the page that displayed South America. Whatever was going on had come from the northwest area of the continent. She placed her hand on her location in Chile and began tracing upward, closed her eyes and allowed any impressions to come through. She well understood the price she was about to pay but there was a need to know where the trouble was coming from. How could she protect the people who were her responsibility if she didn't know where to look for danger?

A prickly sensation ran up her finger, similar to when the circulation was returning after her foot fell asleep. Opening her eyes she saw that her finger was over Columbia. Well, no surprise there; Columbia was a land rife with problems, political and otherwise. Still, the sensation wasn't sharp enough. She looked at the countries around it. She slid her finger over Ecuador but nothing happened. She checked Peru but again, nothing. She frowned. Venezuela? She moved her finger over the country known for a troublesome ruler. Immediately, a burning sensation shot through her finger, straight up her arm, and into her shoulder.

"Jesus Christ, damn it," she hissed and jumped up off the chair. Dancing around the little area she shook out her arm. "Damn it," she yelled again, a hand clamped on her shoulder. She massaged her upper arm and hissed out a breath. She had to get control; she couldn't let anyone else see her like this. She glanced longingly at the crystal hanging in the sunshine but knew it was useless. It had been less than half a day; there was no way it would be of any benefit to her. Well, thankfully, over the years she had been able to build her own psychic first aid kit.

She walked to the bedroom and reached into the nightstand drawer, pulling out a little leather pouch that contained various stones and semi-precious gems. To her immense relief, the burning in her arm and shoulder stopped. She fastened the pouch to her belt and left the camper, not quite ready to go back to work but needing some fresh air.

CHAPTER SEVEN

Spiral notebook in her lap, diet Coke in hand, Kaila sat cross-legged beneath the covers, ready to tackle some of the administrative loose ends. They were just about finished with the cataloguing and needed to arrange for the crates to be taken to the university research and analysis center in Santiago. She had a call in to the adjunct professor who had been assigned as a local sponsor. With any luck they would be clearing out in a week.

She pictured Dan sitting at his little campsite, paperback book and coffee for company. Some nights the students hung out with him long after the sun went down. Rarer still were the nights she would join them.

She smiled. Although she had had her reservations in the early days, Dan had proved to be an excellent member of the team. He was helpful, reserved judgment, and usually acquiesced to her decisions. He was also one of the quietest people she'd ever known and yes, that unnerved her, but not as much as another issue she had with him. She couldn't read him.

All her life, Kaila had been able to pick up on the energies and emotions of those around her. It was a nuisance more often than not, like not being able to turn down the static on a radio, but as she had matured, she'd learned to manage the more challenging aspects of the unusual ability, and had learned to live with it. She had become so used to the constant background noise of other people that when it was absent, the silence was almost deafening. So, when she realized that she was unable to pick up anything at all from Dan Foster, she became curious, then mystified, then uneasy.

So much so that she went out of her way to try and get a read on him. She spent more time than usual in his presence and had even arranged to *accidentally* brush up against him, but no matter what she did, she was unable to get a solid feel for what made up Dan Foster outside using the same tools that belonged to the average human being.

It wasn't the first time she had met someone she couldn't read but it was the first time that she spent any great length of time around them. Usually, if someone was a blank slate, she tended to avoid them and the unease that went with being around such a person. It creeped her out, as if they were a type of zombie or walking vacancy where a person should have been. Well, maybe that would make it all the easier when they had to say good-bye next week. She wouldn't have his residual energy to deal with, only the memory of him.

But that was bad enough, wasn't it? Not being able to read his energy hadn't precluded her from noticing even the smallest details, such as the fact that while his eyes were blue, they were actually three distinct shades of blue. A thin ring of grey surrounded a vivid sea blue while a darker blue encircled his iris. There was the Special Forces tattoo that disappeared beneath his New England Patriots t-shirt, a freckle just to the bottom left of it, and then there was the fact that when he got overtired, he walked with a slight limp; what she guessed was the result of an old knee injury.

He liked his coffee black and his bagels lightly toasted, complaining that they scraped the roof of his mouth otherwise. He was originally from a fishing village in Maine, joining the Air Force in order to escape that life, choosing to become a pilot instead of a fisherman.

"I wanted the wind beneath my feet, not just ruffling through my hair," he'd explained.

Every morning, once he made sure everything was secure, he went through a series of workouts that included a five mile run. He'd lamented not having access to weights like he had on the base, but admitted that he was still challenged by the creative options the wilderness around them provided.

From what Kaila could see, his physique hadn't suffered any since his retirement.

Standing just under six feet, Dan Foster was solidly packed. His biceps, triceps and pecs rippled and moved in a kind of muscular symphony that appealed to her baser instincts. His back narrowed down to a sexy v at his waist and she had to stop herself from being too obvious about being outside when he just happened to be returning from his morning run since he usually had his shirt off by then.

No, energy read or not, there were a great many things she was going to miss about Dan Foster.

Shaking her head, she set the soda can on the night table, picked up a pen and started to make a list of what had to be finished before they could quit camp. She hadn't gotten very far when someone hammered on the camper door. In one fluid motion she rolled out of bed and grabbed up her robe.

"It's Theresa," Derek said, his hair sweat plastered to his head.

"What's the matter?" she asked, pushing past him and running toward the other trailer.

"I don't know, but she's in bad shape. She's all curled up in a ball and she's in terrible pain."

Kaila pushed her way to the front of the trailer where a double bed had been crammed. Sitting on the edge of the mattress, she reached out to feel the young woman's forehead. She frowned as her hand came into contact with heat. Beads of perspiration rolled between her fingers and the student's temples.

"Theresa?" she asked softly, "what's the matter? Where does it hurt?"

In response, the young woman groaned and rolled tighter into herself.

"When did this start?"

Hal was sitting on the other side of the mattress, rubbing the ailing student's back. "She started moaning in her sleep about an hour ago," he said, worry etched in his features.

"Is it her stomach?"

"No, I don't think so, but it's tough to be definitive. She won't let me touch her."

"What's the matter?"

Kaila glanced over her shoulder. Dan was standing in the aisle, a solemn expression on his face.

"I'm trying to figure that out."

He stepped closer. In his experience, people in pain often responded better to direct orders than sympathy.

"Theresa, what's the problem?" he asked, his tone cold but not forceful.

Three sets of eyes burned into him but he kept going.

"Theresa, answer me."

"I don't know," she wailed, "it hurts." As if to emphasize that obvious fact, she groaned and rolled away from him.

Knowing he was risking Kaila's wrath, he gently took hold of her shoulders and eased her away from the bed. Grateful that she didn't protest, he sat in her place and spoke with the voice of authority.

"Is it your stomach?"

"No," she ground out.

"I think it's lower," Hal suggested, "but like I said, she won't let me touch her."

"Theresa," Dan commanded, "you have to roll onto your back. You have to let me examine you."

"No," she cried, and pushed further into the mattress, as if she could melt into it and disappear.

"Hal, help me," he said, and reached out to roll her over. His mouth set in grim determination, he worked silently, reminded of when he was a kid and had tried to move water bugs to places safer than the sidewalks near his home. They always rolled into a tight little ball, making it extremely difficult to relocate them without causing injury. Finally, the two men were able to get her onto her back, although she had her knees drawn to her chest.

"Do you have a history of ovarian cysts?" he asked.

"No," she moaned, pushing his hands away. "Please, don't. It hurts too much."

"Theresa, I will do my best to be gentle but I have to see what's going on. I'm going to press down on your lower right side."

"No," she shrieked and slapped at his hands.

"Okay," he agreed, not wanting her hysterical. He looked over at Hal. "Has she ever had her appendix out?"

"No."

"I think that's what we're dealing with. Regardless, we need to get her to a hospital."

"I'll take her," Hal spoke up immediately.

"I'll go with you," Derek put in, "and I'll drive. You can hold her in your lap in the backseat."

"I'd tell you to use the Jeep, but given the amount of pain she's in, I don't think she'd enjoy the ride," Kaila said. "I think you should take the car."

"Good idea," Derek agreed.

Dan looked down at the young woman, then over at Hal. "I'll carry her to the car and will hand her over to you once you're inside. Derek, grab whatever you think she'll need and follow." He slid his arms beneath the blanket and stood, lifting her. "Theresa, can you put your arms around my neck? I'm going to carry you to the car. I'll be as gentle as I can. Thatta girl."

By the time he made it to the car with the groaning student, Kaila had already opened both driver side doors and was putting the key in the ignition. Hal slid into the back seat and reached out as Dan gently handed the still moaning woman over.

"Okay, I have everything here," Derek said, running up. He tossed a bag into the front seat and slid behind the wheel.

"Call me the minute you know anything," Kaila said, stepping back from the car. "Take care of each other."

"Will do," Derek called, pulling the door shut and speeding away from the dig site.

"Are you okay?" Dan asked, setting a hand on her shoulder.

"You were really great with her. It was clear she wasn't responding to me at all."

He smiled. "It was your tone of voice; too motherly. Come on, let's get you back inside."

"No."

"No? It's almost midnight. Listen, they'll call when they know something but -."

"Too wound up. I need to walk it off. If I go to bed now I'll toss and turn all night. If I find a way to get rid of this energy then I'll be able to sleep. Walking is one the best ways I can accomplish that."

"Kaila, it's dark and -."

"Take me on a walk of the perimeter with you."

"What?"

"You get up at night and walk the perimeter of the camp to make sure everything's fine. Let me go with you. If we walk it a few times I think I'll be able to get to sleep."

"Okay, let me go get the flashlight."

After ditching the robe and changing into jeans, she joined him at the door of her trailer. They walked in silence for twenty minutes.

"How are you doing? Feel any better?"

"A little," she replied. "Are you tired? I think I can do this myself now."

"I'm not leaving you to walk around this camp in the dark. I can handle a few more rounds. Shoot, I'll be able to sleep through the two am shift."

After another thirty minutes she was ready to return to the trailer. "Okay, let's -," but she stopped. The sound of tires squealing and an engine roaring carried to where they were standing at the far end of the camp. In the dark she grabbed Dan's hand. "Who the hell is that? Derek wouldn't have come back for the jeep; I know the car is full of gas since I filled it up myself yesterday, before I came back from town."

"Come on," he whispered, "let's move further back."

Doors slammed and a cacophony of male voices carried to where they were hiding in the bushes.

"Can you understand what they're saying?" Dan whispered.

"It's a bunch of gibberish," she replied. "If I didn't know better, I'd say they were drunk."

"We need to get out of here."

Kaila's heart was pounding. "I have to get something out of the trailer first."

"Are you out of your mind?" he hissed into the dark, grateful that the men were going off as if they were at a rock concert.

"I have to have it," she said and took off in the direction of the camper. She only got about twenty yards when Dan tackled her to the ground. Without saying anything she turned on him, a feral cat in a fight for its life.

"Whoa," he said, holding her hands above her head and throwing all his weight on her, "easy now. Just take it easy."

It required great effort to keep Kaila Ross in his grip. He guessed she weighed all of one hundred and twenty-five pounds, but all of it must have been muscle and all of it was working at escaping him. He tightened his grip and locked his legs around hers, no small feat as they were flailing at him.

"I'll get it," he said, a little breathless. "Tell me what it is you have to have and I'll get it." She didn't stop thrashing. "I promise. Will you stop fighting me?"

"You promise?" She eyed him warily; her knee ready to do bodily harm.

"Yes. What is it and where the hell is it?"

"It's hanging in the window facing south."

"The one near the kitchen?"

"Yes. It's on a hook that is suctioned to the window."

"Okay. What is it?"

"It's a necklace."

"*A necklace?* You want me to risk my life for a necklace?"

"Either you go or I do, take your pick."

Without commenting, he moved silently into the dark, toward the trailer.

CHAPTER EIGHT

Kaila wasn't particularly surprised when Tim Brightman asked that she come to the embassy to make a formal report about the attack on her dig. He assured her that the mayor was unaware of the situation and promised that there wouldn't be a big production made. No one wanted this kind of news to be broadcast, and in any event, it rarely accomplished anything other than trouble.

"When should I expect you?"

"It'll take me at least three hours just to get to the edge of town," she answered, "and I'm not even dressed yet." She mentally calculated. "I would say mid to late afternoon."

"I'll go ahead and reserve a room for you at the Sheraton."

"You don't have to do that."

"I don't, but it's no trouble. If you should decide you don't want to drive back in the dark, you'll have a place to stay."

"And if I don't stay?"

"It's not a problem. The embassy has a retainer with several of the area hotels. They typically keep three or four rooms and one suite available for last minute needs. If we end up canceling, it doesn't matter since the room is already paid for, regardless."

"Then I accept. I'll see you later."

She disconnected the call and walked to the door. She could see Dan's campsite clearly in the early morning light. Clear enough to see that he wasn't in his bedroll.

"Looking for me?" he asked, coming around a corner of the trailer.

She jerked back, a hand to her heart.

"I'm sorry. I shouldn't have done that, especially given what happened last night. Can I come in?"

She opened the door and stepped aside so he could enter. As he walked past, he brushed against her robe, and a shiver ran down her spine. He gave her a bland stare and continued into the living room where he sat down on the hide-a-bed sofa. She took the chair directly opposite, her hands between her knees.

"How are you doing?"

"I'm fine," she replied, stoically.

"I checked the entire site. Although it's been vandalized, as far as I can tell, nothing was taken."

She sat silently, digesting that information and fighting a chill. Telling herself it was just the early morning air, she pulled her robe more tightly around her.

"Pretty damned odd that they didn't steal anything," she said at last. "I thought for sure they were locals looking to make a buck on the black market by selling a few of the artifacts."

"I also think it's odd that they chose the one night when it was just the two of us onsite to attack."

She waved a hand dismissively. "I wouldn't read too much into that if I were you. They had probably been scoping the place out, waiting for an opportunity to present itself. When the crew left for the hospital, they saw the opportunity."

"And if they'd stolen some of the artifacts I would be agreeing with you right now," he replied. "The fact that they didn't says more is going on here than what first appears."

"Any ideas?"

"None. You?"

She drummed her fingers on the arm of the chair. "No. We've been here for the past two months and so far no one has expressed any displeasure, covertly or otherwise, about our being here. Locals are usually pretty happy to see archeologists nearby. Not only do we spend money on the local economy, we often bring fame and sometimes unforeseen wealth with a discovery. It isn't always the case, of course, especially when we're in hostile territory, but Chile hardly falls into that category."

She leaned back and began to cross one leg over the other but stopped when she saw Dan's expression. She smiled.

"Don't worry, I'm not gonna pull a Sharon Stone on you."

He looked at her blankly.

"You know, *Basic Instinct*?"

His brows furrowed.

"The movie?" she prompted, incredulous.

"Never saw it."

For a full minute she just stared at him. "I wouldn't go spreading that around if I were you. If word gets out, your Special Forces buddies will disavow any knowledge of you."

"Hmm, that important, eh?"

"That macho, eh."

"Maybe I ought to go into town, see if there's a Blockbuster."

She smiled. "Or you could just search the Internet. I'm sure there's a clip of that scene out there, on YouTube or something."

"I'll give that some thought," he replied.

"I talked with Tim Brightman. He wants me to come to the embassy to make a report."

"Makes sense," he agreed.

"If I want to get back before dark, I'd better leave before too long. Do you want me to bring anything back for you? Santiago is a modern city with all the amenities from home, more or less."

"No thanks, I have everything I need." He stood. "I'll let you get ready so you can be on your way."

She stood, ready to walk him out. To her surprise, instead of going toward the door he came right up to her. She tried to calm her heart which had chosen that moment to gallop against her chest. He reached into his pocket, slowly drew something out. She held her breath as he leaned forward, his hands going behind her. She worked to keep her breath steady, focusing on the little wing of hair that stuck out over his ear, even as the feathery touch of his fingers on the back of her neck threatened to send her into orbit. Out of an unconscious habit, she licked her lips. When his fingers slid between the folds of her robe she inhaled sharply.

"You wanted this badly enough to be willing to risk your life for it," he said softly, grasping the crystal. His knuckles, calloused, brushed against her chest as he studied it. "I assume this is where it belongs?" He released it and lowered his hand to his side.

Unable to find her voice, she simply nodded. For several seconds he stared at the pendant as it lay between her breasts. "It's not from an old flame," she said at last, her voice coming out rusty, as if she hadn't used it in a long time. She cleared her throat. "In case that's what you were thinking."

"Why would I think that?" he replied, his eyes still on the necklace.

"You're a guy, aren't you?" she answered, her voice steadier this time.

He gazed at her. "What does that have to do with anything?"

She smiled. He reminded her of a little boy trying to hide a frog in a pocket from his mother. "Any man who has the guts to do what you just did, putting your fingers inside my robe like that, has enough proprietary in him that it would be one of the first things that would come to his mind."

He grinned and she noticed he didn't seem in any hurry to let her get ready.

"And if I did have this proprietary as you put it, would that bother you?"

"You're still here, aren't you?"

"So, that means you won't mind if I do this." Before she could blink, he'd put a hand to her neck and drew her to him, his mouth closing over hers.

Kaila put her hands on his shoulders and allowed herself to free fall into his embrace, her mouth opening beneath his. She laughed inwardly as their tongues tangled in each other's mouths. Even in passion they fought for control. She leaned her body into him and happily gave in. This was one time she had no need to be in charge.

He trailed hot kisses down her neck, pushing her robe off her shoulders as he went. She tilted her head back, giving him access to the base of her throat and silently directing him lower. When his mouth closed over her already erect nipples, she dropped her chin to her chest and watched him.

She slid one hand beneath her breast and put the other on his shoulder, guiding him. He backed off for a moment, glanced up at her.

"I like a woman who knows what she wants," he said, and went back to sliding his tongue over her nipples, first one, then the other. Finally, he pulled her breasts together with his hands and put his mouth over both, alternating his tongue with his teeth.

"God," she hissed, then moaned. She shrieked in surprise when he suddenly grabbed her up, wrapped her legs around his waist and carried her toward the kitchen. He set her on the counter, leaned forward and again took her breasts into his mouth.

Having other ideas, she grabbed his shoulders and pushed him back.

"What?" he asked, momentarily confused.

She locked her legs around him and leaned forward, kissing him passionately while her hands slid beneath his t-shirt. "You have the most incredible chest," she whispered, sliding the shirt up over his head. She lightly bit his neck, then his left shoulder, continuing lower until her tongue was over his left nipple. Closing her mouth, she sucked it between her teeth, smiling when he hissed and fisted his hands in her hair.

"Like that, do you?"

"Jesus Christ," he ground out.

"Hmmm, I like a man who says what he likes."

Beside her the cell phone began to ring. They pulled away from each other and Dan handed her the phone even as she turned to grab it.

"Hola." She looked at Dan. "It's Tim Brightman," she whispered. "Anything wrong, Tim?" Across from her, Dan frowned, leaned forward. Understanding, she held the phone away from her ear so he could listen.

"Not at all. I was wondering if you wanted me to have a meal waiting for you at the embassy. I know you've been roughing it and I thought you might like something hot to eat for a change."

Kaila and Dan both smiled, relieved it was nothing serious. Even as she made to answer him, Dan slid his fingers beneath her robe and began to massage her thighs.

"Actually, Tim, it looks like I'm not going to make it this afternoon. In point of fact, I'm not sure exactly when I'll be able to get to the embassy. I hope that's not going to be too much of an issue?"

There was a slight pause. "No, not at all. Is there a problem, Dr. Ross?"

"Please, call me Kaila, and no, there's no problem. It's just that with the students at the hospital I don't want to leave Dan alone. Not when it was three men who ransacked this place."

"Would you like me to send someone out there?"

"No," she answered a little too quickly. She let out a breath. "I mean, that won't be necessary. I'm pretty sure we're safe enough. The local police are aware of what happened and have been driving by periodically to make sure everything's okay. I just don't want to leave Dan out here by himself."

At that moment, he was sliding his fingers between the warm folds of her body, gently spreading the hot wetness with his thumb.

Tim's voice brought her to the present. "I understand. Any idea when one of the students might be back at the site?"

She ignored the sensations surging through her as Dan began massaging that magical nub that held the answer to a woman's sexual release.

"I got a voicemail from Derek," she replied, grateful her voice held steady. "They took out Theresa's appendix and so far so good. They're planning on having her walk around this evening. If everything goes well with that, he'll come back right after, since Hal is with her."

"So, we should see you the day after that?"

"Yes. I'll leave first thing in the morning once I know everything is secure, which means I'll be at the embassy by mid afternoon. If you want to have a meal for me, I would greatly appreciate it."

"Any requests?"

"I love Italian."

"Just give me a call when you leave so I know to expect you."

"Thanks, Tim." She clicked off the phone and widened her legs, giving Dan better access. "Mm, now, where were we?"

He moved his fingers faster even as he leaned down and once again pulled a taut nipple into his mouth. She threw her head back and fisted her hands. If she'd been in bed, she would have grabbed the sheets for leverage. She grabbed the faucet and pushed her body into his hand, moving in harmony against his fingers. Faster and faster they moved, until the familiar throbbing rolled over her, followed by a flood of warmth as she came.

"Wow," he breathed.

She reached down and grabbed his hand, thrusting herself forward and moving against it at a frantic pace, not stopping until the moment of painful pleasure receded. It had taken every shred of self-control she possessed to stop short of throwing the man to the floor, ripping his pants off, and impaling herself on him.

"So, what should we do about you?" She traced a finger down his chest and kissed him lingeringly.

"Well, I -."

Tires crunched on gravel and they both froze.

"You've got to be kidding," she hissed, even as Dan was moving to the door. She jumped from the kitchen counter but had to grab it when her legs almost gave out. She looked up at the sound of laughter. "Very funny. Don't be cocky."

"Pun intended?   Anyway, Derek's back.   Throw me my shirt, will you?"

She tossed it at him and pulled the sash of her robe tighter.

"I'll go talk to him if you want to get dressed."

"I'm going to take a shower, so I may be awhile."

"Right."

CHAPTER NINE

"You really didn't need to go to all this trouble just for me, Tim," Kaila said, twirling fettuccine against a spoon, "but I'm glad you did. This is incredible."

"It was no trouble and besides, this way I get to eat as lavishly as you," he replied, sipping a glass of Carmenere.

"Well, I have to admit, it's nice to have a civilized meal."

"Work going rough?"

"No, actually we're about wrapped up."

"So, the ambush didn't set you back?"

"No," she answered, sighing. "We're actually very lucky in that way. In the end, there was only some minor vandalism. Maybe Dan scared 'em off, I don't know. They didn't steal anything and they didn't really do any damage."

"Sounds kind of strange."

Kaila had arrived at the embassy earlier that afternoon to file a report about the attack on her archeology dig and, won over by Tim Brightman's persuasive charm, had agreed to stay for an early dinner. They sat at a small table in the garden behind his office, a personal server making sure they had everything they needed, including timely refills of their wine glasses.

"Yeah, I'm guessing they were young kids and perhaps were even put up to the stunt. I can't think of any other explanation for why they didn't steal any artifacts."

"Be thankful for small miracles."

"You aren't kidding."

They spent the rest of the meal engaged in pleasant conversation.

"Dessert?"

"No," she answered, patting her flat abdomen, "I'm stuffed. That was incredible; my compliments to your chef."

"We are considering calling him the miracle worker. Listen, I went ahead and reserved a room for you."

"I appreciate that. Now that I've had a couple of glasses of the grape I think it might be a good idea to take you up on the offer."

"Excellent. I'll even have our driver drop you at the Sheraton in a little while."

Something about the way he'd said it gave her pause. Butterflies lit in her stomach and she was grateful she was wearing the pendant.

"There's another reason I'm here, isn't there?"

"I didn't bring you here under false pretenses, Kaila. I really did need you to fill out that report."

"But -?"

"But, by what can only be called a divine coincidence, I was contacted a few days ago by an affiliate organization, inquiring if I knew of your whereabouts."

"An affiliate organization; that's a clever way to put it." Kaila closed her eyes, a sick dread washing over her. Without opening her eyes, she spoke. "Who's down here, Josh?"

"Yeah, as a matter of fact -."

She opened her eyes, stared at him. It was satisfying to note that his face was flushed. At least he felt a little ashamed by the underhandedness of not disclosing that the CIA was in town and would be joining them for a little *tete a tete*.

"Do you have clearance for this?"

"No, I won't be privy to the meeting. They're waiting for you in a conference room. I'll take you there and after the meeting is concluded, the driver will take you to your hotel."

She let out a heavy sigh and stood, offered her hand. "Thanks again for the meal, Tim. I do appreciate it, even if I'll probably wind up with heartburn by the time I crawl between the sheets tonight."

"Kaila, I'm sorry. I can see how much this distresses you. I wish there was some other way -."

She shook her head. "You know the drill, Tim. We all signed up for this when we joined, right? You can do me a favor, though."

"Anything."

"Call Dan Foster, let him know I'm staying over. See if he needs me to pick anything up for the camp. If the answer is yes, leave me a voicemail on my phone, okay?"

"Sure. Listen, Kaila, good luck. If there's anything I can do to help you out here -."

"Forget it. I know you feel bad enough about this. I guess what makes me feel the worst is that now you know."

"Kaila, I've known for six months."

She stared, speechless. He smiled.

"When we discovered the identities of everyone who had been kidnapped, we ran a background check as standard protocol. Your file came up classified so I did a little more digging."

"So, Dan knows?" Her stomach churned.

"No, and neither does the mayor. In fact, no one other than Agent Hernandez and myself know this."

"Juan found out?" *No wonder he had become so distant.* He probably felt she'd lied to him. Well, she thought sourly, she had, hadn't she? "I really didn't want *anyone* to know," she said, emphatically.

"Kaila? You may find this hard to believe, but I understand. That's why I never shared the information with Dan Foster, even though he actually has higher clearance than I do. Shoot, if he were here, he might be allowed in that conference room with you."

"No," she replied quickly, "he's retired."

"He still has clearance, Kaila, I checked."

"I don't want Dan to know," she pressed. "We're almost finished here and he'll be returning to the states, hopefully none the wiser."

He put an arm around her and guided her toward the sliding glass door that led into his office. "Come on, let's get you to that meeting. You know, Kaila, not everyone reacts badly when they learn the truth."

"Provided they're on the inside, sure. But I don't want anyone on the inside, Tim. I could never fully trust them and I would always feel like I was living a lie."

"You could trust Dan."

She stared at him and for a moment her heart stuttered. Had she and Dan been under surveillance?

"Kaila, I have an idea what you might be worried about; don't. The dig hasn't been under surveillance as far as I know, but Kaila? I do have eyes. I saw the two of you together back at that cabin in Talca."

"*Talca?* Tim, he and I were barely civil to each other back there. Hell, I nearly kicked his ass in what basically constitutes as a street fight."

Tim smiled. "You both were shell shocked, I admit, but I think it was more of a reaction caused by the instant and probably intense attraction you felt for each other."

Her mouth opened and closed as if she were a guppy.

"Here we are," he said, opening a door. "Now close your mouth. You look silly." He kissed her cheek and whispered in her ear. "It's going to be okay, I promise."

"Kaila, it's been awhile, how have you been?"

"Hey, Josh." Although she had tried to keep her voice light, she ended up sounding like a violin badly off key; at least to her ears.

"Kaila, I'd like you to meet Jack Porter. He's with the -."

"I know who Mr. Porter is," she cut in.

"You do?"

"His name was all over the paperwork that sent me to Afghanistan in 2003."

"Still," Jack said, coming forward, "we've never been formally introduced. It's a pleasure to meet you, Dr. Ross."

"I wish I could say the same, but I honestly thought you people understood how I left things after that mission. I meant what I said; it was my last."

"Dr. Ross, I am asking you to listen to what we have to say. If, after you hear us out, you still feel as passionately as you do at this moment, we can talk about it."

"You mean you'll threaten me, don't you? That's how it works, after all. You keep pushing until you find the button that sets me off and then you move in for the kill."

"Kaila," Josh interceded, "come over here and sit down."

"Hell, no," she snapped, "I'm not going to sit through this. You two sit down and I'll stand by that window over there, staring out at the night sky. I will not look at either one of you while you explain what the hell it is you're doing here." By keeping her back to them, she could prevent at least some of their energy from invading her system; could maintain her equilibrium; somewhat, anyway.

Ignoring the knowing glances the two men exchanged, she walked to the window and looked out. Keeping her back to the room, she crossed her arms, covering her solar plexus.

"Dr. Ross, I'm going to be completely honest with you," Jack Porter began.

She snorted. "That'd be a first."

"Those in authority sincerely believe that you are not only the most qualified person to handle this crisis, you are the *only one* who can handle it."

"Crisis," she scoffed, leaning her forehead against the window. Her eyes focused on the shadows outside. "It's always a crisis, isn't it?"

"Kaila," he said quietly, "what you did in Afghanistan prevented a blood bath."

"People died because of what we did out there, Jack, people with families." She knew only too well; she'd felt their last moments alive as if she had personally witnessed them. The deep remorse those victims felt over never being able to see loved ones again had just about been her undoing.

"Yes, people died. People die every day in the line of duty, Dr. Ross, and that is exactly what happened to those people. For every life lost there is huge regret but we have to move on. We have to continue."

She stared out the window and willed down the bile rising in her throat. She refused to look at him; either of them. *Heartless bastards.*

"Dr. Ross, are you familiar with the missile shield project in Europe?"

"Me, and anyone who reads the paper."

"A key component of the technology has been stolen, Dr. Ross, and is right now on its way into the hands of the enemy. If we aren't able to retrieve that technology before it's delivered, we're looking at a total collapse of that defense system. It would be as if we'd handed them the entire fucking blueprint."

As the last had been said with such unexpected passion, she turned.

"What is it?" she asked, her eyes on the man who had flown all the way from Washington to plead his case. "This piece of technology. What, exactly, is it?" Although she stood in what Michael Korda had referred to in his book as a position of power, she felt anything but mighty.

"It's part of the laser guiding system that detects the trajectory of incoming missiles and feeds it back to the defense computer. It's a very special component and it's rather small. In fact, it's so small we were able to hide it in a rather ingenious fashion."

"Not too ingenious, it would seem." she countered.

"It was ingenious enough," Josh snapped, but stopped when Jack raised a hand in warning.

Jack continued. "It really was pretty foolproof, Dr. Ross. So much so that we are left with only one possibility."

"Someone on the inside sold you out."

"Exactly."

"Any idea who?"

"As a matter of fact -," Josh started, but again, Jack Porter stayed him.

Now, wasn't that interesting? Josh was fairly high in the chain. If his superior was reining him in, the situation was probably worse than was being indicated; worse, and more dangerous.

"We have a pretty good idea where we lost the link in the chain, and even as I'm standing here asking for your help, we're working multiple avenues to mitigate the damage."

"So, who did it? Who stole your precious technology, and more to the point, why?"

"As to the why," Josh said, "we're pretty certain he's about to sell it to the highest bidder."

"As for the *who*," Jack took back over, studied her. "It's why we flew thousands of miles to speak with you in person, Dr. Ross. The man who took the technology is your old partner, Chad Kroeger."

Kaila's fingers went immediately numb as the name washed over her, bringing shockwaves of pain. Her ears began to ring and darkness descended as if someone were pulling a shade down over her eyes. The last thing she remembered was falling forward.

CHAPTER TEN

When Dan caught himself looking up the road for the umpteenth time he tossed the paperback aside and stood up. He'd gotten the voicemail from Tim Brightman; she'd decided to stay over, which actually should have made him feel better given the distance and the time of day, but damned if he wasn't way past disappointed and fully into pissed off territory.

Derek's arrival that morning had halted any further activity in the amorous department and while that alone would have put any guy in a sour mood, it was her absence alone that was grating at him. He missed her, damn it.

"Hey, Foster, can you help me with this?"

He turned to see Derek trying to get the leverage he needed to lift a crate filled with catalogued artifacts. He walked over, squatted down and helped him get it over to where the other crates were piled into a wagon.

"Thanks. If you could help me load these into the car, I can drive them into town and get them in the hands of the university contact."

"Sure." He followed Derek to the gravel path just off the main road that they were using as a parking lot.

"Do you want to take the Jeep? It might handle the road a bit better."

"No, thanks, but I'd rather keep these locked in the trunk. After what happened here I'd feel a whole lot better. In fact, that's why I'm meeting with the professor today instead of next week. I think we need to get as many of these artifacts as we can to the university as quickly as we are able. Are you going to be okay here by yourself? I can ask the professor to drive out here instead."

"No, you go on ahead. While you're in town, grab some diet Coke, okay? Kaila's out."

Derek smiled knowingly. "Will do." He climbed in the car and gave a little wave before driving off.

Dan walked the perimeter of the camp, actually glad to be alone with his thoughts. So far, everything had been quiet in the aftermath of the attack on the site. He shook his head. Nothing made sense about it other than the fact that Kaila was right, whoever had vandalized the area had probably been scoping the place out, waiting until there were only two of them in camp to strike. Dan might have been more concerned about being on his own if it had been night, but he had a feeling that the perpetrators wouldn't be back. No sooner was the thought completed; the sound of tires on gravel reached his ears.

"Jesus Christ, what now?" He crouched low and moved along the side of the camp until he was in a place where he could easily see the road, yet remain well hidden. A familiar black sedan pulled up. Senor Juarez had someone in the passenger seat. When the door opened and the man got out, Dan did a double take. "You have got to be kidding." He quickly left his hiding place and made his way to the car.

"General," he said, his voice all respect, "I have to say, this is the last place I ever imagined running into you."

General Murphy smiled. "Civilian life must agree with you, Foster, you didn't even salute."

"You didn't see my hand twitch, sir," he replied, smiling for the first time in several hours. He glanced over at the other man, nodded. "Juarez."

"Senor Foster," he replied, indifferently.

"Senor Juarez was kind enough to give me a lift out here to talk with you. Is there somewhere we can have some privacy?"

Dan's smile widened. He swept a hand back toward the camp. "Take your pick, sir. We happen to be the only ones here at the moment."

"I see. I won't take up much of your time."

"Juarez," Dan said, "can I offer you something to drink? There's some beer in the fridge."

The man nodded. "I would appreciate that, thank you."

The General waited until Juarez was seated with a beer and a magazine before following Dan to the camper.

"We can talk in here." He led his former boss to the living room.

"Nice," the General commented, sitting on the sofa.

"Yeah, this is where Dr. Ross hangs out. You saw my bedroll outside?"

"I'm sure you could find your way in here if you wanted to, though," he said meaningfully, and Dan laughed, thinking of the opportunity missed only that morning. Maybe it was a good thing that Derek had arrived when he had. It would have been terribly awkward had they been interrupted by Senor Juarez and the Special Forces commander.

"Sir, can I offer you a beer? Other than that, I'm afraid all we have is water."

"I'll take the beer, sure."

Dan grabbed two brews from the fridge and headed back to where the General looked fairly comfortable in jeans and a t-shirt. Handing him the bottle, Dan sat down in the chair facing him and tried not to think of Kaila's Sharon Stone remark as he set a booted ankle on the opposite knee.

"So, what has you leaving the comforts of the good ol' U S of A and how the hell did you know where to find me?"

"Dan, in spite of the casual dress, I'm on official business." He drank deeply of the beer. He stared at the bottle, his brows beetling. "I understood Chilean beer wasn't so great, that it was watery. This is good."

"It's imported," Dan replied, his entire body tense while he waited for the General to get through the small talk and tell him what was going on. Official business? It had to be bad. Dan was retired; the General knew that.

"Dan, I got a visit from Jack Porter earlier this week."

"What's that old hound up to now? Gotten himself into another mess he wants you to dig him out of?"

"Something like that."

"Something like that or that?"

The General nodded once and took another drag on the beer. "I feel like I'm in a goddamned Frederick Forsythe novel, to be truthful about it. I put in for an emergency leave, told them I had some vacation time coming up and was using it. I then had to ditch my official documentation and come down here as a civilian, turn myself in at the embassy and plead my case to a Tim Brightman in order to get an official ride out here so I could talk to you about unofficial bullshit I learned from a guy who was never there."

"And none of this ever happened and you were never here, right?"

"Got that right. If Porter knew I was here he'd have my ass handed to me by the president. Brightman about had apoplexy when I explained that while I was aware that Jack's organization was down here, I absolutely had to stay off their radar. I guess he was in a room across the hall at that very moment."

Dan laughed, picturing the efficient embassy agent actually losing his cool. "You will live dangerously, sir."

"Get me another one of these, will you? I think I'll need to finish that one before I'm able to get through this."

"Christ," Dan said, "then I'd better have another one too."

"How are you doing down here? Adjusting to retirement okay?"

"Still working your way around to it, eh?" Dan replied, prepared to wait until the ball was dropped.

"Actually, this goes right to the point. How are you adjusting to retirement?"

"Since this is a security assignment -." He shrugged.

"The powers that be in Washington had me put a stop on your paperwork. You haven't been processed."

"Are you telling me I'm still a member of the United States Air Force Special Services team? That I still report to that dickhead back at Hickam?"

"Yes, and no."

"Which?"

"Both, and in that order. Yes, you are still in the Air Force, but no, you don't report to Colonel Thomas. In fact, this is so officially unofficial, you are under the direct report of Jack Porter with a dotted line to me."

"I see."

"There's been an emergency."

"And you couldn't have picked someone else to do this? Someone who is still officially official?"

The General let out a deep sigh and held the empty bottle out. "Another, and make it quick. I've got to fill you in on everything that's going on and get myself back to Santiago, on a plane, and get the hell out of here, all without being seen by Jack Porter or any of his minions."

Dan sat across from the General and unscrewed the cap on the water he'd chosen instead of a third beer. "Spit it out, sir."

"A critical piece of technology that was slated for delivery to Lawrence Livermore Labs at Berkeley never made it and is on its way, if it isn't already there, to Venezuela."

"I see."

"It was an inside job."

"How was it done?"

"They hid the laser crystal in a pendant, like one of those you'd see at a New Age shop."

Dan nodded, thinking of the one that nestled between Kaila's breasts. She'd explained it had been a gift from her mother for her fourteenth birthday. She didn't explain why she was willing to risk her life to retrieve it when they were under attack, which rankled. He didn't like secrets.

"For reasons that are too complicated to go into, the pendant was actually supposed to be delivered by one of the operatives from Monterey."

"SRI guys?"

"No, but close enough. The guy was undercover at some occult store so he could keep an eye on it until it was picked up."

"It wasn't accidentally sold, was it?"

"No, the guy who worked at the store was a weak link. He left the country with it sixteen hours before it was scheduled for pickup."

"How certain are you Venezuela is the destination?"

"Relatively certain. At least, Jack Porter is. So much so that he had me halt the press on your orders and assign you to him. The problem was, he didn't intend to fill you in until long after I felt was appropriate."

"Still getting his ducks in a row?"

The General nodded. "The problem is, I was afraid that with all the unknowns, your life would be put in jeopardy and you would have no warning. I didn't want you ambushed."

Dan's body jerked to attention.

"Has something happened?"

"As it so happens, we were attacked last night."

"Attacked? Here?"

"Yes. One of the three students working the site came down with appendicitis and the other two drove her to the hospital for surgery. Kaila and I were alone when we were ambushed by three Hispanic men in their twenties."

"What did they do?"

"Other than vandalizing the place? Not much. Dr. Ross and I were out of sight when they arrived. I managed to get to my gun and scare them off simply by firing into the air and making a hell of a lot of noise. Definitely seemed amateurish based on that, but in light of what you're telling me, perhaps it was more?"

"A warning?" the General asked, staring out a window at the scenery.

"Kaila doesn't think so. She said the locals seem pretty happy that they're here and before last night, there was no hint of trouble. The fact that they didn't steal anything is definitely peculiar, but it also suggests they were scoping the place out. They seemed surprised by my presence, especially armed as I was, and they scrambled to get the hell out of here. We spent the rest of the night outside but they never came back. Derek, that's one of the students, left about twenty minutes before you showed up to take the majority of the artifacts to the local archeology professor for safe transport to the university."

"Do me a favor, will you, Foster?" the General said, rising and handing over the empty bottle.

"Anything."

"When you are finally contacted, act like you are completely surprised. If they don't tip you off that you are still in the service, don't let on that you know you are. I was never here. But most of all?"

"Sir?"

"Watch your ass, okay? My wife still expects you at my retirement party."

"And when will that be, sir?" he asked as he walked the man to the door.

"If Jack Porter keeps showing up on my doorstep? A hell of a lot sooner than I'd originally planned."

"Why don't you wait for me to let you know what civilian life is really like before you go that route."

"Good idea. Take care of yourself, Foster."

Bob Murphy made his way back to where Juarez waited to take him to the airport in Santiago. He'd done all he could for his friend. He hadn't told him more than he needed to know. For instance, he hadn't told him that Kaila Ross was a CIA operative about to be brought out of retirement, and he hadn't disclosed that the ambush of the previous evening had been paid for by the CIA to lure her to the US embassy. Shaking his head, he got into the car and tried not to think about what Dan would do when he eventually found out. There were few people on this earth Dan hated more than the CIA. After all, they'd been directly responsible for the death of his wife in Afghanistan's Hindu Kush in 2003.

CHAPTER ELEVEN

"Kaila?"

Something cold pressed down on her. A washcloth?

"Is she coming around?"

"I think so."

"Tim?" She swam up through a hazy grey.

"Yep, it's me. Can you sit up?"

"If you help me," she replied quietly.

"Sure." He slid his arm beneath her and lifted her forward. She was happy to see that he kept it there. She blinked several times, still coming to the surface of reality, such as it was.

"Here, drink this."

She eyed the cup, looked over at him. "What is it?"

"Tea; a very strong herbal tea. I made it myself. Drink it," he commanded.

She did. Not bad, she thought, and took another sip.

"Dr. Ross?"

Kaila looked around, trying to get her bearings. Ignoring the other two men in the room, she let Tim maneuver her so that she was supported by the sofa back. He spread a blanket over her lap, tucking it around her ankles and ensuring her feet were completely covered.

"How'd I get in your office?"

"I carried you," Tim replied.

"Thanks." She drank from the cup, thankful her hand was steady.

"Dr. Ross, I'm sorry."

Feeling stronger, she looked up into the eyes of Jack Porter. Josh Coldwell, her handler in the CIA, stood to the side, apparently resigned to the fact that the Washington man was in charge when it came to interacting with her.

"I had no idea -," he continued, his hands out in entreaty.

"You've read my file."

"Black and white ink doesn't translate, Dr. Ross."

She thought back to her hands on the map of South America; how the information caused physical pain. Perhaps for some it didn't translate, but Porter should have understood. She'd worked for him for years, he'd had numerous reports on her abilities, how she'd done in tests, how she'd performed in the field. He should have known.

"Kaila, we need you to understand the gravity of this situation -," the handler began.

"I think Kaila Ross more than understands," Tim retorted. He was sitting on the couch, her hand in his. "In fact," he hurried on when it appeared Josh was about to open his mouth again, "she understands in a way neither of you ever will."

"Be that as it may," Josh snapped, clearly sizing Tim up, "we need to discuss -."

"Later." Tim stood, moved closer to the handler. "As of now, this meeting is adjourned until tomorrow morning at oh nine hundred hours."

"You have no authority -," Josh complained.

Instead of answering, Tim took two steps toward the shorter agent, his eyes menacing.

For several seconds the two men took each other's measure.

"This is the US embassy," Tim uttered quietly, his tone leaving no room for comment. "Kaila Ross is under my protection. I am granting her asylum -."

"That won't be necessary," Jack said, his tone just a hair above condescending.

"It most certainly is, and if I have to have the two of you placed under arrest in order to protect her, I won't think twice."

"Do you know who you're dealing with?" Josh asked, incredulous. At his side, he curled and curled his fingers.

"I know full well who I'm dealing with, Mr. Coldwell, it's you who doesn't."

Although the statement had been directed at the handler, Tim's eyes were locked on Jack Porter, pure challenge in them.

"We'll see you both at nine tomorrow morning," the Washington man said at last. At the door, he turned. "I hope you're feeling better soon, Dr. Ross. Good night and rest well."

Once the men were gone, Kaila let out a shaky laugh.

"Remind me never to cross you, Tim. My knight in shining Armani."

"Actually, it's Bill Blass." He sat down and took the now empty mug from her. "You feeling a little stronger?"

"I am, thanks." She rubbed her eyes with the palms of her hands. "Thanks for chasing those bastards outta here."

He smiled.

"Are you going to get in trouble for that?"

"No, though I think I just got crossed off Coldwell's Christmas card list."

Her laugh was a little stronger this time.

"I'm going to take you to the hotel. Can you walk or would you like me to carry you?"

"I can walk on my own, thanks." They were brave words spoken in folly. The moment she'd taken two steps she began to fall, and would have if Tim hadn't been there to catch her.

"Let's try that again, shall we?" He set her on the couch and grabbed a nearby phone, speaking quietly.

"Put your arms around my neck," he directed.

"Maybe if I wait a few more minutes -?"

"Do it, Kaila. We're leaving."

He carried her out of his office and down a series of hallways, finally kicking open a door that led directly into an underground garage. A black sedan with tinted windows was just outside the door. A man in uniform with a telltale bulge under his jacket opened the back door and Tim got in, never letting her out of his arms.

"You can put me down now."

"Not a chance," he replied, and said nothing further until they got to the Sheraton San Cristobal.

"I already called Roberto," he told the driver. "We're all set," he added cryptically.

"You aren't planning to carry me through the lobby, are you?"

He grinned. "We'll just say we're newlyweds." He laughed at her expression. "Horrified at the thought? Hmm, I'd better work on my charm. Seriously, we're being taken around to the back. There's a service elevator that will take us where we need to go. Trust me, you're in good hands, Dr. Ross."

"Don't call me that. I like Kaila; it's my name."

"You have Porter calling you doctor."

She smiled but before she could say anything further, a man in uniform opened the car door.

"Good evening, Mr. Brightman, Ms. Ross. Welcome to the Sheraton San Cristobal."

Kaila's wobbly smile conveyed her great discomfort with the situation. "Thank you," she said quietly, wishing she could bury her face in Tim's sweater. They weren't that close, however.

"Get Ms. Ross' bag from the trunk, please, Roberto."

"Right away, Mr. Brightman. Everything is as you requested."

"Excellent. Thank you, Roberto." He looked over at the driver. "Have the car sent for us tomorrow morning, at eight thirty."

"Yes, sir."

Once in the elevator, Tim slid an electronic key into a slot and pressed a button.

"You didn't?"

"I most certainly did, and with pleasure. After what the US government put you through tonight, you've earned it."

"Well, I have to say, Tim, you've more than made up for your part in this nightmarish play."

"Hey, I didn't say what I put you through. I was telling the truth earlier; that they happened to call right before you did is pure coincidence. I'm the victim here, as I've been put in the middle of all this crap."

"Victim?"

"I have to sit there, in my very own office no less, and watch a three ringed circus where two lions attempt to attack the beautiful assistant. I have to put pieces of this puzzle together without really knowing what the hell this is all about and knowing that I probably never will. Not your average day at the embassy."

"Hmm, maybe not at the embassy," she replied, smiling, "but in your life? Somehow, I suspect so. In fact, I'd be willing to bet on it. There's more to you than you let on, methinks."

Once Roberto had delivered her bag, Tim threw the bolt on the penthouse suite security door and turned to where Kaila stood looking around her. She wore an expression that was half bewilderment, half appreciation.

"Go in there," he ordered, pointing toward the main bedroom, "take off your clothes and get in bed. I'll be in there in a minute."

"Now, wait just a -."

"Get in there," he ordered, and though he hadn't raised his voice, it was clear he intended to have his command obeyed. "Strip down to your underwear and climb in bed."

He slid a finger beneath her shirt collar, lifted the chain.

"Does this bother you? I can put it in some salt water. It should be good to go by morning."

Kaila's eyes widened. "You -." She swallowed. "You're like me."

He slid the index finger of his right hand beneath his own collar and lifted a heavy gold chain, jiggling it. "I'm a member of the club," he confirmed, "but I'm not the same as you."

For several seconds she stared at him, turning over what she'd just learned. Finally, she reached behind and undid the clasp and handed over the necklace. "I feel so naked without it."

"That's a good start," he replied, his voice empty of any humor. "Now, get in there and strip down to your underwear while I put this in the solution."

She walked toward the bedroom and its king bed.

"And take off your bra," he yelled after her.

Ten minutes later he pulled the covers aside and slid in behind her. "I see you don't follow orders," he observed, and began undoing the clasp on her bra. She started to turn but he easily held her still. "Trust me."

"Tim, I'm not having sex with you."

"No, you're not. That won't be necessary. I can still help you. Now, be quiet, take this off, and let me." He waited while she slid her bra off and tossed it to the floor. "Now, scoot over and stay on your side like that, facing away from me."

"What are you going to do?"

"Kaila, please trust me." He kept his voice soft. "I haven't hurt you before now and I'm not going to. I kept my boxers on." He slid his body forward, his bare chest sealing warmly against her back so that there was complete skin to skin contact. Immediately, all the tension went out of her.

"Wow," she whispered into the dark.

He slid one arm beneath her and the other over her, bringing his hands together to rest on top of where hers were clasped over her solar plexus.

"Now," he whispered into her ear, "relax into me and let go."

After several minutes, just when he thought she'd fallen asleep, she spoke.

"How did you do that?"

He smiled into her hair. "That's my gift, Kaila, my ability. I'm a psychic healer. I can diffuse the pain left by psychic onslaught. I'm also an intuitive, like you, though not nearly as strong or sensitive. The wire in your bra would have interfered, which is why I had you take it off."

"Thank you. What you did, however you did it, it really helped. I'm still tired, but I'm no longer in pain."

"Good night, Kaila."

The next morning, Kaila found herself tightly wrapped in Tim's embrace, her head nestled between his shoulder and his jaw. They were skin to skin but instead of feeling turned on, she felt restored and whole again. For awhile she was content to lay there, eyes closed, a smile on her face, absorbing the healing sensations that cascaded through her. He truly had the touch.

"That's a beautiful sight to see first thing in the morning."

She opened her eyes and smiled up at him. "Good morning."

"Good morning yourself. That's quite a smile."

She let out a contented sigh. "I don't remember ever waking up in the arms of a handsome man, not having had sex, and yet still feeling this good."

He laughed and sat up, bringing her with him as he maneuvered them back against the headboard. He kept an arm around her, his embrace more affection than anything else.

CHAPTER TWELVE

"We will miss you and the students, and of course, Senora Ross," the Chilean grocer said from behind the counter.

"I hope we weren't too much trouble for the town?" Dan asked as he paid for the gas.

"Not at all. You spent money at my station and my market, and you gave our townspeople something to look forward to in their day, outside of the ordinary. You could do me a favor, however."

"Sure, what is it?"

"Could you take the rest of this off my hands?" He pointed to where a couple of cases of diet Coke were stacked on the floor. "Senora Ross is the only reason we carried it and now that she is leaving, I'm afraid I will be stuck with it forever."

Dan laughed and slid more cash across the counter. "I'm happy to take it off your hands."

"Thank you. It was a pleasure doing business with you. Please give my best to Senora Ross and wish everyone a safe journey."

"Will do."

Dan took a look around before getting in the car. He would miss the small town, he realized. It had been a peaceful little slice of the planet with people who were happy to see him, who didn't care that he was American, and who had had only good things to say about the country he was from. As he was Special Forces, it had been too long since he'd had such an experience on foreign soil. He was about to turn the key in the ignition when he caught sight of Senor Juarez pulling into the town's only gas station. There were two men with him and Dan sighed as they pulled up alongside. This must be the contact the General had flown some five thousand miles to advise him of. He waited patiently in the Jeep. Juarez stayed just long enough for the contact to reach Dan's car before driving away with his other passenger.

Well, well, well, so the old hound dog himself had shown up to deliver the assignment. *Must be more of a crisis than Murphy let on.* Dan made sure the doors were unlocked. When Jack Porter got in, he drove off toward a café at the edge of town. The place was pretty much always deserted at this time of day so the two men would be able to talk in relative privacy. Neither of them spoke until each was seated with a drink, his water, Jack's, coffee.

"Major Foster," the man started.

"Not anymore."

"Actually, still."

So, they were going to tell him that at least.

"Oh? Brad Thomas miss me that much?"

The other man smiled and slid a manila folder across the table. Dan picked it up and read through the contents.

"I didn't realize the CIA drafted people."

"According to the President of the United States, you are still a member of our armed forces. Until he releases you from that duty, you report, ultimately, to him, as Commander in Chief. Since he has more pressing matters than overseeing your day to day duties, he has asked that I be put in charge. I'm here to give you your orders."

"And if I refuse?"

"You haven't even heard what it is yet."

"I have a pretty good assignment right now. I'm guessing that whatever you have in mind doesn't include a beautiful woman and probably *does* include my ass getting shot at. Somehow, that just doesn't seem to measure up." Dan sipped at his water.

"Well, you're wrong about one part of that," he answered, his smile almost feral.

"I won't get shot at?"

"It comes with a beautiful woman. In fact, the very same beautiful woman you are helping right now, Dr. Kaila Ross."

Dan's entire body jerked. "Kaila's involved in this?"

"Let's just say that Dr. Ross is going to be your cover."

"You're putting an innocent out as my cover?"

"There is a professor in the anthropology department at the University of Caracas who needs some help cataloging aboriginal artifacts recently brought in from Cubagua. They have petitioned for Dr. Ross to assist since she has an expertise in pre-Columbian antiquities of the area."

"What is Cubagua, some sacrificial temple in the middle of a Venezuelan Rainforest?"

"An uninhabited island located off the coast of Venezuela; its role in archeological history is profound. They need Dr. Ross and we need you in Caracas."

"What do you need me in Caracas for?"

"A valuable piece of weapons technology has been stolen and is being auctioned to the highest bidder. Our information tells us that the auction is to be held in Caracas this week. We want you there."

"To bid on the thing?"

"To steal it back for us."

"And apprehend the bad guy?" he inquired, his tone mocking.

"No, we actually aren't as concerned about Dr. Kroeger at this point. We simply want that technology back in the hands of the US government."

"What is it, this technology that I'm supposed to steal?"

"Part of a photonic crystal laser."

"Never heard of it."

"The technology is based on nano-structures -."

Dan held up his hand. "When you start talking nano technology, I start thinking of Michael Crichton's *Prey.*"

"Let's stay on the ground, shall we, Major Foster?"

"So, just how am I supposed to find this stolen technology, and more importantly, what am I supposed to do with it once it's in my possession? Venezuela isn't exactly the friendliest or the safest place for Venezuelans, let alone an

American soldier who has something I'm guessing old Hugo himself wouldn't hesitate killing for."

"There's a U.S. naval carrier parked in the Caribbean Sea, should the need arise. You'll also have support personnel in Boa Vista, Brazil, Georgetown, Guyana, and Paramaribo, Suriname." He sipped at the coffee. "When Senor Juarez arrives to pick me up, I will transfer your readiness kit to you. You've been issued a SAT phone, new weapons, your orders in full, a dossier on Kroeger, a photo of the missing technology, and any other essentials."

"And Kaila?"

"She will be busy at the university."

"Won't she be suspicious if instead of returning to the United States to get on with my post military life, I follow her to Venezuela?"

"It's been taken care of."

"How?"

"As you pointed out, Venezuela can be a dangerous place and very inhospitable for Americans. A woman as beautiful as Dr. Ross certainly needs personal security and alas, the university is unable to provide any."

"What about the US Embassy?"

He shook his head and stood as the black sedan drove up. He pulled a backpack out of the trunk and handed it over. "Everything has been taken care of. Dr. Ross will not have a problem with you accompanying her to Venezuela."

* * *

"Josh, I have a problem with Dan Foster coming to Venezuela with me." Kaila frowned at the CIA handler. She stood, her back against the camper, her arms crossed in front of her. "I don't want him involved in this."

"Foster is the perfect person to ensure this goes off without a hitch. You need security protection, the university can't provide it, and Foster is not only available for the foreseeable future, he's already on the job."

"Venezuela is an entirely different situation," she argued. "We're not talking Chile, we're talking hostile territory and Dan's ex-military. Anyone and everyone will sniff that out and it will just invite trouble. It will be more than conspicuous that I have a body guard as it is. Some people will take a shot at me just to challenge him."

"The idea is not to have you two there any longer than it takes to get the crystal back. The auction is set to take place in Caracas at the end of the week."

"And just how do you know this?"

"The Russians and the Iranians both have people arriving today. Our operatives are tailing them and keeping us up to date."

"I take it I'll have a contact in Caracas?"

"Dr. Sanchez is your contact."

"*You have an operative at the university*?"

"He's a visiting professor."

"If he's visiting, what help can he be?"

"He's been on assignment for a year. Kaila, this isn't Kotal-e Salang," Josh assured, referring to a strategic mountain pass near Kabul where bad information had resulted in a failed mission and the deaths of several people, across multiple security and military forces. "We've done our homework here. Foster is going to have your back and he is Special Forces."

"*Was* Special Forces."

"Retired less than six months and is currently on a security detail." He paused. "You."

'I'm not a mission, for chrissake."

"I'd ask Foster about that if I were you," he said, one side of his mouth going up.

For a moment Kaila just stared at him. Her stomach tightened. "You guys are responsible for that attack on the site." It wasn't a question. "You knew I'd contact the embassy and Tim would ask me to come in to make a report. You set the whole thing up."

"Would you rather we strolled up to you and briefed you in there?" he asked, pointing to the camper.

At that moment Kaila knew several things. She knew that they had indeed been under surveillance. She knew that the CIA had waited until the students left and attacked her site, probably using local henchmen. Worst of all, she knew that the man standing in front of her was well aware of what had taken place in the camper between she and Dan Foster. And finally, Kaila knew that she despised Josh Coldwell like no one and nothing else in her young life to date.

"Still getting off as a voyeur, eh? You should find someone real next time. Try it, you might like it."

His face flushed, but otherwise he showed no reaction to the slam. Without saying another word, he stalked toward the black sedan where Jack Porter was waiting to be briefed on the meeting with the reluctant operative.

Kaila waited until the sedan was out of sight before walking over to a large boulder at the edge of the site. She rested her back against it, wrapped her arms around her knees, laid her head down, and growled in frustration. She was still doing it when Dan Foster walked up.

"Is this some new meditation thing?"

She took several breaths and looked up.

"Is something wrong?" he asked, squatting down.

"No," she replied, unconvincing even to herself.

"All set to go?"

"As soon as I turn over the keys to Hermosa, we can leave."

"When is she going to arrive?"

"Any time."

Dan stared at her thoughtfully. Most people would see her sitting with her back against the boulder and think she was just chilling out. He had been around her enough to see the tension held in check. Something had happened.

"Mind if I take a last look around?"

"Still on duty?" she asked, smiling. It was a tired smile.

"Let's just say we don't need to leave anything behind, tick off the locals so that we aren't welcome back."

"We, huh? Okay, have at it." She waved a hand in the general direction of the camp.

Dan made an extra effort to relax his body as he walked toward the Jeep. His eyes swept the gravel in front of him, searching. Aha, he thought, someone had been there. There were fresh tire grooves in the gravel. He was no expert in tire marks, but he was pretty certain it had been a car. Trucks and Jeeps left different impressions, deeper impressions. Not wanting her suspicious, he continued circling the camp in his typical security walk, stopping in front of where she still leaned against the bolder.

"Everything is a-ok."

"That's cool. Thanks for the last minute check. I'm guessing you would have noticed if we'd accidentally missed a tool or something."

He smiled.

"Listen, Dan -."

He tensed. Was she going to tell him who had been by, what happened to upset her? He hoped so, because that meant trust.

"I got a call while you were in town, from the next stopover."

"Venezuela? You got a call from Venezuela?" She had told him about the request to assist with the Cubaguan artifacts.

She nodded, sighed. "The university is unable to provide any security while I'm there, outside what every tourist has, which isn't much in reality. Let the traveler beware, ya know?"

"So, what does that mean? For you?"

"Well, they said I'm still welcome, but they are pretty upset. They don't want to be responsible for my safety and if something happens it would be a media nightmare."

"How nice of them to care about you," he drawled.

"No, actually, I understand. Political relations are badly strained between our two countries as it is. Education and research have often been able to skirt around that but if students or faculty start getting caught in political cross-fire, everyone loses."

He sighed, waited.

Venezuelan central range. The campus itself was surrounded by lush green with the coastal mountain range a breathtaking backdrop. It was a relatively peaceful place in a country beset by violence and crime. From his window he had a view of the anthropology building where Kaila had been holed up alongside Dr. Sanchez from sunup to sundown.

The day they arrived he had gone to the anthropology lab with her and even helped uncrate and organize the latest batch from Cubagua. To his untrained eye, it seemed like little more than beach junk found anywhere an ocean washed up on sand. Kaila had explained to him, in a rather condescending manner, that the shells had been cut or carved in a way that suggested they were actually tools for a civilization that had existed millennia before.

He sighed. He really had no reason to complain about her frosty demeanor. It kept it a hell of a lot simpler that way. If they had continued down the avenue they'd begun that morning in the camper, he would not have been able to keep the objective mindset that was not only essential to any mission, but that had been drilled into him as part of Special Forces training. It was all about the mission. Emotions, outside those related directly to instinct, only got in the way. Still, he preferred a passionate, vivacious Kaila with laughing eyes to the solemn, professional archeologist he had breakfast with every morning, and dinner with every evening.

As security jobs went, he couldn't have had it easier. Dr. Sanchez was acting more of a personal guard than university professor and if he didn't know any better, was definitely allowing his personal feelings to overshadow the job. The man rarely left her side and if she hadn't been staying in the adjacent suite, Dan suspected he may even have attempted a midnight liaison. As a man, that made Dan want to smash the guy's face into one of the cinderblocks that made up the student housing. As a soldier, it made his job all the easier, freeing him up to focus on retrieving the stolen technology.

On the desk his SAT phone vibrated. He grabbed it up and read the coded message. Auction location moved to La Gran Sabana, some eight hundred miles southeast of Caracas on the Brazilian border. He punched in a response. How was he supposed to justify taking off if his assignment was protecting Dr. Ross and she was in Caracas? The answer shocked him.

Kaila was on her way to notify him that they were going to La Gran Sabana?

Dinner was a tense affair. Dan would even go so far as to say barely civil. They had run out of small talk before their appetizer had been served and Dr. Sanchez had not joined them like he had on the previous evenings, so most of the meal was spent in silence.

He could stand it no longer. "Kaila?"

"Mm?" she answered, staring at the dessert menu. The strained relationship between them certainly hadn't affected her appetite, and damned if she never seemed to gain an ounce. One of those people who had a fast metabolism, he guessed.

"Can I ask you something?"

She set the menu down, folded her hands in front of her, and gave him her full attention, which actually startled him. He'd expected her to blow him off.

"Have I done something wrong?"

"No, why do you ask?"

"No reason," he replied after several seconds.

"Listen, I know I said this assignment wasn't going to last more than one or two weeks, and I meant it, but it does appear it's going to take us out of Caracas."

"Really? Where are we off to next, Columbia?"

She smiled. "Thank God, no. Actually, southeast of here, to Santa Elena de Uairen."

"Where?"

"It's in the heart of La Gran Sabana National Park."

Lest he give himself away, he pinned his eyes to a distant point just to the top of where her hair was pulled into a ponytail. How the hell had his ops known that Kaila was going there unless someone close to her was an informant of some type. Dr. Sanchez? It had to be, unless there was someone else.

"Does Dr. Sanchez have an assistant?" he blurted.   She blinked in confusion.

"What?"

"A grad student, lab assistants, is there someone working with you two on this project?"

"Of course."

Good, he had a way to back pedal from that outburst.

"Why can't he send that person down there and let you go home?"

For a few seconds her mouth hung open and she appeared legitimately surprised by his question.

"I take it that means no, you won't be going with me then?"

"I didn't say that," he snapped, "I just don't know why it has to be you."

She scoffed.   "This is the opportunity of a lifetime, Dan. Do you know what this is going to do for my career?   How often do I get the chance to be in Venezuela to begin with, let alone have two separate archeological opportunities?"

Hell, he thought, what was he supposed to say to that?

"I -." He shut up. The less he said, the less likely he was to compromise the mission, and it was, after all, about the mission.

"It is an incredible opportunity," she continued, enthusiastically.   "We'll be going to the headquarters of the Peace Villages Foundation in Venezuela, using it as a home base, and making trips to see all the area has to offer, which includes visiting the Pemon aboriginals."

"I see."

"Look, you don't have to go at all. I was actually going to suggest that while Dr. Sanchez escorted me to the various sites of archeological interest, you could do the tourist thing."

"The tourist thing?" he echoed, stupidly.

"There are flights over Angel Falls. As a pilot yourself, I would have to think you'd find that of interest.   There's hiking tours to Monte Roraima, which would answer your need for fitness, and there's the breathtakingly beautiful Canaima National Park."

"I'm supposed to be protecting you."

"Dr. Sanchez can do that while we are there, although you are certainly welcome to come with us. I just figured you might want to do something fun instead of something academic that isn't even your field of interest."

Dan leaned back in his chair and crossed his arms over his chest. "So, when do we leave?"

"First thing in the morning."

"Okay, I'm game."

"Do you want dessert?"

He did, but he was on a diet. A diet no man liked to be on, but the kind of diet that would help him survive the mission.

"No, thanks, but go ahead if you want."

"No, actually, I'd like to turn in early. I need to pack up and be ready. I'll come by your room around five, alright?"

"See you then. Sleep well."

Once in his room, he punched the update into the SAT phone. He received confirmation and assurance that he was moving closer to the support ops stationed in Guyana. While this should have bolstered his confidence, it didn't. Something was damned wrong. How had they known about Kaila's plans? Who was the spy?

He vented his frustrations by slamming his clothing into the backpack. Obviously, Porter hadn't told him who all the players were. He shouldn't be surprised. The CIA was known for not caring who got hurt, so long as their ends were met.

He knew it would be a long night because he was so pissed off, but he also knew that if he was going to be worth a damn the next morning, he'd better get his ass to sleep. After all, five am would come around sooner than later.

"Here." Kaila handed him a book and a pamphlet.

"What am I supposed to do with this?"

"Look it over. By the time the plane lands, you'll have a better appreciation for where we're going."

Dan looked down at what she had passed across to him. The book was an aged copy of Sir Arthur Conan Doyle's *The Lost World.*

"I got that copy from the university's library," Dr. Sanchez said from where he sat between Dan and Kaila. "It's an original release from October, 1912, which is why it isn't translated into Spanish."

"Wow," he replied, trying to put appreciation in his voice, "thank you."

The pamphlet she had given him was a treatise on the story, a sort of cliff notes, apparently written in the mid twentieth century.

"Canaima National Park was the inspiration for that book," Kaila said. "I thought it might be more meaningful to you if you had a bit of trivia to go with it."

"It was Dr. Ross' idea to have you read it on the flight down," Sanchez explained. "She wanted to go to a bookstore to look for a copy but I told her the library at the university was a much likelier place to find it in English."

"Thanks," he said in her general direction. "That was thoughtful." He refused to lean forward or across Dr. Sanchez in order to talk to her, so she could take it for face value. It had been thoughtful, but a guy had his limits.

If Dan thought Caracas was humid, he had no idea what humidity was. They were basically in the heart of rain forest territory. The moment he stepped off the plane his clothes began to stick to his body as perspiration slid over his skin.

"I have rented a vehicle suitable for the terrain," Dr. Sanchez said, "for when we visit the geological wonders of this area. First we will go to the Foundation. After checking in, the day is ours. It would be my pleasure to show you some of the sights."

"That would be great," Kaila replied before Dan could weigh in.

"Is there a restroom?" he asked.

"This way."

Dan was glad to find the bathroom deserted. He quickly tapped an update into the SAT phone. An affirmative was his only reply. While he washed his hands, he stared at himself in the cracked mirror.

"This is fucked up, Foster."

He held his peace as he rode shotgun to the Foundation. He had to admire Dr. Sanchez's choice. The H3 was well suited for the environment they were in, capable of handling the worst road conditions, its independent front suspension a definite advantage. Kaila sat in the back and talked about the archeology of the Orinoco River Basin as well as the geological uniqueness of La Gran Sabana. Dan let her voice wash over him as he observed Dr. Sanchez. If the man was who he claimed to be, he should participate in avid, if not passionate conversation about the topic.

"Does our occupational conversation bore you, Major Foster?"

Dan jerked. *Major?*

"I'm retired, sir. You don't need to -."

"He prefers to go by Foster," Kaila put in from the back. Dan replayed the sentence in an attempt to gauge the smart-ass factor. It was at least an eight on his scale.

"Does our occupational conversation bore you, Foster?" Kaila asked from behind him.

"No, though it probably doesn't drive me to the emotional highs it does someone such as you or Dr. Sanchez. How long have you been in anthropology, doctor?"

"I earned my doctorate in nineteen seventy-nine," he answered, proudly, "although I have only been at the university in Caracas for a little less than a year. This is my third time in Venezuela, the last being for a conference in 2004."

Dan stared ahead as the Peace Villages came into view. It wouldn't surprise him one bit to discover that Dr. Sanchez was working for Porter's organization. The CIA loved to brag how they filched from the intellectual alphabet soup. What really pissed him off was that they turned around and treated the armed services personnel like they were nothing more than lemmings, incapable of interpreting data or making split second decisions beyond the one to pull the trigger at the appropriate time, be it a trigger that dropped a bomb or one that sent tracers into the Afghanistan desert.

"Please," he said, amiably as he jumped from the driver's seat, "wait here."

"What do you think?" Kaila asked from the back. "A bit more beautiful than even Caracas, wouldn't you say?"

"It's definitely in my top ten," he admitted. "I had no idea Venezuela was so beautiful."

Of course he knew, but that wasn't anything Kaila Ross needed to be aware of.

"Okay," Sanchez said, climbing back into the driver's seat. "We're all set. Shall we be on our way?"

At noon they pulled off the well beaten path in order to have lunch.

"Dr. Ross, you will be happy to note that I got you two diet Cokes."

"Thanks, Carlos."

Dan was glad he hadn't eaten yet. If he had, *Carlos* would be wearing his lunch.

The anthropologist opened his mouth to reply, but never got the chance to finish his sentence. The side of his skull was blown out, splattering blood all over the emerald grass.

CHAPTER FOURTEEN

Dan dove for Kaila, slamming her back and rolling her into nearby shrubbery as bullets peppered the ground around them.

"What the hell -?" he hissed, his body curled protectively around hers. Occasional gunfire broke up the otherwise peaceful sounds of nature, although the forest had gone ominously quiet after the first onslaught.

"That was an execution, Dr. Ross. Would you like to explain that to me?"

"He's dead," she answered, pushing herself to her knees and breaking cover, making a run for the H3.

"What the hell are you doing?" he roared, following. "You're going to get yourself killed."

"We have to get out of here," she yelled, flinching as bullets sprayed the ground near the front tires. She yanked the door open and slid into the driver's seat. "Foster, get in here," she yelled as she turned the key in the ignition.

"Do you know how -," but his words were cut off by the roar of the engine as she drove straight into the rain forest. Dan barely got the door closed, let alone buckling himself in. As the H3 bounced through the jungle, he braced a hand against the dash, praying the air bags wouldn't deploy and mess up her ability to see. Not to mention he wasn't looking to get nailed by one opening at some two hundred miles an hour, and receiving powder burns from the trigger mechanism.

Kaila drove like a demon, not speaking to him and never once glancing in his direction. He quit watching her and turned to see where they were going. It was obvious she knew what she was doing. Why in the world that shocked him, he couldn't have said, but he was damned well going to find out once they got out of this. It was obvious there were many things about Kaila Ross he didn't know.

Kaila maneuvered the SUV beneath a canopy of trees and cut the engine. Letting out a pent up breath, she kept her eyes and hands on the steering wheel.

"Are you hurt?" she asked quietly, not looking at him.

Instead of answering, he climbed out of the vehicle, his sidearm drawn, and walked a quick perimeter of the area. She knew they were safe enough but suspected that wasn't something he would want to hear without a pretty strong explanation as to how, exactly, she knew that.

"What the hell was that all about?"

"We were being shot at," she replied simply, her eyes focused on her fingers which were wrapped around the steering wheel. "Getting out of there seemed like a good idea."

"That's not what I meant," he growled from where he stood next to the driver's door. "Where the hell did you learn to drive like that? And don't give me some bullshit story about it being something a real archeology student would do."

She kept her eyes fixed on the steering wheel. She wasn't ready to meet his gaze, to enter into the discussion she knew was coming.

"Look at me," he shouted and she obeyed.

For several seconds they just stared at each other. Her eyes lit briefly on the gun he held. His stance was deceptively at ease but she could see the storm brewing behind his blue eyes. She debated only a moment further before answering.

"I felt it was a good skill to have," she replied, her voice calm enough, if filled with resignation.

"Why?" he snapped impatiently.

"Several years ago I was on a dig in Africa; my first international opportunity." She recalled the details dispassionately; as if it were someone else she was talking about. "We were told we were far enough behind the protected zone, that we'd be safe."

"Who told you that?"

"Our guides," she answered, her voice void of emotion. "We came under heavy attack early one morning. Rebel forces poured into our camp. Several members of the team were shot."

"Were you?"

She nodded, continued. "Our guides were armed. They put up a good show, acted as if they were protecting us." She was staring past him, her eyes focused on a distant time and place, seeing it again, only this time in black and white, as she'd learned to do all those years ago.

"They'd sold you out?"

Again, she only nodded.

"One of the other students managed to steal a Jeep," she continued. "The keys were in it. Three of us were able to climb in and pull away from the fighting."

"How many were on your team?"

"Not including the guides, seven. Including them, there were thirteen of us."

"Go on," he ordered, though his tone lacked the bite it held moments before.

She took a deep breath, let it out. "The guy behind the wheel, he hadn't been injured but he was scared; real scared." She was frowning, her eyes unfocused. "It cost him his judgment. He drove straight through the rebel line."

"I would think," Dan cut in, "that would be a normal reaction for a kid in a foreign land without the experience to handle such a situation."

She nodded. "He drove straight through them," she repeated, "and paid for that mistake with his life. I had to push his body aside and take his place," she explained. "It was hard to steer, my hands kept slipping from the wheel."

"Because they were shaking?" Dan had taken several steps closer to the H3, so that he stood beside her.

"Because the wheel was slick with blood. They'd decapitated him, you see." She swallowed. "I could hear

Kelly screaming, but it was like it was in a tunnel or something, far away."

"Kelly?"

"She was still in the back seat."

"And the driver?"

"His body was in the passenger seat. His head -?" She shrugged. "I drove toward the helicopters."

"Helicopters?"

"The marines had arrived; the British marines."

"What happened next?"

"They pulled Kelly and I out of the Jeep, pushed us into the back of another one and drove like hell for the nearest safety zone. I remember watching the officer behind the wheel as he drove. He was calm, focused; he made no mistakes. He got us out of there and to a hospital."

"And?"

She blinked, looked at him as if just realizing he was there.

"And they evacuated us to Germany, then home."

"And Kelly?"

"She spent some time in a hospital and ended up leaving school. I thought it was better to lose contact with her rather than be a constant reminder.

"How many students died that day?"

"Four."

"So, another student survived?"

She smiled, a bittersweet expression. "Ray was an artist and had crawled away just before dawn in order to get a head start on sketches before the site was disturbed further by the day's digging. I guess the guides forgot about him long enough that the marines were able to liberate the camp. They found him hiding nearby and rescued him."

"Did you see him again?"

"Oh, sure, we continued to run into each other in various classes. He graduated and moved to the Midwest somewhere. I think that's where he was from, Indiana or something like that. Last I heard, he'd given up on archeology."

"What a terrible experience. How old were you?"

"Twenty-five."

Dan thought of where he had been at twenty-five. No wonder he felt an odd connection to the woman still seated in the H3. They'd survived similar experiences even if his had been in the line of duty.

"So, you decided that learning to drive like you're in the CIA was a survival skill for the soon-to-be graduated?"

She flinched and he grimaced. His attempt at humor had gone over like a lead balloon. "Sorry."

"Back to the present," she said suddenly, her tone brisk. "We can't stay here." She psychically scanned their immediate surroundings. "They probably won't be too far behind; they'll follow the tracks."

"You bought us a little time with your expertise, but you're right, we can't stay here. How well do you know this area?"

"Pretty well," she answered, nodding and turning the key. "I studied a map while we were on the plane, to get a feel for the areas we would be traveling with Dr. Sanchez. If we continue in this direction, we should come to a main artery that will take us where we need to go."

"Which is?"

"Out of Venezuela, that's for sure. If we keep on this road, we'll reach Brazil. Boa Vista isn't that far over the border. We can get help."

Dan got into the passenger seat. "Do you want to let me take the wheel?"

She smiled, shook her head. "I'm fine." She put the H3 in gear and stepped on the gas.

Dan studied her profile in silence. He had no doubt the story she'd told was true but he felt she'd held something back. For all the information she had provided, she'd left out an awful lot of detail.

"Where were you? In Africa, where was the dig?"

"Lunsar."

"Why would a group of college students go to an area that was war torn?"

Her mouth turned up in irony. "Name an archeology location that isn't," she said by way of an answer. "Outside the United States, that is."

"How were you notified of this dig and why did you go?"

"What, are you interrogating me?"

An interesting choice of words, he thought grimly. Had she been interrogated before?

"I just think it's awfully odd that a young graduate student would purposely endanger her life by going into a part of the world so rife with violence that her odds of being killed would be quite high. Especially given your appearance. The enemy could find you in the dark."

"Look, Dan, I think I've gone far enough down memory lane. Take it for what it's worth because you aren't going to hear anymore." She let out a sigh, grateful to see a reprieve before he really dug in. "The road."

"Stop here."

"Why?"

"I want to check things out. Turn off the engine."

They sat there in silence, each scanning the area visually and listening for any sounds that suggested they'd been followed.

"I think it's safe," she persisted.

"Do you know which way to go?"

"We can go either way and get to a town, but I think we should move south, toward the border. There's an airport in Boa Vista so we can get out."

"Kaila, do you trust me?"

She glanced over at him. "That's an odd question. You wouldn't be sitting next to me right now if I didn't trust you; I wouldn't have asked you to come to Venezuela with me."

"Don't drive over the border."

"What? You think I'm going to stay in Venezuela after what just happened?"

"We're definitely going to go to Brazil but we are going to sneak over the border."

She said nothing while she digested that. "Just how are we going to manage that? Dan, this is not the United States, the borders -."

"There are hikers everywhere here, right? The Canaima National Forest, the rivers that run through here, hell, just hiking in the rain forest is the sole destination of visiting tourists, right?"

"Yeah, okay."

"So, we stash the H3 a ways in the opposite direction and hike south. Thankfully, we didn't unload our bags back at the Peace Villages Foundation so we have everything we need."

She stared at him.

"Hey, it won't be much different from when you're on a dig, right? Camping doesn't always come with a nice camper, am I right?"

"True, I've camped outdoors before, including in the rain forests."

"We both have mosquito netting and survival gear and we're both in excellent shape. Trust me, this will be better."

"And if we get caught?"

"Caught at what? Hiking? We haven't done anything wrong. The car wasn't rented in your name; we were off the beaten path when we were ambushed. Even if whoever was responsible for Dr. Sanchez's murder calls the border authorities, we have done nothing wrong. We can say we weren't with him, we can say whatever. Given the options before us I say we have to risk it."

Of course, he knew he could call in reinforcements if he needed to, but alerting Kaila to that fact would mean he had to explain all of it and he was trying to avoid that.

"Okay. I don't have a better idea and you're right, if we can avoid a border checkpoint we'll be better off." She studied him, smiled. "You know, it could be tough going through the forest."

He smiled. "We're up for it. Let's go."

She put the car in gear and drove away from the border.

CHAPTER FIFTEEN

Somehow, Kaila had to get away from Dan, at least for a little while. They'd been hiking for three hours and while they'd made steady progress, she was beginning to rethink the plan of hiking over the border. It seemed like they would never get there. What worried her more, the longer they went side by side through the jungle without her having any privacy, the longer it would be before she could report the death of the operative to Jack Porter's organization.

"I need to go to the bathroom," she blurted. "I won't go far."

"Okay, I may as well take advantage."

Moving in the opposite direction, Dan breathed a sigh of relief. Now that he was away from Kaila, he could update Jack Porter that Dr. Sanchez had been killed and that they were on the run. He demanded that the support team be moved closer to the Brazilian border and that they set up a meet in Boa Vista. They needed current intelligence and a debrief. The response was coded and predictable. Keep moving; they would get back with him soon.

As he made his way back to the path they had been on, Dan mulled over what he knew. Although he had no proof, he was certain that Sanchez had been more than just a university professor. It certainly explained a hell of a lot, including the execution style hit. What it didn't explain was Kaila. How did she fit into all of this? Was the CIA just using her archeological project as a conveniently timed cover for tracking down Chad Kroeger and the stolen technology? It seemed more than plausible. He wondered if she realized she was being manipulated, that her sponsorship was orchestrated by the security organization.

Kaila stared at the screen and rolled her eyes. How typical; await further instructions but continue toward the border. She wiped her brow. The heat and humidity were definitely starting to take a toll.

"Kaila? Everything all right?"

"Coming," she answered, closing the SAT phone and shoving it into a little zippered bag that was attached to the inside of her pack with a plastic hook. She made her way toward his voice.

"Sorry if I worried you."

"You don't look so good, why don't we take a rest?"

"It's the heat and humidity," she answered, walking over and sitting next to where he rested on a fallen tree. "I'm not used to it being this thick. I feel like I'm breathing liquid air."

"Here, have some water," he said, offering a canteen. While she was drinking it, he soaked a clean rag with water and handed it to her.

"Thanks," she replied, returning his canteen and mopping her forehead. "I think it might help if I put my hair in a braid."

"Let me. I want you to rest."

"You know how to braid hair?"

"With three sisters, are you kidding?"

She sat still while he worked long blonde strands through his fingers and began the familiar weaving. She was amazed at how relaxing it was. Her lids grew heavy and she worried that if it took much longer, she would fall asleep right there.

"Rested?" he asked, suddenly, and part of her cried out at the unfairness of being jolted from the comfortable place she'd been slipping into.

"Sure, let's go."

"Kaila, are you sure you're alright? We can stay here a little longer."

She shook her head. "I'll be more than happy to close as much of a gap between us and the border as we can. Let's move."

She didn't want to think about it, but she was starting to feel a bit queasy. She'd already been going through the post trauma eye routine that had helped her so many times before. Known as EMDR, or Eye Movement Desensitization and Reprocessing, it was part New Age and part scientific in basis. What was true was that it helped the brain recategorize events in such a way that although the person still remembered them, they no longer experienced the horrible impact of when the event first transpired. The key to making it work was to move the eyes in specific directions while simultaneously replaying the traumatic memory.

She had learned her own twist to the technique. By repeating the eye movements a second time, being sure the memories were painted in black and white in her mind's eye, it further distanced the events so that it was almost as if they had actually happened to someone else.

The benefits were immense. She was better prepared for debriefs, able to recount details without getting caught up in the emotions of them. In fact, she was so distanced from the events that more than a few people in the CIA had suggested she had ice water in her veins. Only a select few, members of *the club*, were actually aware of the truth.

Kaila let her mind wander since it helped distract her from the fatigue that was beginning to drag her down. The rain forest made for a challenging environment with its fallen trees and thick vegetation.

Who would have guessed that Tim Brightman was a member of the small team that circumvented the traditional reporting structure within the CIA? In point of fact, most of the people who were members of that elite organization, known as the club, reported directly to Jack Porter, although everyone had been assigned a handler. What made members of the club so unique was that they were all highly gifted psychics.

She snorted derisively. More than once she had argued that what she possessed was far from a gift. A gift implied that, like music or writing, it was a talent to be developed and used to some benefit, to be enjoyed. From the beginning, her talent had brought little but grief.

At its simplest, her capability enabled her to detect emotions, much like the ship's counselor in *Star Trek: The Next Generation*. For Kaila, however, the more common experience lay at the other end of the spectrum. She was able to literally get inside of someone and feel what they were feeling with a granularity that was frightening.

She had actually spent a good part of her life trying to get rid of the ability since she had found it so exhausting. It was like living between stations, never able to turn off a radio that only picked up static.

As the day wore on, the intensity of the heat and humidity grew, forcing her to focus on her breathing, which was becoming increasingly labored.

"Why don't we quit for the day?"

Since she had been on autopilot, she didn't realize he had come to a stop. She plowed into him, and since there was a thick tree root at his feet, he tripped and went down, and she proceeded to land right on top of him.

"God, Dan, I'm sorry," she said, rolling away from him.

"It's alright," he replied, pushing himself to his knees, "I kind of saw it coming at the last minute. No harm done."

She unhooked the belt that secured the bottom of the pack around her waist and pulled her arms from the shoulder straps. She reached for the water bottle sitting snugly in the netted pocket on the side and guzzled its contents, swishing some of the water around her mouth and spitting out what she didn't swallow.

Blowing a breath out, she dragged her arm across her brow, only half surprised when she detected heat and excessive perspiration.

"I'll set up a camp for us," Dan stated. "I want you to sit right where you are. You look like you could more than use the rest."

She smiled wanly, nodded, and took a bite of a protein bar. *God, I feel so wiped out.*

Dan walked deeper into the forest and checked his phone for messages. The Ops contact stated that the support team was close to the border and would rendezvous with them whenever Dan and Kaila were ready. He told them that barring any unforeseen difficulties, they should be at the border the following night. As he closed the phone and slid it into his pocket, he grunted in satisfaction. It felt good to know the Ops team had his back. Almost too good, but he refused to follow that line of thought.

By the time he got back to the site with a bundle of kindling, Kaila had already dug a pit, lit a fire, and was roasting vegetables leftover from lunch.

"I threw some of the turkey on there, too," she informed him.

"Thanks. Listen, why don't you go sit with your back over against that tree and let me finish up with this?"

She crawled over and made sure no unfriendlies were in the area. The last thing they needed to be dealing with was illness from a snake or spider bite, or worse.

God, but it felt good to sit down. Ignoring the shaky tremors that occasionally rolled down her spine, she watched lazily as the flames bent and twisted through their hypnotic dance.

"Here." Dan handed over an aluminum plate and sat down next to her, using his fingers to scoop food into his mouth. "That was smart thinking, holding some of the food back in case we need it later. By the way, how are you doing?"

"I'm beat," she admitted, "how about you?"

"I'm definitely feeling it," he agreed. "I think we'll be at the border tomorrow night."

"Good. The sooner we get out of this god forsaken country, the better."

He nodded in understanding. He knew all too well what it was like to hate a place simply because of what had happened there, regardless of whether or not it was beautiful. In fact, it was amazing, in his opinion, the hypocritical cruelty that carnage could wreak upon the otherwise pristine beauty of nature's landscape.

"I was married once," Dan blurted out suddenly.

She nodded, her eyes going to his.

"You knew that, right?"

Again, she nodded.

"You never ask me about it."

She smiled. "Why would I?"

"You mean you aren't curious?"

"Dan, I know you were married a very short time and that your wife died. That has to be a terrible thing to live through so no, I don't ask about it simply because I don't want to bring up painful memories. If you want to talk about it with me I'm more than happy to listen, but I don't seek out topics that may cause trouble for a person; that's not my style."

For several seconds he simply looked at her, then, finally nodded.

"I just thought it curious."

Her smile widened. "Because most women would have asked by now?" *Especially given what they had happened between them in the trailer.*

"Yeah, something like that."

"Something like that or that?" she asked, her tone teasing and light.

He laughed.

"I like you, Kaila. You've got a good sense of humor. You work harder than almost anybody and yet I don't recall you ever complaining."

She bit out a laugh. "Don't let my folks hear you talk like that else they'll feel compelled to disabuse you of your good notions about me."

"Listen," he said, rising, "I'm going to walk a perimeter. Why don't you get some sleep? We'll set out when we are both awake and able to see where we're going."

"Sounds good to me."

Dan's stomach was in knots as he strode away from where she was crawling beneath mosquito netting. Whatever had possessed him to bring up that he'd been married? Afraid he might be losing perspective, he decided to tap the one resource that had never failed him.

"This is Andrews."

The tone of voice his friend used when talking on a cell was what some would call abrupt, others indifferent, yet others would call professional. Dan was just glad to hear it come through crystal clear over the satellite connection.

"Do you think Staci would have liked her?" *No hello, no is this a good time to talk?*

The question had been foremost in his mind throughout the day so he wasn't completely shocked when he blurted it out. Then again, he knew full well that Sean would understand like nobody else, that explanations would never be necessary.

"No," Sean answered after a moment, "I don't think so."

"Why not?" He kept his tone even.

"Because she wouldn't follow an order," he replied, easily. "Kaila Ross is a passionate woman who listens to her own counsel. She would never have made it in the military, where obedience is every bit as important as leadership. Staci knew the importance of following the chain of command, the need for discipline. Kaila Ross doesn't know the meaning of that."

Instead of saying anything, Dan grunted.

"She's gotten under your skin, huh?"

"Yeah, you could put it that way."

"Are you asking me if I think you two could make a go of it? Whether your personalities would mesh or if you'd end up spending eternity trying to kill each other?"

He laughed. His friend understood him well and knew how to cut past the bullshit of small talk.

"I want honesty," he replied.

"And when have I ever given you anything else?" He let out a sigh. "Alright, I'm going to tell you straight. I've thought you and Kaila would be well suited to each other from the moment I met her. She mouthed off, butted in, and was a general pain in the ass at times, not unlike yourself."

"And you wish this for my happiness?"

"You asked for honesty, right?"

"Well -."

"Then let's just say that I'm glad you aren't sitting across from me right now, because after you hear what it is I'm about to tell you, you would probably try to plant your fist in my face."

Dan's stomach tightened.

"For the last seven years, no one, including me, has been able to say thing one about Staci because you've had her up on a pedestal."

"Go on," he said, his hand clenching at his side.

"Because of what happened, how it happened, the fact that it happened when she was young, you have blinded yourself to a lot of realities."

"I'm listening."

"No one deserves what happened to Staci, no one. Everyone agrees with that. But that didn't blind us to her faults or from seeing what was going on between you two."

"What do you mean, what was going on between us two?"

"Dan, I was your best man. I am saying with all honesty that if Staci hadn't died, you not only *wouldn't* have been a happily married man, you probably would have ended up divorced."

"She was pregnant," he snapped, "I wouldn't have walked out on her or my responsibility to her."

"Listen to yourself, what you're saying. Your responsibility, your duty. Like your duty to the military. Look, a lot of what drew you and Staci together was that each of you understood that part of your lives, but there were other things going on, Dan, things that you both blinded yourselves to."

"What things?"

"You fell in love with Staci because she was like the girls back home, in small town Maine. She was a girl you could take home to your mom, to your sisters. She was a way for you to get back in your dad's good graces. For Staci? You were the security she never had."

Dan paced, listened; remained silent.

"She needed to escape a crappy home life, so she joined the military," Sean continued. "It got her far away from where she grew up and enabled her to build a new family in the military. What it didn't do was give her the security she craved because that was a hole within herself she hadn't filled. She should have found a way to fill it herself. Instead, she transferred that unrealistic and completely unfair expectation from the military to you.

She had an empty place in her that needed love badly and she thought you could fill that, too, Dan. When reality started to set in, when she realized that maybe she might have made a mistake, instead of facing that, what did she do? She got pregnant."

"That was an accident," Dan defended.

"Was it? Dan, you were in the middle of your rising star in the Air Force. A baby was not what you wanted at that point in time and as I recall, you made that more than clear to Lieutenant Staci Foster. I think she got pregnant on purpose. I think she felt having a baby was the answer to all of it, the emptiness inside of her, a way to fix your marriage, a way to walk away from the military."

"Why would she want to walk away from the military? She had just been promoted."

"When it didn't fill that emptiness inside of her, she felt betrayed. She only re-up'd when she realized you came with it. She didn't care about the promotion. She wanted security and love, and rather than giving them to herself she looked for them outside. That is always a losing proposition."

Dan unclenched his hand and pushed it through his hair, let out a sigh. His heart was pounding, but instead of wanting to lash out in fury, he wanted to crawl away somewhere and digest what had been said, what he'd suspected, in a deep dark part of himself that he had hidden away long ago.

To admit his wife had had any faults, that she had done any wrong, not only betrayed her memory, it suggested that somehow she deserved punishment. It was ridiculous, of course, and didn't bear thinking about.

"Dan, the fact that you are willing to listen to this, that you've gotten to this point, tells me you are ready to live life again, and that maybe a part of living that life includes another person."

"I've gotta think on this," he said at last.

"Dan? I have never spoken of this, of Staci, with anyone, not even Kian. What I can tell you is that Kian has told me a great deal about her sister and I can't say that I've heard anything that makes me think you and Kaila Ross don't suit, that you wouldn't be able to make a life together, if you so choose."

"Thanks, man. I've gotta get going."

"When are you two going to be back in California?"

He snorted, looked around at the eerie shadows cast by a rain forest at night.

"As soon as I know, I'll let you know."

"If you need anything, don't hesitate."

"I know." It was one of the things Dan had learned to count on about his friend. "Later."

CHAPTER SIXTEEN

Not taking time to figure out what woke him, Dan instinctively drew his gun and rolled over to where Kaila slept. Only she wasn't. She was thrashing her head side to side, her hand on the necklace.

"Kaila, what's the matter?"

"Get it off," she whimpered, pulling on the chain.

"The necklace?"

"The headache, get it off."

"The necklace is giving you a headache?" he asked even as he unclasped the chain and slipped it into his pocket. "Easy now, it's off." He reached out and touched his fingers to her forehead. He frowned; she was burning up. "The necklace didn't do this."

Kaila pressed her hands to her head and began to roll from side to side. "I've never had a headache this bad," she moaned.

He unzipped her sleeping bag and shoved her t-shirt up, closely inspecting the skin of her upper body.

"Does it hurt anywhere else?"

"My whole body aches; it feels like I have the flu."

"Hmm, no rash."

"What?"

"Dengue fever."

"What's that?"

"Yellow fever's cousin. I assume you've been vaccinated against that."

"Of course," she answered, managing to sound indignant in spite of the situation.

"I actually have something I can give you for the pain." He went back to his bedroll and reached into a zippered bag he had hidden there. He withdrew a brown bottle and shook out two pills. Grabbing his canteen he crawled back over to where she lay still, hands to the sides of her head.

"Are you allergic to anything? Codeine?"

"No," she moaned.

"Take these."

"What is it?"

"222's; I keep them around for the times my knee gives me grief." Dan knew that if she did have dengue fever, aspirin or an NSAID would be the worst thing he could give her. He also knew if she had contracted the fever, he had to get her to a hospital. He sure as hell didn't want her at the local clinic which left him only one option.

"Hey, will you be okay here for about thirty seconds? I gotta take a leak."

"Sure," she replied weakly, chewing the pills.

Staying long enough to see her swallow the last of the pain medication, he walked into the woods on the opposite side of the camp and moved as far away as he dared; what he hoped was out of her hearing range but still close enough that he would be able to get back quickly should she call out. He drew the small SAT phone from his pocket and punched in the numbers, working to hold anxiety at bay.

"Hot Lips, are you there?" he hissed into the phone.

"What is it, Burns?"

"Got a white cross," he said, referring to the code word for medical emergency.

"Roger that, Burns. Key in."

"My little soldier," he replied. The reference would alert them to his suspicion of some sort of tropical fever. The line he'd used referenced a MASH episode in which hemorrhagic fever was a central part of the plot.

"Roger, out."

He made his way back to the campsite knowing that they would send him coded transmissions detailing the pickup site and time.

"Miss me?"

She didn't answer.

"Kaila?" he spoke, soft, yet firmly.

"Hmm?" she replied, her voice so soft he barely heard her. She turned to look up at him. Her eyes were glassy and as he knelt at her side, she began to shiver.

"Shit," he said and quickly stripped down to his underwear. He opened the sleeping bag and got her down to hers. He slid in next to her, zipped them in, and repositioned the mosquito netting. He grabbed all their clothing and shoved it down toward their feet. Her body was shaking violently and he all but smothered her in his attempt to warm her.

"Kaila? Listen to me. It's going to be okay, help is on the way." Beads of sweat glistened across her forehead. He wetted a t-shirt and proceeded to wipe her down as best he could. Against his leg his phone vibrated.

They were on their own for six more hours. He quickly punched in a carefully worded acknowledgment; they'd better not be much longer than that. He set the phone down and pulled Kaila into his embrace, surprised when his own body shook alongside of hers. Taking a deep breath, he closed his eyes and willed a calm to spread throughout his body, hoping the effect would be transmitted to her. He wasn't sure if he was successful, but she did seem to relax a little after minutes of being in his tight embrace.

Dan dozed on and off, his arms always around her, his body half on top. Because they were skin to skin, he became acutely aware of when the fever began to spike. He rolled away from her at the same moment she began pushing at him.

"Hot, hot, hot," she chanted. He glanced at his watch. Thirty minutes. He had thirty more minutes to go before the insertion team would be nearby.

Knowing the challenge of trying to carry her through the jungle to any rendezvous point, they had decided to send a retrieval team to their location. Fortunately for everyone involved, they were near three friendly countries, Brazil, Guyana, and Suriname.

He continued to wipe her down and prayed the team wasn't much longer.

When a foreign sound carried to him from the jungle, he didn't bother to check his SAT phone. He pulled his weapon and aimed.

"Major Burns, good to see you hale and healthy. How's Dr. Ross?"

"Not good, she's burning up." He backed away, giving the medic room.

"Well, help's here," he replied, kneeling. He pulled out a syringe and jabbed it into her arm. "The name's Koski, Lieutenant Michael Koski, at your service."

"What's that?" He indicated the shot.

"Ribavirin. It's still in the early stages of development but it seems to interfere with the replication of RNA metabolism." He looked up at Dan. "The virus can't replicate."

Dan nodded as another man carrying a stretcher made his way toward them.

"Let's get her out of the sleeping bag and loaded up," Koski said.

"No, wait."

Both men looked up at his sharp tone.

"She isn't dressed."

"Hell of a time to do the nasty, Foster," the second man, Lieutenant Steve *Leopard* Perry, said, shaking his head.

While some would find the remark in poor taste, Dan appreciated it for what it was; an old friend using his stunted sense of humor to try and ease the tension.

"Good to see you, Leopard. How's the leap these days?"

"Sherry's pregnant again, Tad and David are doing well. All three of them are hoping it's a girl; the boys because they want someone to protect, the way dad does, and Sherry because she says between us and the dog, there's too much testosterone in them thar house."

They talked quietly, yet companionably while they broke down camp. By the time they were finished, Koski had Kaila out of her sleeping bag, into her t-shirt and shorts, and well covered on the stretcher. He'd also started an IV which lay on top of the blanket.

"She's unconscious," Koski said, lifting one end of the stretcher as Dan grabbed the other.

Leopard provided cover as they moved through the jungle toward a Jeep that would take them to Guyana. A helicopter was just across the border, ready to fly them to an aircraft carrier stationed in the Caribbean Sea. Equipped with the latest in technology, it had a hospital and full diagnostic laboratory aboard.

In the helicopter, Dan sat next to the stretcher, Kaila's hand in his. Koski and Leopard exchanged meaningful glances before buckling in and giving a thumbs up to the pilot.

"She's gonna be all right, Foster," Leopard shouted, "the naval doctor is ready and waiting."

He nodded but kept his eyes on Kaila. What was eating at him wasn't just that she was ill, but the way things had been the last few days. They hadn't been able to thaw the frost that had settled between them. Oh, they were polite, even cordial at times, but for two people who had been so damned close to coming together in passion and perhaps a little bit more, the hollow emptiness that had descended was now churning up inside of him. She had to pull through, damn it.

The helicopter set down on the naval carrier and two men rolled a gurney up, loaded the stretcher and wheeled it away with incredible efficiency.

"This way, Foster," Leopard shouted, grabbing his arm and indicating a doorway. "I'll take you to the hospital."

"Hey, Digger, long time, no see."

"Manic Man," he replied, shaking the hand of another former teammate.

"Why, Digger?" Koski asked.

"Because," Manic replied, "Maine boy here taught us how to dig for clams, which can come in handy when you want to impress the ladies with a romantic, oceanside rendezvous."

Dan smiled, but shrugged. "How's Kaila?"

"Too soon to know what's going on," he replied seriously. "I just dropped off a blood sample for the lab. The doc is with her right now. She hasn't regained consciousness. Right smart of you to start the IV. If it is dengue, dehydration is a problem."

"When was the last time you had anything to eat?" Leopard asked.

"I'm not hungry," Dan snapped.

"That's not what I asked."

"I want to be here when she wakes up. She won't know what happened, why she is aboard a ship -." He paused. "Shit. She gets seasick. Tell -," but Manic was already disappearing through a doorway.

"I guess it would be redundant to ask what your feelings are toward Dr. Ross," Leopard said, letting out a sigh. He had seen his comrade like that before, and therefore, knew better than to get in his way. Until he knew the woman they'd brought aboard was out of danger, Dan Foster would be the immovable object.

"She's awake," Manic said, returning, "and asking for you."

Dan shot up as if someone had set a bomb off under his ass. Leopard pursed his lips and watched as the man practically mowed over the medical officer in his haste to get to her. It appeared it was time to start the matrimonial pool, for as sure as God gave him eyes, Digger was sunk.

Looking around as he stepped through the doorway, Dan smiled and wondered if Kaila realized she was being given the queen's treatment. Her quarters were luxurious by military standards and although they weren't large, they were more than comfortable. Thanks to a porthole letting a good amount of light in, they were also somewhat cheery.

"You have quite a bit of explaining to do." Her voice was so hoarse it came out a croak.

He wasn't ready to get into the discussion he knew was imminent so he sidestepped the question.

"How are you feeling?"

"She's weak but stable." The man checking the IV tubing appeared to be in his sixties. "I'm Lieutenant Colonel Craig Harper, ship's physician."

It was all Dan could do not to salute. He nodded. "Doctor."

"I hear you two have had quite a day." His brown eyes held compassion but also polite curiosity as he focused first on the woman in the bed and then on Dan where he stood at the foot of it.

"That's the truth."

In the bed, Kaila snorted and for a moment, he worried she would say something like, *well, duh.*

"I'm still waiting on the lab report to confirm what this is, but definitely looking like a virus of some sort. If it does end up being dengue, there isn't a whole lot we can do outside common sense supportive care until it passes."

"Which is how long?"

"Six or seven days."

Where did that leave the mission? Dan didn't want to leave her aboard the naval carrier while he went off to chase bad guys. He would talk to Porter, see what it took to have her transferred to a hospital in the US.

"Thank you for everything, doctor." Kaila's voice was weak.

"If you need me, press that button there. I'm going to go see if the lab report is ready."

"I'd start explaining if I were you," she snapped the minute they were alone.

He sighed, realizing it was time to face the music. Well, he thought, might as well do this right. He made sure to leave the door open. He suspected that it wouldn't exactly stop her from yelling if she felt the need, but he hoped it might at least encourage her to try for discretion. Taking the chair next to the bed, he got as comfortable as he could and gave her a look he hoped was honest, if not innocent.

"Guests of the US Navy?" she snapped, indicating their surroundings. She leveled a glare at him. "You're still in the service, aren't you?"

Blowing a sigh between his lips, he nodded. This wasn't going to be good.

CHAPTER SEVENTEEN

Jack Porter set his coffee on a conference table and walked over to stare through a porthole at the horizon. What a contrast the calm sea was to the tempest brewing aboard the carrier.

"I have the lab report."

Jack turned.

"It isn't dengue, just influenza."

"She has the flu?"

The doctor nodded. "The symptomology can actually be very similar, especially when milder -."

"Mild? From what I was told -."

The doctor shook his head. "I didn't say she wasn't sick, just that she has a fairly mild case." He entered the briefing room but remained near the doorway.

"What happened to her didn't sound very mild to me," Jack responded, skeptically, "and it sounded a lot worse than the flu."

The doctor nodded patiently. In his experience people often thought having the flu was the same as getting a cold. They had no idea just how lethal the infection could be. Even its deadly history, that it was cause of death for tens of millions of people in the early twentieth century, didn't bring the appropriate perspective.

"I've got her on fluids and anti-viral medication. She should be able to return to service in a couple of days."

"Have you updated her, told her what it is?"

"Yes, and as you can imagine, she was relieved it wasn't dengue fever."

"I'll tell you, Craig, I have a hell of a mess on my hands, having both her and Foster aboard under these circumstances."

The doctor smiled. "Not to mention you aren't going to get much of an opportunity to talk with Dr. Ross without him looking over your shoulder. He's extremely protective of her."

"Which is what we needed when they were in Venezuela, but I'm finding it damned inconvenient at the moment."

"Well, then I can be the bearer of good news. At this moment, Foster is eating in the officer's mess with a couple of his former teammates. I also heard them talking about a movie, so I would venture to guess you'll have her to yourself for awhile."

"Thank god," he replied, hurrying past the doctor.

Craig Harper stared at the empty doorway, rubbing his chin thoughtfully. It had been awhile since he'd been able to witness something so entertaining, yet so mundane. For too long he'd been caught up in his responsibilities to the men and women fighting the war on terror, keeping them alive, doing what he could to set their bodies and minds, if not souls on the road to healing. To watch two people fight love as if it were an enemy to be conquered would be a treat. He had fifty bucks riding on Foster in the marital pool. Smiling, he went to find the ship's commander so he could update him on Dr. Ross' condition.

Dan looked around at the officers laughing and talking and wondered if he were in a *Twilight Zone* episode. How many times had he been the guest of the US navy aboard an air craft carrier on his way to some mission? How many times had he sat in an officers' mess, talking and joking with some of the very people seated around him? Now, sitting among them but not one of them, he felt like he was walking through his own shadow. It was eerie as hell.

Most of the men and women serving aboard the carrier didn't know the details surrounding his presence, but they were all treating him with a great deal of respect. The word had been put out that he and Dr. Ross were civilian advisors and part of a top security mission, which was partially true. He, at least, was an advisor to the military. That he was still officially one of them was not a part of the plot here, and therefore, that information had been reserved for a very select few.

He smiled. Jack Porter underestimated the military mind, definitely intelligent and often suspicious. He had no doubt that many more people suspected the truth, but understood the need to play the game because in this game, playing by the rules meant the mission would succeed, so everybody wins.

"Come on, Digger, let's go watch the movie. It'll get your mind off things for awhile and after what you've been through, you could use the break."

He smiled across at Major Lucinda Anderson, affectionately known as Prowler because of her ability to gain information in stealth ways that had even the most hardened of her superiors in awe.

"Your friend is in excellent hands with Dr. Harper, so let her get her rest. With the flu, that's what she needs; rest."

"Okay, you've convinced me," he answered, ignoring the emphasis she'd put on the last part of that sentence.

"Besides," she added, with a wink, "from what I hear, you're probably the last person she wants to talk to right now."

"I'm not even going to ask what it is you've heard because I'm sure I don't want to know."

She laughed and preceded him into a lounge where *Lethal Weapon Four* was playing. At the end of the scene in which Leo explains to Detective Martin Riggs that marrying Lorna wouldn't betray the memory of his dead wife, you could have heard a pin drop. No one dared to look in his direction.

He stared blandly at Prowler, who wore her most angelic countenance. "Movie; nice idea." He stood and walked to the door.

"Foster, where are you going?" she hissed. "The movie isn't over."

"I've seen the ending. *We're family.* G'night, Prowler."

The minute he was out of sight, the men and women in the lounge were pulling out their wallets, anxious to get in on the pool.

Dan froze in the hallway just outside Kaila's room, tension coiling within him. Jack Porter was standing over her, pointing to a folder resting in her lap. It was obvious from the body language that they knew each other quite well. The security liaison glanced at his watch.

"I'd better get out of here before -."

"Before -?" Dan queried, coming to stand on the other side of the bed. "Don't let me interrupt. You were saying?" He folded his arms and looked directly at Kaila.

Porter grabbed up the folder and walked to the door.

"I hope you continue to feel better, Dr. Ross." He gave Dan a cursory nod. "Foster."

"Well, Dr. Ross, it would appear there's more to you than meets the eye."

Kaila could have done several things. She could have told Dan a lie. She could have told him to leave. She could have remained silent, claiming the fifth. Instead, she sighed and gestured toward the chair he had been in earlier that day, only the roles had been reversed.

"When were you going to tell me?"

"Tell you what?" she asked, resignedly.

"You're goddamned CIA, aren't you?"

She nodded, her eyes fixed on the place in her lap where the folder had been. It had contained the latest intelligence on the stolen technology.

"So?"

She looked at him, her expression blank. "So, what?"

"So, just when the hell were you going to tell me?"

"Never," she answered, her voice barely above a whisper.

Dan's face morphed through several emotions, surprise, hurt, anger, disbelief.

"Come on, Foster, you're Special Ops. You know that kind of knowledge can get people killed. Hell, no one who doesn't absolutely need that information knows about this."

"Your family doesn't know?"

"Good god, no."

Kaila forced herself to relax when she realized she was clutching at the hospital sheet. She'd be damned if she'd let this man make her feel she'd done something wrong by not endangering his life. When she looked at it that way, fear transformed into frustration which ran dangerously close to anger.

"So much for honesty," he spat.

"Oh, spare me the self pity, Foster. I mean, what's good for the goose is good for the gander, right? Or have you so quickly forgotten our earlier discussion?" It was a good thing for the major she was hooked up to so many tubes, she decided. She took a deep breath, but before she could continue, they were interrupted.

"I think it's a bit late for Dr. Ross to have visitors," Dr. Harper said, coming to check her IV He grabbed her wrist and looked at his watch. "She needs her rest."

Dan stood. It was obvious he had more to say, but equally as obvious he wasn't going to cause a scene. "I hope you get a good night's rest, Kaila," he called as he stepped into the hallway and disappeared.

"How are you feeling, Dr. Ross?"

"Please, call me Kaila," she responded, "and I'm doing okay. I still feel a little weaker than I'd like."

"Yes, well, that shaky feeling might last another day or two, but I think you're well on your way. Did you eat?"

"I had a hot turkey sandwich." She smiled. "It was really good."

"You seem surprised."

"I guess I figured military food was bland and awful."

"Oh, but it can be," he assured, smiling and scribbling medication changes on an HP tablet PC. The information would be uploaded wirelessly and the medical officers on duty would be able to access it. He looked up at her. "It depends where you are and what you're eating. Life aboard an aircraft carrier can have its advantages. Out in the field, that's a whole different ball of wax. It isn't always possible to get more than the most primitive of meals."

"Kind of like when I'm out on a remote dig. At times like that, beans from a can are a luxury."

He nodded, smiled. "If all continues up and to the right, we'll be removing your IV tomorrow afternoon."

"Interesting timing," she murmured.

"Not a coincidence," he replied, and walked to the door. "Have a good night, Kaila."

She stared at the ceiling and thought over the day's events. According to the latest intelligence, Chad hadn't yet carried out his plans to auction off the laser technology. The crystal, so far as everyone understood, was still in his possession and no longer in Venezuela.

What had been most interesting to Kaila was Porter's reaction to all of this. For a man who had been panicked at the possibility this technology would end up in the hands of the wrong government, he was awfully calm. It could be that he had a great deal of confidence in her ability to anticipate Chad's next move, to stop him, but she didn't think so. Normally, she would have used her gift to determine what Porter was really up to, but to use that kind of energy draw when she was so sick, would only leave her with a psychic hangover. Totally, not worth it.

The migraine, nausea, and shaky weakness that came after a heavy drain on her psychic resources was identical to how she felt when she'd had one too many margaritas.

She closed her eyes and leaned back, trying to make herself comfortable. Between the tubes taped to her left wrist, and the starched sheets, not to mention being sick, it was more than difficult. She knew she could ask for something to help her sleep but she didn't want to risk having any residual in her system the next day since it interfered with her ability to focus her intuitive energy.

Besides, she thought grimly, she knew what was really wrong; how badly she and Dan had left things. He was hurt because she hadn't told him the truth. He probably felt that because he'd been in Special Ops, she should have trusted him more. Maybe he was right. Maybe Tim was right. She smiled. How could she bring herself to trust Dan Foster when she wasn't sure she even trusted herself? *Especially after what happened all those years ago.*

"Kaila?"

Her eyes snapped open. Dan was standing in the doorway.

"Can I come in?" he asked, softly.

She nodded.

"Listen, I don't like how we left things."

She was so startled at hearing her own thoughts expressed she was unable to do anything but stare.

"It looks like we're in this together and I would much rather we get along than not."

She nodded. "Agreed."

"I'm not going to stay because I know you need your rest. I just didn't want -." He shifted uncomfortably. "Have a good night."

"Foster?" she called softly. He stood by the door, head turned so that he wasn't looking at her but letting her know she had his attention.

"Thanks for coming by."

He nodded and stepped into the hallway.

Smiling, feeling much better, she leaned back and fell asleep.

CHAPTER EIGHTEEN

"I can ask them to come in here," Dr. Harper offered. "It might be a tight squeeze, but everyone who needs to be part of the briefing can fit."

"No," Kaila grit out, leaning on him heavily, "I can do this."

"Kaila, you're shaking like a newborn fawn. Let me -."

"Let me help."

They looked up as Dan came into the room.

"I told her we can hold the meeting in here -."

Dan snorted. "I wouldn't waste my breath," he said tersely, coming to stand next to Kaila. "Once she gets her mind set on something -." He shrugged.

"Stubborn, eh?"

Dan chose to ignore the smirk being directed at him by the doctor.

"Put your arm around me."

"I don't have to -."

"Do it," he growled, "or I'll carry you."

By the time the three of them maneuvered their way clumsily to the conference room, Dan decided to do just that. He swept her into his arms and stepped over the threshold.

"Put me down," she hissed once they were inside.

"I can see I'm no longer needed," the doctor said, bemusedly, and pulled the conference room door closed.

"Sit down and behave," he hissed back.

"Don't be an ass," she countered.

Ignoring the mirth buzzing about the table, Dan sat down at the opposite end, next to Jack Porter.

"Kaila, since you aren't feeling one hundred percent," the security liaison stated, "I'll make sure we keep this meeting short. Everyone here has been brought up to date, so I'll go ahead and turn things over to you."

"Thank you. You'll all understand if I remain seated. If my voice doesn't carry, let me know. I'm sure we can get a microphone in here."

Prowler brought over a pitcher of water, filled a glass, and handed it to her.

"Thank you."

Kaila indicated that the officer could dim the lights. She pressed a button on a data pad set into the table and a screen descended silently from the ceiling. She hit a few keys on the HP laptop she was using and a map appeared on the screen across from where she sat. She waited until the officers had situated themselves before proceeding.

"We know that Kroeger has left Venezuela," she began. "We know that he has alerted the Russians and Iranians about the stolen technology. What we don't know is why he chose to delay the auction after moving it south of Caracas." She hit a few keys and Chad's face appeared. She didn't miss the appreciative hiss that escaped the woman seated to her right, but she also didn't fault her for it.

Acting as if she were simply massaging her ribs, she pushed the crystal beneath her shirt into her skin with such pressure she knew it would leave a mark. Still, the protective talisman was not enough to shield her from the shock of seeing her former lover's image.

Someone who could easily pass for Mel Gibson's double, Chad Kroeger was beyond handsome. He had a disarming smile that, paired with dark hair and blue eyes, gave him a boyish appearance that made him seem harmless. The problem was, he was anything but, something she had learned only too well. Avoiding the eyes staring back from the screen, she continued.

"Our experience with Kroeger is that he is a thrill seeker, which led to his enlistment into the CIA, but he is also a narcissist, which is why he had a failed track record. While some have suggested that money, or selling to the highest bidder, is Kroeger's primary motive, I'm inclined to disagree. Money never mattered to him."

"How do you know that?"

Kaila turned her attention to Foster as she answered his question, staring between his eyes rather than directly into them.

"Kroeger was raised with money. He spent his childhood educated at the finest international boarding schools. He was a Rhodes Scholar and spent several years wandering and living off his trust."

"Are his parents still living?"

"No. They were killed when a hurricane overtook their yacht."

"So, they just disappeared?" he pressed.

"Along with three other couples, none of whom have surfaced. I know what you're getting at. They're not pulling a Bob Marley."

More than a few officers smiled at the term used in intelligence circles to describe those who faked their own deaths. Dan, however, bristled.

"No disrespect, Foster, but the information I'm sharing is solid," she pressed.

"How old was he when this accident happened?"

She sighed. "He was already working for the CIA when his parents died. His psychological profile does not indicate any of the regulars, such as Oedipus." Not willing to continue down that path, she hit a few keys and a new map appeared.

"We believe he is in Russia, that he entered through Georgia as part of a humanitarian relief group delivering medical supplies."

"Does he have a medical background?" Dan asked, his eyes boring into hers.

She wiped her brow and took a sip of water before answering. "His field of expertise is cultural anthropology." She shifted.

"Dr. Ross, are you feeling okay?"

She smiled at the officer to her left, Captain Ron Vegas.

"Thank you, I'm holding my own. I'm almost finished, anyway."

"What did he do for the CIA?" Dan asked.

"Perhaps I'd better answer that," Jack spoke up, effectively pulling the major's attention away from her. "He was a cultural attaché to the Middle East."

"I see. Any chance we can get a more detailed briefing of his service in the year prior to his decommission?"

"Dr. Ross, would you be able to put something together?"

"I'll have something ready to present tomorrow morning, if that works for you," she replied.

"Is there anything else you feel we need to know?" Jack asked, not unsympathetically. "I think you'd better get some rest. I'm sorry if this has overtaxed you."

She shook her head, smiled weakly.

"I think that right now we need to assume he is playing a game of cat and mouse. My guess is the players are the Russians, the Venezuelans, and the Iranians."

"So, you don't think he'll remain in Russia?" Prowler asked.

"I'm still reading intelligence data. Kroeger has been off my radar for a long time. It's going to take me a bit to come up to speed on things and to form a conclusion. In the meantime, we have to assume that he is arranging a potential auction in Moscow, since it's a safer venue than the Middle East."

"I take it we have people in place there?" Prowler asked.

"Jack is a better person to address that than I am."

"It seems to me a guy like that wouldn't be able to hide easily," she theorized, and Kaila winced. Damn Chad's good looks to hell.

"You'd be surprised," she replied, ignoring blue eyes boring into her from the opposite end of the table. "He has worn colored contacts and grown a beard, totally transforming his appearance."

"Foster?" Jack said, "why don't you escort Dr. Ross back to her quarters? The rest of you, remain here and I'll continue the briefing. We'll reconvene tomorrow morning at ten hundred hours, provided Dr. Ross is feeling up to it."

She was already at the door before Dan managed to reach her.

"Don't make a scene," he whispered, "let me help you." Once they were out of sight of the conference room, he picked her up and carried her to the infirmary; the two of them silent all the way. He dumped her unceremoniously, if gently, on the bed.

"I'll get you something to eat."

Without waiting for a response he left.

"How are you feeling, Kaila?" The medical officer inserted a thermometer under her tongue. "Hell of a thing to do with having the flu like you do; a security briefing."

She smiled. "Manic, you worry too much," she managed around the thermometer.

"Here, take this."

"What is it?"

"Acetaminophen," he replied, dumping two white capsules from a tiny plastic cup into her palm and handing her a glass of water.

"What's the purple pill?"

"Anti-viral. You'll take it with food."

"Foster went to get something for me to eat."

"I know, I heard him, which is why I am giving this to you now." He put a blood pressure cuff around her right tricep and put two fingers on her wrist. She held still until he'd finished.

"It's a bit high," he said, removing the cuff, "but I'm not surprised. Security briefing -." He shook his head and scribbled onto another HP tablet PC. "Anything I can get for you?"

"No, but thanks. You've all been just terrific. I appreciate how you've taken care of me. I know you've spent extra time here and you didn't have to do that."

"Are you kidding? Miss an opportunity to spend time with a beautiful woman of intelligence?"

"Out, Manic Man," Dan snapped, stepping up to the bed. "And don't be an ass."

He set two trays on a rolling table and lowered it over her lap. He took one of them, sat on the edge of the bed, and cut into broiled cod. "That must have worn you out."

"I'm probably not as bad off as you think," she countered, spearing a piece of broccoli.

"Why were you the one to brief us on Kroeger?"

"We worked in the same organization."

"So did Porter, why didn't he give it?"

"Ask him."

"Do you ever give a straight answer?"

"I just did. If you want to know about Kroeger, ask Jack. Like I told Prowler, he's been off my radar for years."

"When was the last time you saw him?"

"The exact date?"

"Stop answering my questions with a question," he snapped.

"I don't answer to you, Foster, so I'd consider your tone before continuing down this path." She took a sip of water and worked to rein in her temper. It sapped so much energy; damned flu.

"Kaila, how are you feeling?"

"Hey, doc, I'm hangin' in. Good fish."

"Take your meds?"

"Two white tablets and a purple horse pill."

Excellent. Your recovery is right on. I hope the meeting didn't overtax you?"

"I'm fine."

"I understand you'll be back at it tomorrow morning."

"Yeah, and if I'm going to be ready for that one I'm going to have to work on the material tonight." She looked meaningfully in Dan's direction.

"Then I'll make sure you're undisturbed," the doctor replied, glaring at the major. "Make sure she doesn't get over-excited, Foster," he snapped before going back to his office.

"Looks as if I've been given my orders," he commented, chugging down the rest of his water. "Is there anything I can get for you before I leave?"

She was about to tell him he could bring her the laptop she'd inadvertently left in the conference room when a young seaman appeared just outside the door.

"Ma'am? Mr. Porter asked me to deliver this to you. Is it okay if I bring it in?"

"That would be great."

He set the portable computer on a table, and, wishing her a speedy recovery, left.

"I can't believe how well I'm being cared for," she said, pushing her now empty plate away. "They're spoiling me. I feel guilty -."

"Don't."

"No, these guys are busy and have enough to do without watching over a civilian."

"They don't mind. Trust me."

One side of her mouth went up. "Meaning that if I had buck teeth, crossed eyes, and couldn't string two sentences together they would bitch, but because I'm blonde and intelligent they're all fighting for the chance to talk to the circus side show?"

"Circus side show?"

"Oh, come on Foster, don't tell me you don't have a repertoire of blonde jokes. No intelligence in there? God knows I've heard my share of that crap since I was nine years old."

He smiled, but shook his head. "Even if I did, I know better than to throw them in your face. You'd kick my ass."

She gulped down the last of her water, avoiding his eyes. *Would he ever get over that?*

"Listen, I'd better let you get to it. Tomorrow morning will come around soon enough." He gave a wave and stepped out into the hall.

CHAPTER NINETEEN

Kaila stared at the screen on the laptop and wondered how in the hell was she going to get through this assignment. A summary of Chad Kroeger's last year of service? Why didn't Dan just ask for six pints of blood? It would have been easier to give.

Her fingers were poised over the keys and as she searched for the right words, she wondered if she would throw up. It wasn't motion sickness from being on the aircraft carrier; they had given her medication for that. It was Kroeger.

His photo was in the upper right corner of the monitor and while she never looked directly at it, the energy coming from it, from him, was wreaking havoc and leaving her feeling as bad as she did in the rain forest. She drew in a shaky breath and wondered if she should ask for a reprieve. Would Jack accept a doctor's note? In spite of how awful she felt, she smiled at the thought.

"Knock knock."

"What the hell do you want?"

The security liaison strode up to the bed. "I came to see how you were?"

"Oh, and like you care. If you cared about my well being, you would have left me alone down in Chile and we wouldn't be having this conversation right now."

"Kaila, trust me, I know how hard this must be for you."

"Don't patronize me, Jack. Since when has the CIA ever given a shit about anyone's feelings? It's always about the mission. We're always told it's about a cause greater than ourselves, right? Ignore the pain, ignore the -."

"Okay, so I don't understand," he conceded, taking a seat and resting a booted leg on his knee.

"Why me, Jack? Why did you drag me into this? There are plenty of other people in your organization that could have handled this."

"You were his partner for three years. No one knows Kroeger the way you do."

In that moment she understood a great deal.

"You son-of-a-bitch."

"You wouldn't be the first one to think so," he said, sighing.

"This isn't about any stupid piece of technology."

"The hell it isn't," he snapped.

"This isn't about the Russians or the Iranians, it's about Kroeger."

Porter steepled his fingers beneath his chin and studied her, but didn't respond.

"How did he get a hold of the laser, Jack? If Kroeger was out, how did he get access to the technology?" When the liaison didn't reply, she sneered. "You reintegrated him, didn't you?"

"Kaila -."

"You conceited, stupid bastard. Didn't I tell you something like this would happen? Didn't I warn you? What, after what happened in the Middle East, you lost confidence in me? You thought it was personal? That I wanted revenge on him?"

"No, trust me -."

"No wonder you didn't hesitate when I told you I wanted out, that'd I'd had enough."

"It wasn't like that."

"The hell it wasn't. I saw the looks on your faces when I got back from Afghanistan. You all blamed me for what happened in the Hindu Kush. You decided that because of my previous relationship with him, I'd lost my perspective out there; that I wasn't able to see clearly."

"I admit, back then, there was a great deal of question about what really happened that day, but we've since come to realize that it wasn't you, Kaila." The last came out as a plea for understanding.

"You came to realize it wasn't me," she spat. "Didn't you think that might have been something I would've liked to have been told? Perhaps something that would have helped with the guilt I've been carrying on my shoulders night and day since that goddamned mission?"

"We didn't come to understand the truth until very recently. Honestly? We weren't even sure what to do at first. We were still trying to figure it out when he ran on us."

Kaila's heart pounded. For over six years she had relived that day, the despair of the soldiers, their knowledge that they would never see loved ones again, never hold them. It was the one trauma that nothing in the world could ease, not the EMDR, nothing. She had replayed those last hours endlessly, wondering what she could have done differently, and she had always come to the same conclusion. Other than killing Chad Kroeger, there was nothing she could have done to stop the events that transpired.

She swiped at tears that streamed down her cheeks and worked to control the rush of hatred threatening to overwhelm her. She had to get it under control or she would never be able to think clearly, and she needed all her wits about her to deal with the man sitting across from her. The man who sent her to that hell all those years ago and who let her think she was the one responsible so that he didn't have to admit he was wrong in trusting Kroeger instead of trusting her. She took a deep, shaky breath.

"I'm here, right now, and I want to hear it from you. That day, that mission. All those people died because Kroeger didn't listen to *me*, right?"

"I'm here, right now, looking at you and telling you yes, those people died because Kroeger let his feelings about you mar his judgment. If he'd listened to you, to your psychic intuition, none of those people would have died."

She put her face in her hands and let the tears flow; tears for herself and for all those who lost because of Chad Kroeger.

Outside the door, Dan Foster stood staring into the eyes of Manic Man, his hands fisted at his sides.

"I've heard enough," he growled, and spun on his heel.

"Foster, wait -."

Dan shook his head and stalked toward the passageway that would lead him topside. Ignoring the men on duty, he pushed against the wind that whipped across the deck until he stood at the railing. So far away from city lights, millions of stars were easily visible, and every few minutes a shooting star would streak cross the horizon. He took several deep breaths and tried to sort through the emotions clamoring through his brain. Blood thundered in his ears. She was a goddamned psychic.

Worse than that, she was one of those bastards they trained to work with the military, to provide intelligence that supposedly couldn't be gained by other methods.

The US government had been using psychics in national security since World War II. At the height of the Cold War it was decided to have them trained alongside and by the military in order to ensure communication and cooperation between the different security agencies. As a result, specialized intelligence centers were established. Although many of them had either closed their doors or consolidated over the years, the program remained a priority in the name of national security.

There was such a school down in Monterey and as Kaila Ross was from the Bay Area, he imagined she had trained there. Hell, maybe she'd even attended one of his lectures. Part of his climb through the ranks required that he give lectures to the misfits, to teach them the skills they would need to work with military intelligence.

Dan sneered. Misfits; it's what they were, too. Often intelligent to the point of genius, they tended to lack appropriate social skills and definitely carried chips on their shoulders when it came to the chain of command. It wasn't that he couldn't appreciate bucking authority; it was their self-entitled superiority, their arrogance. They rarely accepted that maybe they didn't know everything. Maybe they were wrong. Maybe someone else knew better. He shook his head. She was one of them.

He wasn't all that surprised when he noticed Prowler making her way toward him as he stared out at the night sky. Since the wind would drown out her footsteps, she'd made sure he saw her coming.

"Manic Man send you after me?" he asked, resignedly.

"Would you be upset if he did?" she replied, standing companionably next to him and staring out at the calm sea.

"Look, I appreciate your concern, and his, but this -."

"There's more, Foster."

The way she'd said it sent a wave of apprehension over him. He turned.

"She's not an analyst."

"No shit, she's not an analyst." He laughed at her expression. "What kind of a moron do you think I am? Any fool can see that she's being played by Porter just like the rest of us. Who knows what the bastard is really after, but we're all in the game til we find out, right?"

She continued to stare at him.

"I've known for awhile that there was more to this thing than is on the surface, but isn't that always the way? Especially with the CIA? Need to know, right? They worry if they give us too much information it might crowd our brains, screw up our judgment. Hell, we might start making decisions without their permission."

She blew out a sigh, stared out at the horizon.

"Prowler, if you know something you think I should be aware of, spit it out. I'd rather hear it from you, one on one, than have it brought out in a conference room full of people tomorrow morning."

"Kroger's last year of service was in 2003. He was put on administrative leave after a mission failed badly."

"What are you saying, that Chad Kroeger and Kaila Ross are responsible for what happened in the Hindu Kush?" *Where Staci had died a brutal death.*

"I'm saying that there's more going on here than Jack Porter is telling any of us. Whether or not Dr. Ross knows what that is -?" She shrugged. "I suspect she doesn't."

"You think Porter is withholding information from her?"

She nodded. "The relationship between the two of them certainly seems adversarial, so it wouldn't surprise me that he's holding back. From what I understand, he is the one who relies on her to give him the details."

For several seconds, he digested that.

"You think he is waiting for her to tell him what he needs to know, then he deploys us to recover the technology?"

"I think the technology is a small piece of this. I think he wants Chad Kroeger and he is using Dr. Ross to do it. It's more than likely Kroeger is already aware she has been enlisted for this."

Dan thought back to the day Dr. Sanchez had been killed. Whoever had been shooting at them had peppered bullets at her feet but hadn't killed her when it was obvious they could have. Had it been Kroeger out there that day?

"Dan? Do you think her judgment might be clouded by the fact he used to be her partner? Maybe she can't reconcile the fact that she somehow missed his true character?"

He thought back to what he'd overheard. It hadn't sounded like Kaila's judgment was impeded when it came to Kroeger. Still, she was an enigma when it came to how she felt deep down. She was too good at keeping her true feelings hidden. He had a hunch that if he had enough time with her he could learn the subtle nuances that unlocked who she was, inside. There had even been a point in time he assumed that was in his future. Now, he wasn't so sure.

"I like Dr. Ross," she continued, still staring into the distance. "I would hate to see her get hurt because two asshole males are fighting over her."

"Tell me I'm not one of the two assholes in that statement."

"Of course not. I'm talking about Jack Porter and Chad Kroeger."

"You think -."

"I think I've told you what I need to tell you. No more speculation. Take it for what it's worth and make the information work. Gotta go."

For several minutes he stood and stared out at the night sky. Although it was familiar to him, standing on the deck of a naval carrier awaiting orders, this time it was different. It was surreal, as if he were a ghost walking among familiar faces, familiar objects, but unable to connect with them.

Not that long ago this was his life and he felt very comfortable in it. Now, however, there was a sharp disconnect, as if he were merely a spectator to the events taking place. Oh, the instincts were still there. His mind still clicked in place, analyzing, sorting information. His radar was on full alert. He hadn't lost his edge. This was something else; something deeper.

Maybe it was that the players were different. He let out a deep breath and brushed the thought aside as soon as it formed. It wasn't the first time different governmental departments had teamed up in the name of national security. More than once he had worked alongside men and women from all branches of the armed services and Lord knew, being in Special Ops, interacting with the Central Intelligence Agency was as common as getting a cold in the winter.

Some of the guys in his unit hit the gym when troubled by something they couldn't understand but that wasn't his style. He always felt better after he'd slept on a problem since morning light usually brought new clarity. Nodding, comfortable with that course of action, he turned and made his way back to his quarters.

Although his intention had been to go right to sleep, he found himself staring up at the ceiling, listening to the familiar sounds of life aboard an aircraft carrier. He smiled. One thing the military had taught him, how to be a light sleeper and still get rest.

Maybe what he needed to do was to try and connect with the pieces of his past that were at hand; the people. That must be what had been eating at him. For the most part during the last few weeks, the people he had been around were people he didn't know that well and therefore, didn't completely trust. Especially Kaila Ross, who was a kaleidoscope, continuously changing definition before his eyes; he never had time to adjust.

He thought over the few people aboard he did know, did trust. He hadn't seen Leopard since the day the chopper set down on the carrier. Manic Man seemed to know more than he let on but he was such a smart ass, sometimes it was difficult to distinguish between when he was fishing for information and when he was sharing it. That left only Prowler as the continuity point between his old life and his new one, and as far as he could tell, she was trying to push him into his future.

He hadn't missed the not so subtle messages she was sending his way about Kaila. Problem was, she didn't understand. It wasn't just a simple matter of boy meets girl, boy likes girl, boy goes for girl. It was different now; in a short time the stakes had completely changed.

The woman wasn't just an archeologist innocently caught up in a bad set of circumstances. She was a fucking CIA operative and part of the freak show group of psychics the security agencies liked to pull out and show off when it made them look good. Circus. No wonder she had used that term when describing herself. She understood full well who and what she was.

He sighed, turned on his side and stared at the door. In spite of the fact that she was virtually a stranger to him, a member of a group he had come to despise for more reasons than he could list, he couldn't bring himself to despise her. For that matter, he couldn't bring himself to see her as part of that circus freak show he had interacted with more than once during his years in Special Ops. He wasn't able to drop her into that category. Some part of him said she was different. She wasn't like them; couldn't be.

Aw, hell.

He grabbed up a paperback he'd been reading and tried, unsuccessfully, to put her out of his mind.

CHAPTER TWENTY

"I'm sorry, man, doctor's orders; no visitors."

Dan stared at Manic Man and considered using physical force to get in to see Kaila. The medic smiled. It was an evil grin.

"I appreciate the delicacy of this situation, Digger, but I wouldn't try it. You'll lose. Badly."

He blew out a sigh, clenched his fists. "Can you at least tell me how she is?"

"She's sick, okay? We had to put her IV back in and pump a bunch of meds into her."

Dan caught it when the medic's eyes slid guiltily away.

"What meds? What did you pump into her?"

Instead of answering, the medic grabbed his arm and dragged him into the doctor's office, conveniently empty since the good doctor was off taking a meal. "Sit down," he ordered, indicating a chair and taking a seat on a sofa situated against one of the walls. "Since the only other patient currently in here is a seaman first class who broke his leg this morning, we have a bit of privacy."

Dan sat stiffly in the chair and waited. His instincts screamed for him to go to her bedside. It was all he could do not to rage at the man sitting across from him, even though he knew he was just doing what Dan himself would have done, were the roles reversed.

"We had to sedate her."

"Why?"

"Shortly after Jack left last night, she started throwing up. We were afraid she was going to become dangerously dehydrated. The doc tried just giving her anti-nausea meds but it wasn't enough. Whether it was what Jack told her, seasickness, or the flu, it's hard to say, but over a very short amount of time she got sicker and sicker. When she became delirious, started saying some off the wall things, I hit her with sedation. She's been asleep ever since."

"Off the wall things? Like what, for instance?"

"She started out asking for an iPod, then asked to take a shower, then said something about an amethyst. As it got worse, she started talking about Kroeger and someone named Karina. She broke out in a sweat and started thrashing. When she took a swing at the doctor and began yanking at her IV tubes, I gave her the sedation."

"You gotta let me see her, Manic."

"No. I will not disobey the colonel. He said that no one, and I mean *no one* was to see her."

"Meaning especially me," Dan growled. "Just what does he think I would do to her? I'm guessing my name, as well as that of Jack Porter, were listed very specifically on that list of who not to let in, right?"

The medic smiled. "I -," he stopped. "Look, if you want to see her, you need to get permission from Dr. Harper."

"And he is going to need one hell of a good reason to let you in there," the doctor said, walking around his desk and sitting down to face Foster. "I see you two have been having a nice chat."

Dan's mouth dropped open. The man had a black eye. "She did that?"

Manic snorted. "I told you, she swung at him."

"And connected, I see." When the doctor's face colored, he laughed. "Remind me to tell you about when she nearly kicked my ass." Both men wore expressions of disbelief. He sobered. "You have to let me see her."

"Convince me that doing so won't make the situation worse," he countered.

Dan let out a sigh. "I can translate that gibberish that was making her hysterical," he replied, tiredly. "At least, some of it."

"Talk," Manic said. The doctor leaned forward, his elbows on his desk, and nodded.

"I'm not going to say I understand the whys of it but I am somewhat familiar with her kind. I used to lecture at MRSI, in Monterey." The acronym stood for Military Research Scientific Institute; spook school.

Both men nodded.

"I've also spent some time around her and her environment; enough to have figured a few things out. She surrounds herself with some pretty odd things. At first I thought she was just one of those New Age kooks that likes to burn candles and incense. You know, the modern day hippie?"

The men nodded, smiled.

"But I realized after something happened that this stuff has more meaning for her. That necklace she wears. It's some kind of talisman, but for her it's more than a good luck charm. She thinks it has some kind of power. She would have risked her life to get it from her camper-trailer during an ambush if I hadn't stopped her and retrieved it for her." He turned to Manic. "You said she mentioned an amethyst? She had a little group of them on a nightstand near her bed in the camper. When we were in the forest and I crawled into her sleeping bag to keep her warm when she was shivering so violently? She had them spread out near her head."

The doctor picked up a manila folder from his desk, opened it and scanned the contents. He looked at Dan. "You were right; those items do have special significance. I guess they are all a part of her toolkit. Many of the people in her organization have different charms and tricks that help them do their jobs, get through life, as it were. The iPod has a couple of playlists that help her regain her equilibrium after a bad episode. The shower probably meant she wanted to douse herself in apple cider vinegar. Apparently, it is an emergency remedy for clearing the effect that violence has on her."

"Where did you get that?" he asked, pointing at the folder.

"Jack Porter brought it by this morning. He thought it might help with her treatment. He's worried about her."

Dan snatched it from the doctor's grasp, read it. He looked up, furious.

"Kroeger authored this."

The doctor sat back, stared up at him, nodded.

"Why did Kroeger -?"

"They were partners for three years," Manic reminded him. "He would know her habits."

Dan's heart slammed off his chest. He snorted. "Partners? I'd say they were a hell of a lot more than that."

"Now, Foster, you don't know -."

"The hell I don't. Taking a shower with vinegar and the other crap in this report? No partner would know that kind of stuff unless the relationship was a hell of a lot closer than just working together on assignments. It's too personal." He tossed the folder back on the desk and sat down.

"Kroeger was a psychic, too," Jack Porter said, resignedly, stepping into the office and closing the door behind him. "Can I join you?" He sat next to Manic on the sofa.

"I had no idea the situation would get this out of hand," he started. "Foster's right. They were lovers. For how long, I'm not exactly sure. I do know that they had broken off that level of the relationship by the time we assigned them to Afghanistan. They weren't even physically in the same location at that point. We had them each assigned to different Ops teams."

"What happened over there?" Dan asked. His heart continued to pound. Would he finally get an answer as to why his young, pregnant wife had been murdered?

"We had obtained information that was considered vital to the security of our armed forces. A new informant had shown up on the radar, only too willing to sell out the Taliban. The person was not someone we planted, so we went through the tests you would expect, putting him through trials to assess his loyalty, the accuracy of the information. He passed with flying colors. We assigned him to a special task force." The security liaison stood, paced a small square before leaning against a wall, arms crossed, and continued.   His eyes were unfocused, seeing through a distant memory.

"He came to us with information that a caravan of terrorists was moving a huge cache of weapons through the Hindu Kush. They were using women this time, cleverly disguising the weapons by mixing them in with provisions the American Red Cross had sent as part of a UN relief effort. We went to great lengths to verify the tip through alternate sources." He closed his eyes. "Neither Dr. Ross nor Chad Kroeger initially had any reservations about the validity of the information."

"You relied on two psychics for that?" Dan bit out, clenching his teeth. "You risked the lives of men and women based on what a couple of freaks told you?"

The security liaison stiffened. "I assure you we had every reason to believe whatever either Kroeger or Ross ever shared with us. They were highly respected operatives. That they were gifted psychics was not the sole reason for their placement over there."

"You used their academic backgrounds," he accused.

"Of course we did," he snapped. "A cultural attaché and an archeologist would fly under the radar. But to address your original comment, no, we didn't just rely on their opinions. We did not make the decision to try and intercept the weapons cache until we'd obtained multiple sources of corroboration."

"So, what happened?" Manic asked. He'd been there in the aftermath of that disastrously failed mission.   He'd zippered too many bodies into bags. He wanted answers.

One of the women in the caravan had infiltrated our intelligence network."

"Through Kroeger," Dan guessed.

"They had become lovers. No one was aware; at least, not initially."

"Kaila found out."

"She said she sensed that someone in the group of women was a problem and that we needed to abort the mission."

"And you didn't listen to her, because -?"

"The only thing she had going for her was a hunch, a gut feel."

"Something you had been paying her for and following religiously until that point." It was the doctor who spoke.

"We're talking about a woman who used to be Kroeger's lover. We believed the breakup had affected their working relationship, that it had impaired her judgment, her ability to be impartial."

"And you automatically assumed it was Kaila who was wrong, not Kroeger?" Manic asked.

"We had no other information that suggested she was right," he hissed, exasperated. He thrust a hand through his thinning hair. "Christ, don't you think if we suspected for one minute that she was right we wouldn't have called it off?"

The three officers remained silent.

"The fact that we didn't have one shred of evidence to support what she was saying should tell you how badly we were breached."

And what a strong a psychic she was, Dan thought.

"How soon before the caravan was scheduled to traverse the Kush did Dr. Ross come to you?" Dan asked, finally.

"The day before they were set to move the weapons through." He let out a sigh. "Now, maybe you can understand why we had trouble believing her. She came to us hours before a vital mission was set to go off and told us we had to cancel it because she had a bad vibe about it. That's how she put it," he snarled, frustration at its peak. "That she had a bad vibe about it. We had to abort. No other reason than that she had a bad vibe about it."

"How old was she?" Dan asked, working to keep his emotions from getting out of hand. Facts, he reminded himself, stick to the facts.

"How long had she been working for you?" the doctor added, "and was this her first major assignment?"

"She was twenty-seven years old, had been working for the agency since she turned twenty-one, and no, this was not her first international assignment."

Dan's body jerked. The doctor had asked if it was her first major assignment, not international. While that may not be relevant to some, especially since the CIA only had jurisdiction off US soil; for him, it was significant. He was trained to examine every nuance of speech for tone, tempo, body language, and definitely words used. He stared at the liaison. His mind sifted through everything he had learned in the last few days.

"Lunsar. You sent her to Lunsar."

Porter nodded.

"I'd say you have a pretty poor track record with Dr. Ross as a psychic," he said, his voice dripping contempt, "since people died there too." He looked briefly at Manic, then the doctor. "She was shot on that mission and four people died that day."

"Many more would have if it weren't for her. She radioed that morning, before dawn, said she'd woken up with an incredibly strong premonition that they were about to be ambushed. She'd already sent one of the students to hide until help could arrive and while we were trying to figure out how to get them out of there, the rebels moved in. We were cut off. We gave the information to the British who had marines stationed close by. They moved in, but by the time they were able to get to them, four people had been killed and Dr. Ross had been shot."

"And the guy she sent into hiding?" Manic asked.

"Because of her he is alive to tell about it. The British knew right where to look for him, not only because she told him where to run, but because she was able to remotely detect his presence." He sneered at Dan. "Psychically."

CHAPTER TWENTY-ONE

Kaila opened her eyes and tried to figure out where she was. Her brain was swimming in a fog. She tried to rub sleep from her eyes but something was wrong with her hand; it wouldn't move.

"What -?"

"Hey, you're awake."

"Foster?" Her mouth tasted like sawdust. "Can I have some water?"

"Sure. Here."

She tried to reach for the glass but couldn't. She blinked rapidly and saw why.

"Here, I'll help you."

When he took the cup away she frowned. "Why are my wrists tied down like this?"

He smiled. "Because you took a swing at the doctor. You got him, too. Gave him a black eye."

Her brows knitted as she searched her memory. She shook her head. "I don't remember. What happened? What day is it?"

"You've been asleep for the past thirty or so hours, mostly because of heavy sedation, though some of it simply because your body needed the downtime. The flu, remember?"

"I remember the briefing." She closed her eyes. "I remember having a conversation with Jack Porter." She opened her eyes and glanced at Dan, away again. "After he left I tried to put together a few facts about Kroeger's last year of service."

"Kaila, you're awake."

"Dr. Harper, hello. I'm sorry for the black eye," she finished sheepishly.

He smiled kindly, his eyes dancing with mirth. "I'm the talk of the ship. Prowler thinks you're a hero."

In spite of the situation, she laughed.

"Foster, get out."

"Hey, I thought we already went through this," he countered.

"I need to remove a few of these tubes. Out. You can come back when we're finished." He looked at Kaila. "Are you hungry?"

She nodded.

"Good. Foster, make yourself useful. Go get her something to eat."

The doctor closed the door and came over to the bed, sliding his hand beneath a corner of the blanket. "Let's get this catheter out, shall we? Take a deep breath and when I say, blow it out."

He placed a thermometer under her tongue and took her blood pressure, entering the results on the tablet PC.

"Good, completely normal. I don't think we need these anymore," he said, removing the restraints.

"I really am sorry."

"You were delirious, don't worry yourself about it. How do you feel?"

"Fine. I mean, tired, and a bit discomfited from sleeping so long, but I actually feel better than I have in days."

"Excellent. I love to hear things like that from my patients."

"Thanks for everything you've done."

"Any time," he replied, "all part of the service here at the floating casino."

She smiled, grateful to have landed in such a wonderful place. Thanks to Dan Foster, she reminded herself.

"Chicken and rice," Manic called, carrying a tray through the door. "Dan had to go to a meeting or something; said to tell you he'd be by when he could."

"Glad to see I didn't plant one on you, too," she observed, taking the tray.

"Well, it wasn't for not trying. I'm just faster than the doc here at ducking."

"Kaila, if you're up to it, I'd like you to try and get out of the bed this afternoon."

"Hell, yes. I've got more important things to do than lounge around with you people waiting on me," she said, tongue in cheek. And she desperately wanted a shower.

"We'll come back when you're ready," the doctor said. "In the meantime, eat. Can I get you anything else?"

"Could you get my iPod from my backpack, please?"

Both men scrambled to where the pack rested on a chair.

"Okay, you guys, knock it off. You're spooking me."

The doctor handed her the iPod. "What are you going to listen to?"

She smiled. "AC/DC, *Black Ice.*"

He shook his head. "Enjoy your food and we'll see you later."

Two hours later, Dan found her rummaging through her backpack. She was shaking so badly she had to brace herself against the wall to keep from falling.

"What do you think you're doing?" He came up and put an arm around her, steadying her.

"They told me I needed to get out of bed and move around," she snapped, irritated at being caught. She desperately wanted to get into that shower. She tried to unobtrusively drop her hand to her side but he was too observant. He reached across and pulled at her wrist.

"Um," she said, looking at the small plastic bottle of vinegar. "I use it as a rinse for my hair."

"Which would make sense if you were a redhead," he countered. "Blondes use white vinegar."

She stared at him.

"I told you, three sisters."

She blew a breath out. "I need a shower, Foster. I've been in that bed for days and I feel worse than grimy."

"I'll help you."

Her eyes flew to his.

"I promise I will be on my best behavior. Besides, I have a feeling it's either me helping you take a shower or Manic Man giving you a sponge bath. Between the two of us, I think you're better off with me."

"Because of what we did in the camper?" she asked, quirking an eyebrow.

"Because he's a grade A letch; he'd be lusting after you the entire time, nothing professional about it."

"Oh, and you're telling me you wouldn't have any lust?"

He kissed her quickly. "I can see you enjoy causing trouble. Seriously, I will help you get a shower." He moved the backpack to the floor. "Sit down, I'll be right back."

"But -."

"I don't want you falling and hurting yourself. I'll be right back. Sit down."

Through the open door she heard him tell Manic Man that no one was to be admitted to the room until he opened the door. She smiled as his voice carried clearly.

"And Manic? If you disobey that order for any reason other than to tell us this carrier is sinking? I will come up with something much worse than anything the colonel could ever devise, do I make myself clear?"

She was still smiling when he returned, shut the door, and came to the chair.

"Ready?" He took the vinegar and helped her over to the shower. There was a handicap bar on the wall, a fold down seat and a hand held sprayer. "Now that's convenient," he murmured. "Sit down."

He stepped out of the small space and stripped to his underwear.

"What are you doing?"

"I don't want to get my clothes wet and it might make you feel a little more comfortable if we're dressed in kind."

"Whatever happened to being on your best behavior?"

He grinned. "This is what I'm best at; my behavior." He reached around and pulled the tie that held the hospital gown closed. The top fell forward, exposing her breasts. He leaned over her and reached around, untying the ties securing the gown around her back. He grabbed it and pulled it away, tossing it on the bed. When the door opened behind him, he turned, blocking Kaila's body, a snarl on his face.

"Here." An arm holding a fresh gown and towels was thrust through a small opening.

"Thanks," Dan growled, grabbing the linens and slamming the door, barely missing the medical officer's fingers. He set them on the bed and returned to where Kaila sat.

"How are you feeling?"

"I'll feel a hell of a lot better once I'm showered."

"How does the vinegar thing work? Do I just dump the whole thing over you?"

Eyes wide, she nodded.

"Before or after you get clean?"

"Before."

"Do you have to be standing or can I get you while you're sitting there?"

"You can do it while I'm sitting here, but can you turn the water on first? The stuff is icy cold and it's nice to get rinsed quickly."

"Here goes," he said, removing the cap and pouring the contents over her. Her nose wrinkled and in spite of himself, he smiled. She reminded him of a pissed off elf. He sprayed her with warm water.

She sighed deeply, closed her eyes. "Thank you."

"What next?"

"I -," but she stopped, apparently at a loss.

"Never mind, I'll figure it out," he said, grabbing a bar of soap. He efficiently slid the small white bar over her skin, fighting the sensations that were swimming through his blood as it rushed straight to his waist. Biting the inside of his cheek, he reached for a washrag and held it under the spray. She took the soap from him as he moved the warm cloth over her face.

He mentally recited military protocol as he poured shampoo into the palm of his hand, making sure he'd have enough to spread through her long locks. She rubbed the soap vigorously in her hands, working up a good lather. He imagined she wanted to wash between her legs herself.

He started to whistle as he began washing her hair, gasping when she reached out with soapy hands and grabbed him. Already hard, she set his body throbbing.

"As I recall," she said impishly, her fingers massaging between his thighs, "I owe you."

"I wasn't keeping score," he answered, hoarsely.

"Of course you were," she countered, sliding his boxers off. "Ever since we were interrupted, you've been as prickly as a hedgehog."

"Kaila, soap is going to get in your eyes -."

"They're closed."

"Oh."

He grit is teeth and threw his head back as her hand grasped his shaft, moving back and forth, the soap a wonderful lubricant.

"Ouch," she squeaked.

"Sorry." He let go of her hair and focused all his energy on where her fingers were alternately stroking and squeezing him. He growled as he spurt hot liquid into her hands, his arms braced against the walls of the shower.

"There, now, all clean. Feel better?"

He grabbed her under the arms and pulled her onto his knee as it rested on the shower bench. "I'll show you just how much," he replied, and brought his mouth down over hers, thrusting his tongue inside. When she wrapped her arms around his neck and pulled him toward her, he slipped and fell sideways, pulling her, laughing, with him as he went.

When Manic opened the door they were sprawled on the floor, half out of the shower. Water was spraying at the wall and bouncing out, quickly forming a puddle on the floor.

"What did I tell you?" Dan called out, half yelling, half laughing. "Shut the damned door."

"I wanted to make sure everything was okay, that you two weren't killing each other," he replied.

"We're okay, Manic," Kaila replied. "We're totally, o-." she kissed Dan before continuing, "kay."

"I think that would qualify as conduct unbecoming an officer, Foster."

"Manic, unless you want to go for a swim with the sharks, I'd shut the damned door."

Laughter could be heard from the hallway.

"Pervert."

"I think you owe your friend. He's right. This kind of behavior would never be tolerated by the military under normal circumstances. Why, what would an admiral say?"

Dan thought about General Murphy's comments back in the trailer.

"If he didn't give me a thumb's up, I'd think he was six months in his grave."

"Foster, I have a feeling you've had quite an interesting relationship with authority." She wiggled against him. "I think we should finish up in here. We're making a mess."

They sat cross-legged on the floor of the shower, the seat folded against the wall, warm water trickling between them.

"Would you like me to return the favor?" he asked, reaching out and stroking her nipples.

She smiled, shook her head. "I'm still a little shaky. I think it'd only make things worse."

"I think it'd be just the thing to put roses back in your cheeks."

"How 'bout a rain check?"

"Okay."

Someone pounded on the door.

He sighed. "Looks like the party's over."

CHAPTER TWENTY-TWO

"Commander." Kaila nodded respectfully and took a seat at the conference table as far away from Foster and Manic Man as possible without seeming obvious.

"Dr. Ross, I'm glad you're well enough to join us."

His smile said it all. It was clear he had been briefed on the afternoon's activities, and while he was amused, he was also appreciative in a way only a male who had been out to sea, away from female companionship, could be. If she was going to be bombarded by those feelings for the entirety of the briefing, it was going to be a long meeting. Sometimes, her psychic abilities were a real pain in the ass.

"Thank you, sir." She didn't have to salute the man but she certainly knew to treat him with the respect he not only deserved, but had earned. But damned if she didn't feel like a kid caught with their hand in a cookie jar. She cleared her throat. She was not a kid, damn it.

"We have received confirmation that Chad Kroeger is currently in the former Soviet Union," the Commander began, "in Moscow; just as Dr. Ross predicted."

She winced. It had been common sense and not a premonition that had led her to that deduction. Russia was not only one of the players in Chad's little game, they had been his escort into Venezuela. It was logical to assume that he would lead them to believe that in return for protection from the United States government, they would have priority in the bidding process. She wondered if they realized he likely had no intention of allowing them to have the technology. She smiled. They probably had no intention of letting him leave the country alive. Her smile slipped. He was a psychic; he would know that.

"He has not given any indication that he intends to conduct the auction from that location."

"Iran?" Dan inquired.

The Commander nodded. "Good guess. However, we believe he will try to move the auction somewhere a little more neutral, perhaps somewhere more in his favor in terms of safety."

"There's not a whole lot of friendly territory in that part of the globe," Captain Vegas stated from where he sat on her right. "What is he hoping to accomplish?"

The Commander shifted and a wave of guilt and concern from him washed over Kaila. She shivered. His concern was for her.

"Dr. Ross," Dan stated, his gaze momentarily shifting to her. She stared back to where he was sitting between Jack Porter and Manic Man.

"Kroeger wants her and he is using this auction as a way to do that," he continued. "He knew that Porter would bring her out of retirement to track him down." He turned his gaze on the security liaison. "Is there even any stolen technology?"

Jack nodded. "That's a legitimate concern. We didn't consider that he had any motive other than financial until our analysts suggested, as did Dr. Ross, that it wasn't a logical conclusion, given that the man is independently wealthy."

"Rich people declare bankruptcy too," Prowler put in.

"Yes, but we checked. He has no need for money. By the time we had done the research, we'd already engaged Dr. Ross' help."

"He wants revenge," Dan concluded.

"For what?" Prowler asked.

Kaila stared at Dan. Everyone else but him had their gaze trained on her. He looked directly at Lieutenant Anderson when he answered.

"In 2003, she and Kroeger were partners, assigned as a team, yet deployed separately, to Afghanistan. The military had received information that a large weapons cache was being moved through the Hindu Kush and they were set to intercept and retrieve. Dr. Ross discovered a security breach, that one of the women involved with moving the cache was a spy. She tried to have the mission called off." He took a sip of water.

"When Kroeger gave the okay to continue in spite of her warning, she suggested that her partner's integrity had been compromised, and again tried to convince those in charge to cancel the mission.   Unfortunately, Kroeger was more persuasive; he convinced the powers that be that it was actually Dr. Ross whose veracity was in question.   The mission was not aborted and was a disastrous failure, as many of you at this table are aware."

"No one better than you," someone muttered.

What the hell did that mean?

Kaila stared across the table. Dan's face had colored, and although he said nothing, his fingers were interlaced on the table, his knuckles white. He still wasn't looking at her.

"Dr. Ross, were you aware of this, that Kroeger might be motivated by revenge?" Manic asked quietly, his eyes full of sympathy, even as his tone was completely professional.

"I was not aware of this until two nights ago," she replied, flatly.

The medical officer's brows moved toward his hairline. She couldn't help but feel satisfaction that he finally understood. When she had realized it, not because Jack Porter had told her, but because she felt Kroeger's intentions, she became so violently ill that she had to be sedated.

Several people at the table stared and for several seconds no one said a word.

"Wait a minute," Vegas interjected, "are you telling me that this guy is pissed off because she was right -." He jerked a thumb in her direction. "He wants revenge because she made him look bad? What kind of a psycho are we talking about?"

"Maybe she should answer that," a young man at the end of the table said, "since she worked with the guy."

"That's enough, Yellis," the Commander said gruffly from where he'd taken a seat across from her.

"It's a logical request," Kaila replied, her eyes still on Foster. That he refused to look at her was turning her blood to ice. Unfortunately, that was one mystery that would have to wait. She turned her eyes toward the officer, a lieutenant who was new to the Air Force Special Ops.

"I have not seen Kroeger since before that day. When I received word that the mission had failed I was evacuated from Afghanistan."

"Why?" It was Foster who spoke, and he directed the question at Jack Porter. The liaison didn't immediately respond. "Because you suspected Kroeger would harm her if given the chance," the major surmised. "This whole thing is a cluster fuck, you know that?"

"That's enough, Foster," the Commander snapped.

"The hell it is," he roared, standing. "I am sick of this cloak and dagger bullshit. The men and women at this table are being told to risk their lives over what is basically amounting to a goddamned soap opera. It would certainly serve the best interests of those here that it all get out in the open, since I certainly think *there's a need to know.*"

He strode over to an easel, flipped the pad to reveal a clean sheet of paper, and grabbed up a marker.

"Fact -," he snarled.

"I think you'd better sit down, Major," the Commander said, his voice quiet, yet full of authority.

"No," he snapped. "I mean, no, sir. No disrespect, sir, but we need to review the facts. That's what a briefing is, am I right? Fact -," he continued, a little less belligerent. He wrote the number one at the top left side of the paper. "Kroeger and Dr. Ross were partners. Fact," he snapped, writing the number two immediately below, "they were lovers for some duration of time."

Kaila closed her eyes briefly as sadness and regret washed over her. No wonder he refused to acknowledge her. She ignored the sympathetic looks several people leveled at her and continued to look at Foster.

"Fact, they broke it off before they were assigned to Afghanistan. Fact -." He continued listing everything he knew, filling up three sheets of paper. Each time he ran out of room he would tear off the sheet and use masking tape to hang it for everyone to see. When he was finished, he looked directly at her, his expression cool.

"Have I missed anything, Dr. Ross?"

She stood and walked toward the easel, making sure she took a route around the table that let her avoid him as he made his way back to his seat.

"Most of these facts are correct," she said quietly, her back to the men and women seated at the table. Their emotions slammed off of her, invading her, abusing her, punishing her. She took several deep breaths and pretended she was studying the words and phrases for accuracy. When she felt the sting of their initial reactions begin to ease, she turned.

"I am not going to go into the details of my personal relationship with Kroeger, as I do not believe it would provide any valuable insight into his personality or motivation. Suffice it to say that he was bitter when it ended, and that fact certainly contributed to his adamant plea with Porter and the other commanders that I was nothing more than a woman scorned, and the mission should go forward as planned."

"Who called it off?" Lieutenant Yellis asked. "The relationship, I mean."

"I did."

"Why?" It was Prowler, her tone not unkind. "Did you sense instability in him? Did you feel you were in danger? You had to know that it would bring repercussions in your professional dealings."

She let out a deep breath. "His professional envy was getting in the way of our personal relationship."

"Dr. Ross was higher in the organization than he was," Jack put in. "She was younger than him and that always rubbed him the wrong way."

"Especially since he recruited me," she added.

"He was a predator," Prowler said, her gaze on Kaila. "He probably seduced you and flattered you, pretending admiration and wanting to learn from you when in reality his resentment seethed quietly beneath the surface. He made sure you felt that resentment in dozens of petty, painful little ways, correct?"

For a moment, she didn't know what to say, how to respond.

"In addition to my talents as chief bottle washer," the officer explained, "I'm a psychologist with a specialty in criminal profiling."

A bit more at ease, Kaila nodded. "When I realized the extent of his jealousy, I called it off, with as little drama as possible. That alone infuriated him. He got quite nasty at that point and I tried going to my handler for help. He was, to say the least, unsympathetic. I was reassigned to another team as it was felt that I needed to be kept away from Kroeger."

"Seems kind of a backwards way of handling things," Manic murmured.

"It is what it is," she said, sending a brief smile in his direction. "My point is that the agency was aware long before Afghanistan that I believed Kroeger's judgment was - ." She stopped, considered. "Compromised, I guess you might say. I didn't know how to make them understand. Every time I tried to express it in terms I could identify with, feelings, my concerns were dismissed, swept into the scorned lover category. I finally quit trying."

"Why were they kept as partners?" Yellis asked Porter.

"We felt that as she matured, Kaila would be able to get beyond her issues with Kroeger."

"But why keep them as partners in the first place? Why not just reassign each of them to someone else?"

"For better or for worse, Dr. Ross and Kroeger were the most successful team we had in our organization. Their track record, up until what happened in the Hindu Kush, was phenomenal. Statistically important, as those on the White House scientific oversight committee used to say."

"I honestly didn't know, when I was first sent to Afghanistan, that Kroeger was there."

"How did you find out?" Dan asked, his gaze trained on a clock several inches above her.

"I don't think that's relevant," she answered.

"Let me rephrase the question. When did he find out that you were there and that you were trying to supersede his orders?"

"I can't answer that as I was never directly engaged with him. I interfaced with my local contact. When that got me nowhere, I contacted Porter directly. When that didn't work -."

"I think they get the idea, Dr. Ross," Jack said, the pitch and octave of his voice higher than normal.

"Let her finish," Manic Man snapped. "What did you do when Jack Porter didn't listen to you?"

"I called the Pentagon, even contacted someone on the Joint Chiefs of Staff. They told me to take it up my chain of command." She stared in turn at everyone in the room. Foster was looking at the table. "I tried everything I could think of to stop that mission from going forward."

"I'm calling a break," the Commander said, looking at his watch. "We'll reconvene at eighteen hundred hours. I'll have dinner brought in. Until then, dismissed."

Kaila remained standing at the head of the table while the members of the team filed out. Jack cast a sorrowful glance in her direction before leaving.

With the exception of one person, she had been able to read everyone in that room. Every emotion that washed through them, every time they switched gears, she felt it. Sometimes it was a stabbing pain, sometimes it was like a cool cloth on her forehead.

She turned back to the charts on the wall, stared unseeing at the words. Dan had been so cold and calculating as he'd brought the marker in contact with the paper, slashing words and phrases as if they were a sword he could cut her with. Her body jerked and she focused on the writing. *Psychometry.* She hadn't been able to read Foster through her normal channels; perhaps if she touched the marker he'd written with, ran her fingers over the words.

Letting out a deep breath she stared at the marker. Was she ready to find out the truth? No one knew better than he that the mission went so badly. What did that mean? Did she really want to know? She stared up at the words, smiled at the irony. A year of her life summarized in black and white; without emotion, without meaning.

She looked back at the marker. As she grabbed it with one hand, she reached out with the other, running her fingers over the second point Dan had put down; that she and Kroeger had been lovers.

CHAPTER TWENTY-THREE

"Dr. Ross, can I ask you something?"

Major Anderson had returned to the conference room just as she had been about to leave. She wanted to spend some time with her iPod, tuning the whole world out. It appeared that pleasure would have to wait.

"Sure."

"How is it you didn't feel Kroeger's true intentions before now?"

Kaila reached out and grabbed a glass of water from the conference room table. Taking a long swallow before speaking allowed her to gather her thoughts.

"There are billions of people on this planet, major," she said by way of an answer.

"Yeah, but your relationship with Kroeger is unique. Even if you hadn't been intimate, he was your partner and he's another psychic. Didn't that make a difference?"

"You're forgetting that I also had an adversarial relationship with him. I've spent the last six or so years actively shutting him out." She took a deep breath, reminded herself that the major, a psychologist no less, probably wouldn't understand how her abilities worked.

"Even after Porter showed up on my doorstep, as it were, I didn't focus on anything other than the location of the stolen technology. I purposely shielded myself from most of the feedback from Kroeger. I did," she added, holding up a hand so she wouldn't be interrupted, "work to determine his motivation with regards to the technology. I told Jack that he thinks this is a game. Like I said, he's a thrill seeker."

"So, he's doing this just for the fun of it?"

"Stealing the technology? Yes. In fact, that is a game specifically aimed at Jack Porter for some reason."

"What do you mean?"

"I told Jack that I'm not the only one Kroeger wants revenge on. Something about this particular piece of technology relates to Porter, though I'm not sure just how."

"Why didn't you bring this up during the meeting today?"

She smiled sadly. "Do you really think it would have made a difference?"

"It's a piece of the puzzle. We are after locating that technology and if it involves Porter, specifically, then that is an angle someone should be looking into."

"Someone is. When I told him that I sensed Kroeger wanted revenge on him, he assigned some people to follow up on that."

For several seconds, neither woman spoke. The major stared out at the sea, turned back to Kaila.

"He doesn't hate you, you know."

Kaila stared at the ceiling. Her fingers tingled where she'd touched the letters he'd written. "Oh, I don't know about that."

"He's confused is all. You're making him rethink almost everything he's held onto for the last seven years."

She looked at the officer.

"He's used all those thoughts, that hatred of the CIA, as a shield so he didn't have to face certain realities. Constantly thinking of Staci as a victim keeps her a hero, untouchable, elevates her above us humans."

"That was her name, Staci?"

She nodded. "How much do you know?"

"Not as much as most people think." She snorted. "I spend most of my time trying to shut people out. I haven't read anything, haven't seen any file on Foster or his wife." *I can't read him.*

"So, after Afghanistan -?"

"I told Porter I was burned out, tired of being bombarded by violence and hatred in the name of national security. It was at that point that I decided to go back to school, get a doctorate in archeology."

"You didn't consider your profession tainted, dirtied by the way the government had manipulated it to their advantage?"

"Heck no. I have a true passion for archeology."

For a long moment the officer studied her. "Does it have something to do with your psychic thing?"

"I know you didn't read that in my file because I've never told anyone."

She just smiled. "I haven't read your file. I'm just very good at figuring people out."

"Then you must be awfully good at your job. Which is?"

"Not that much different than yours, actually; providing information to the powers that be in an effort to keep us all safe." Her smile widened. "That, and the fact that I'm a kick-ass sharpshooter."

Kaila laughed. "Where did you learn your skills?"

"Not the same way as you. Where I come from, two things are imperative to survival; being able to read a person's intentions and knowing how to use a gun."

"Where are you from?"

"Chicago; south side."

"Wow, and you made it out alive. Good for you, major."

"Prowler works for me if you're good with it."

"Prowler, it is, if you'll call me Kaila."

"Okay, Kaila. Since we're gettin' ourselves in the way of being friends, I'll tell you this. That man not only doesn't hate you, he cares about you more than he has cared about anyone in the last few years. If he didn't care, he wouldn't have gotten mad at you. Try and remember that."

"Thanks for talking with me, Prowler. I'm going to go see if I can get relocated out of the infirmary to regular quarters. I'll see you back here at six."

Kaila insisted on moving her belongings to the room they had assigned to her, which irritated Manic Man. She knew he wanted to pick at her, the way Prowler had come to pick at her. She didn't necessarily mind; they were just looking out for their friend. She really couldn't blame them, either, since she probably would have done the same herself. Still, she needed the time alone, to decompress after everything that had happened. Grabbing up her iPod, she headed topside.

Gavin Rossdale's raspy voice washed through her, drawing out the poison that negative emotions turned into once they got inside. Sorrow, anger, and frustration all had varying effects, none of it good. It wasn't that she needed to live in a Pollyanna world; it was just that when the volume of negative emotions increased and cascaded through her, it dragged her down, driving her to the edge of despair. She had spent a lifetime learning how to counteract and neutralize the effects.

Music had always had the ability to soothe her soul, from the time she was a child. Ironically, the louder and more discordant the sounds, the better she felt, which is why her iTunes library consisted almost entirely of heavy metal and rock and roll. Although she did have some instrumental and what might be classified as New Age, she left the classical music to people who thought listening to it would turn their kids into geniuses.

She shook her head. Most people had no idea what they were asking for and would be completely unprepared if their kid was a genius. People wanted conformity, sameness. Parents dragged kids to doctors constantly in order to be reassured that their kids were average, behaving like everyone else. If the kid did act different, fear and apprehension had them searching for answers, drugging the kid until they ended up normal, whatever that was, and acting like everyone else.

It was incredibly challenging to be different from everyone else. Fear and insecurity brought out the worst in people, regardless of their age, and over the years, Kaila had withdrawn socially, pouring her energies into activities that kept her on the fringes of society. Afraid their isolationist daughter would end up part of some cult, her parents had sent her to a psychologist when she was a teen-ager.

If she hadn't believed in a Higher Being that looked out for innocents before then, she certainly did after. The doctor was himself a psychic and immediately recognized what was happening. He turned their sessions into a place of refuge, using them for training instead of trying to make her over into a carbon copy of the average teen.

He had recommended she find a way to use her talents for something productive. He reasoned that helping others may enable her to let go of any resentment she felt at being burdened by such uniqueness. He put her in touch with someone at the local police department who agreed to keep her identity and ability a secret in exchange for information that helped the law enforcement agency solve crimes.

She wasn't the only psychic helping the police, but she was a minor, and had kept her parents unaware of her activities, so she was given special consideration. When she graduated from high school, her contact suggested she apply to the police academy after completing a degree in criminal justice.

By then, she understood only too well the toll such a career would take on her, so while university was definitely in her future, continuing to work with law enforcement wasn't.

Unfortunately, the road to hell was paved with good intentions. Even though she'd kept to herself and poured her energies into her academic career, she wound up on the radar of people who were more than interested in her unique talents.

Over the years she had wondered if she shouldn't have relocated out of the Bay Area since it was a mecca, not only for New Age movements, but for psychic research. Something told her, however, that it wouldn't have mattered. Somehow, she knew, her ability would always catch up to her. It had set her apart from others from the time she was a child, keeping her from living a normal life or having normal relationships of any kind.

How many times had she gone through break-ups made all the more traumatic because she could feel every emotion from everyone involved, including another female if that ended up being the reason a guy left. For awhile she avoided dating altogether since the emotional roller coaster it put her through was more than she could handle. Even the euphoria at the beginning of a relationship, the *honeymoon period*, had been too draining.

By the time she was near graduation, Kaila had become a very lonely young woman. She was on the honor roll at Berkeley and had won several awards in martial arts competitions, but nothing could fill the emptiness inside. Knowing she needed to figure out what was next, she attended a job fair where she met Chad Kroeger.

Staring out at the calm sea, Kaila turned up the volume so Nine Inch Nails' *Closer* was blaring, and thought about that fateful day.

"Ms. Ross, I know this is going to sound like an odd request, but would you have lunch with me? I have a break coming up in fifteen minutes and I have something very important to discuss with you, a career opportunity I think you should consider seriously."

"Why can't we talk about it here?"

"When I explain it to you, you'll understand."

Fast forward the clock thirteen years and here she was, standing on the deck of an aircraft carrier, helping the US government locate a valuable piece of stolen technology and the very agent who had recruited her for the CIA all those years ago.

The last notes from her playlist faded away, and as she scrolled through, searching for another grouping of songs to listen to, she glanced at her watch. She didn't have to be back in the conference room for several hours, which was good since she wasn't yet ready to face Dan.

"Dr. Ross."

She jerked in surprise. She hadn't heard him come up. Not willing to feel as if she had done something wrong, she went on the offensive. She sneered.

"Awfully formal for someone who just had his fingers between my legs, don't you think, *Major* Foster?"

Satisfaction swelled when he flinched. When he spun on his heel and stalked away, satisfaction turned to shock, then anger.

"Don't you dare walk away from me, you hypocritical coward."

He spun back, his face a mask of fury.

"Did you call me a coward?"

"What would you call someone who ran away from you rather than face up to the truth?"

He strode back to her until they were standing toe to toe. "What truth is that, Kaila?"

"You can't handle who I am, what I am. You're afraid of it and you can't get past it to even be civil toward me. I went to Porter, told him we can't work together. We're being separated, put on different task teams. You won't have to see my face much longer."

"You're the one running away and you're calling me a coward?"

"I don't see that I have any choice, major. It's either do what I do in relative peace, or stick around you and feel nothing but anger and resentment emanating from you."

That wasn't exactly true, since she hadn't directly felt any emotion from him. She wasn't able to read him.

"What's the difference?" he taunted. "Whether or not I'm around, all you feel are the negative things this world has to offer, isn't that right? Violence, hate; what do you do, seek it out? Does it make you feel powerful to feel other people's pain?"

Tears blurred her vision and she seethed, needing to lash out, to hurt the way she was hurting.

"You shallow bastard. There's so much more to me than that but you can't look past your own self wounding to see it. I can feel so much more than what's wrong with this world. I can feel the joy from a woman who puts a hand on her flat stomach yet still connects with the life growing there. I feel the pride of a man when his son learns to ride his bike without training wheels, the satisfaction of someone when they finally land a fish after fighting with it for what seems an eternity."

She jabbed a finger toward a doorway that led to the living area of the ship. "When someone in the cafeteria on this floating city laughs, their energy bubbles inside of me as if it were my own private joke."

"Kaila -."

"Shut up and hear me out. When anything happens that brings a surge of emotions, relief, joy, hell, even ecstasy, I can tap it. Can you imagine what it's like for me to have sex, Foster, to feel that place where passion and joy collide?"

His fists clenched and his mouth became cruel, his lips nothing more than a thin line, white around the edges.

"Is that why you fucked him?" he ground out, his teeth clenched.

She gasped. As if she'd been struck, she stumbled and would have fallen had he not reached out and grabbed her. Instinctively, she slapped at his hand but he tightened his hold.

"Let me go, you sanctimonious bastard."

"Kaila, I'm sorry. I had no right -."

"No," she snarled, "you didn't. Get your hands off me." She swiped at her eyes. "Get away from me."

"Kaila, please. I didn't mean -."

"I know what you meant, or do you forget? I can see inside of people. Now get away from me, Foster. Spew your bitterness at someone else, you venomous puff adder."

Chest heaving, Dan stared at her, though she knew he wasn't seeing her. No one could see when they were so consumed by anger and self-pity.

"What a fool I was, to think you might be different, that you might actually be able to just accept me for who I am."

He opened his mouth to reply, but closed it again and stepped toward the rail so she could get past him.

Blinded by confusion, anguish, and outrage, she didn't see Manic Man until he was pulling her against his chest.

CHAPTER TWENTY-FOUR

From Honolulu to Hell, was all Dan could think of as he tugged at the collar of his coat, trying in vain to buffet some of the wind. His eyes watered. His cheeks had gone from icy cold, to stinging raw, to numb as he walked the streets of Moscow. Being from Maine, he wasn't a stranger to harsh winters, and visions of what he would do to Kroeger once he caught up to him provided some warmth. Still, memories of South America, with its summerlike temperatures, were beginning to become a serious distraction.

A young boy, about twelve, approached. He was the third in as many blocks, all selling for the black market. It didn't matter that he was dressed as a peasant; Dan knew that he was easily made as an American and therefore, someone with money. He shook his head and waved the kid away, continuing toward his destination on Novinskiy Bulvar.

Dan pressed the intercom and forced himself to hold still while he waited; no easy task when his body wanted to shiver uncontrollably in the bitter wind. When there was no answer he rang it a second time and cursed his contact for making him wait.

"Mr. Foster?"

He turned to see a tall woman, probably in her late thirties, coming toward him. She had dark, piercing eyes and, as he'd seen on more than a few Russian women, dirty blonde hair with dark roots. The contrast against Mediterranean skin was startling. She was approaching the apartment building, her arms loaded down by grocery bags. In two steps he was beside her, taking the burden.

"Thank you," she replied, her accent thick. "I'm sorry I'm late."

"Fortunately, I haven't had to wait long."

She smiled and preceded him into the lobby. She led him to a freight elevator. "I hope you're hungry," she said, nodding toward the bags in his arms. They rode the elevator to the fourth floor and walked down a sterile hallway that reminded him of a hospital.

"Wow," he commented as they entered the apartment, "this is nice." He knew it wasn't occupied, only rented out by the US government and used for meetings, so he was surprised by how well it was maintained. It was a one bedroom unit, but still fairly spacious, definitely clean, and nicely, if sparsely furnished. He set the bags on the counter and began unpacking.

"If you would start browning the beef and chopping the vegetables? I'm going to go have a cigarette on the balcony."

"You don't have to go out in the bitter cold; I don't mind the smoke."

She sent him a smile over her shoulder as she stepped out. "I live here. The cold doesn't bother me the way it does you."

By the time she joined him in the kitchen ten minutes later, Dan had poured the wine, set the table, and warmed up enough that he could remove his coat.

"How long have you been out of the military?" she asked and laughed at his expression. Her eyes raked over his very fit body. "You realize if you stay much longer, you'll be made for a spy?"

"Which is why I'm meeting with you now. I can get what I need and be on my way."

He'd checked in at the embassy as instructed, but had gotten the usual red tape runaround. When nothing of consequence turned up, he'd reached out to Jack Porter's contacts in St. Petersburg. They had directed him to the woman standing before him now, Ilsa Vanokavic, information broker.

She stepped up to the stove and began adding diced peppers and onions to the beef. She picked up a glass from the counter and sipped red wine.

"Moscow is not happy with your friend's actions. They do not like to be led like a donkey after a carrot."

"If it were up to me I'd let Moscow do with him what they would. Unfortunately, I'm not the one making those decisions."

She worked the pepper grinder over the pan and stirred in tomatoes.

"I'm not entirely certain who is playing who," she said, her eyes on a knife as it sliced through potatoes, "but he is making a lot of enemies. He will not accomplish anything by continuously moving the auction."

"So, it's no longer set for Moscow?"

She sighed. "He says he does not feel it would serve the interests of the Federation by holding it in Moscow, or even in Russia."

Dan watched her set a pot of water to boil. Kroeger had to be up to something more than just trying to sell a crystal laser or even revenge on Kaila Ross, but what?

Does Moscow know why he wants to sell the technology to them?"

"He said he is alarmed by the destabilization of Central Asia and the migration of Islamic militants into Russian territories. He feels that the United States has contributed significantly to this problem and that if Russia has the technology, it would force the US government to rise to a new level of negotiations with the Russian Federation. He said that only a joint Russian-US alliance can stem the tide of terrorism and that by having the technology only in the hands of the Americans, Moscow will remain threatened and negotiations will never proceed."

Dan frowned. Hadn't that been the same rationalization for selling nuclear secrets to the Soviets during the Cold War? Balance the power and then everyone has to deal and negotiate? He shook his head. Kroeger really was an egomaniac if he felt that he could dictate foreign policy and swing the tide of terrorism.

"Any idea where he is?"

"As of this morning he was in Omsk, but he was on the move. They believe he is headed for Georgia. They will let him go; with an escort, of course."

"Of course." Inwardly, Dan swore. He'd told Porter that he should remain in Georgia, but Jack wanted him to follow Kroeger's trail exactly.

Ilsa emptied the beef mixture into a bowl and set it aside before pouring the diced potatoes into the hot pan and frying. "What have you got for me?" she asked, her eyes on the potatoes.

He removed an envelope from beneath his sweater and handed it over.

"Hmm, nice and warm."

Dan didn't miss the hunger in her eyes as they roamed over him. Maybe this was just what he needed to banish the image of green eyes that had been haunting him for longer than he wanted to admit. He set his wineglass on the counter and pulled her into his arms. "Don't let the potatoes burn," he murmured, and brought his mouth down, covering hers.

Two hours later, he was pulling a blanket around his waist as he sat back against the headboard. "Thank you." He grabbed his wineglass from the nightstand, drank deeply. "For the meal. It was delicious."

"Subtlety isn't your strong suit, is it, Major?"

"I'm not a major anymore."

"Hmm," she replied, pulling a brown turtleneck over her head.

For several seconds he remained silent. He had a feeling she knew the truth. It simply amazed him how quickly news traveled in the world of espionage. "Will it be enough?" he asked, finally, indicating the envelope atop the dresser.

"It will be enough," she confirmed.

"There's more, if -," but he stopped as she waved a hand dismissively.

"They know I keep twenty percent for myself. Besides, the information you provided is worth more than the American dollars in there."

She had waited until they were dining by candlelight before opening the envelope he'd brought. In exchange for valuable information regarding the whereabouts and activities of one Chad Kroeger, the US had supplied her with something of equal value to the Moscow government, sandwiched between dozens of American ten and twenty dollar bills. After reading the two sheets of paper he'd brought, she had lit their edges from a candle and allowed them to combust in an empty plate before flushing the ashes down the toilet.

He continued to study her as she pulled pant legs down over ridiculously high heeled boots. She glanced over at him.

"Don't," she said, smiling.

"Don't what?"

"You feel sorry for me, for living the way I do, where I do. Don't. If I didn't like it, I wouldn't do it." Her eyes flashed. "We have more options than you Americans seem to think. Especially in the age of the Internet."

"Why do you stay? You could work anywhere."

"My life is here," she said, as if that explained everything. When he didn't respond, she sighed. "This is who I am, Foster, what I am. I am a Russian citizen and I love my country, so much so that I work in one of the most hated fields; the gathering and brokering of information. I went to college, studied fine arts, and yet chose to serve my country this way. That should tell you something."

He grunted. He respected the truth when he heard it. He also respected that she had pride, for being a Russian, for being a spy. Perhaps a means to an ends but also something she believed in.

"Well, then, it looks as if our meeting is concluded. I'm going to stay awhile, make a few calls. I wish you well, Ilsa, and if we don't meet again, then we're both fortunate, right?"

"As it would mean our world found peace, you would be correct. Good luck to you, Major."

When he heard the door click shut he pushed himself from the bed and went to throw the bolts. He checked the locks on all the windows and doors before stepping into a hot shower. He sighed as the heat broke through the tension, dropped his head forward, and enjoyed the water pounding on the back of his neck, so many hot needles stinging and healing at the same time.

"This is who I am, Foster, what I am."

Kaila had said those same words before they'd left the carrier, each destined for a different corner of the planet. She'd accused him of being incapable of accepting that her psychic gifts came with the package. He sighed. Why was it he had the ill fortune to run into women who could look him in the eye and say that, daring him to reject them outright? He slammed a fist against the wall of the shower. That's exactly what he'd done to Kaila, though, wasn't it? Turning off the spray he stepped out and prepared to leave.

He was scheduled to travel on an evening train to St. Petersburg, where he would rendezvous with one of Porter's minions. Maybe he was naïve thinking he could trust Special Ops more than CIA operatives, but the fact remained he was always uneasy when he had to deal with someone in Porter's organization. He suspected they told him just enough that he didn't wind up dead, but that was a far cry from being cooperative or even helpful.

Long ago he'd given up using the argument that they were all on the same side. The sentiment rarely made a dent. Too often, due to the hostile territory his own missions took him to, the people he interacted with were members of the CIA's Special Activities Division, or SAD. They were the people that the US government would deny any knowledge of or complicity with, should things go bad. As a result, it was just about impossible to warm up to, let alone relate to them. They were an enigma, and since he never spent any length of time around them, remained such.

He was in the kitchen checking his itinerary when the doorbell rang. He grabbed the P226 from where it rested on the counter and moved to the side of the door. He knocked on it twice and breathed a sigh of relief when the visitor answered with the expected verification code. A glance through the peep hole showed a man standing back from the door, one side of his coat open to reveal an ID and a .45. Dan opened the door.

"Ah, a Sig-Sauer; nice." The agent, in his fifties, stepped into the apartment.

Dan set the gun on the counter. Increased velocities from using hot loads caused more chamber pressure which could break the sides of the M9 that was the more standard issue for the Air Force. As a result, a lot of Special Ops guys had a preference for the Sig P226.

The two men stood in the kitchen. Dan went through the cupboards, frowning when he wasn't able to find what he was looking for.

"Try the freezer," the other man suggested.

Dan smiled and withdrew the bottle of Stoli. He filled two glasses and handed one to his visitor, a man with a beefy build and a crew cut.

"Here's your new itinerary."

Another change of venue. He downed the vodka. Kroeger was getting to be a royal pain in the ass.

"Where am I going?"

"Kazakhstan, by way of Silk Route railways."

"Silk Route railways, what's that, some smart-ass name for the prison train to Siberia?"

The agent shook his head. "Such cynicism." He handed over the envelope and Dan spilled the contents on the counter.

"Your entry visas," the agent said, pointing, "and a ticket for a private berth. You're lucky; I had to travel in the open plan dormitory car."

"What's this?" He held up a book titled *Silk Route by Rail*. "The tourist thing?" Dan asked, skeptically.

The other man shrugged. "In case you have any free time."

Speaking of free time, Dan thought, glancing at his watch. He had a few hours to kill before the train left Moscow. He looked up at the agent. "Can you suggest anything local?"

"Red Square," he answered, smiling, "since you've already availed yourself of other pleasures."

Dan kept a stoic expression. He didn't want to think about it, but couldn't help wondering where the cameras had been located.

"Good luck."

"I take it you'll lock up?" Dan asked, gathering the documents and stuffing them back in the envelope.

"Of course."

Grabbing up his gear, Dan headed out, toward the Smolenskaya station.

CHAPTER TWENTY-FIVE

For Kaila, the worst thing about returning to Afghanistan wasn't the memories it elicited. It wasn't the way she and Dan had left things before he was sent to Russia to follow in Kroeger's footsteps, while she and Prowler were shipped to Bagram Airbase. It was the knowledge that for the next several days, if not weeks, she would be enduring some of the most punishing conditions anyone should have to endure. Between the climate, the harsh landscape, and the lawless environment found outside the base, she would be facing unbelievable challenges.

The high elevation meant that temperatures could drop well below zero. Sand and mud were constant companions, and since water was scarce, showering was not considered a priority. As a result, staying clean was a virtual impossibility. She surveyed the area she would be calling home for the foreseeable future while Prowler went in search of their sponsor.

About twenty-seven miles south of Kabul, in the Parwan province, next to the ancient city of Bagram, the air base had changed significantly in recent times. Run by the US Army, it had grown to serve the needs of the military, the civilian contractors, and the locals, many of whom took advantage of the presence of the Americans to help them improve their quality of life.

She was heartened to discover that the quarters afforded the men and women employed in the interest of national security had improved from when she had last been there. Instead of tents that didn't hold up well against the elements, that were occupied by personnel piled atop one another, the soldiers and civilian contractors stationed here now lived in B-huts. The temporary housing, basically a small plywood shack, was a relative luxury by comparison, to what she'd had before.

"Come on, we're over here."

She followed Prowler toward a cluster of huts away from those occupied by the soldiers. Although Bagram was run by the US Army, there were quite a few civilian contractors in residence and it was among them that the two women would be staying.

"Hmm," Prowler said, scanning the barbed wire fence that surrounded the base, "I wonder why more people don't honeymoon here."

Kaila smiled. "It was beautiful, before decades of war took its toll."

"If you say so," she replied, and entered the hut they would be sharing. "Perry said he'd be by in half an hour. While we wait, we're to get comfy, settle in."

Kaila dropped her duffle bag on a cot. "I'm settled in. Let's walk outside."

"Too cold, let's wait in here."

Kaila smiled. "You wait in here, I'm going out. After all those hours on the plane, I need to stretch my legs, regardless of what the mercury says."

"Dr. Ross?"

She turned to see a man in a heavy coat coming toward her. He was handsome with shaggy black hair that lent an air of youthful mischief.

"I'm Perry Garfield, welcome wagon."

She shook his hand and called for Prowler. "Nice to meet you. Some place you have here."

"Home crap home," he replied, grinning. He greeted the lieutenant and led the women on a brief tour.

"This place sure has changed," Kaila observed, noting the stores that sold food and clothing. "None of this was here before. Hell, you couldn't find a pack of smokes, let alone a bag of Doritos or a diet Coke unless someone was just arriving, or just getting back from somewhere more civilized."

"Anywhere has to be more civilized than this," Prowler said, emphatically.

"When were you here?" Perry asked.

"2003."

"Ah, the hell years, or so I've heard."

"What's different?" Prowler asked, eyeing the two of them as if they were nuts.

"Why were you here?" he asked.

"Bactrian horde," Kaila said absently. She pointed toward a cluster of buildings on the other side of the barbed wire fence. "Old Russian barracks?"

He nodded. She continued to stare, her brows knit in concentration.

"They were here before," Perry offered, his expression wary.

She shook her head. She was getting psychic interference; something. "Any way I can get a look inside?"

"I don't know; you'll have to speak to someone in the military. It's outside the base; they may use it for something specific."

Prowler was staring at her. "I'll clear it," she said after several seconds.

"Shall we continue?" he asked.

"Please."

"Compared to when you were here before, things are a lot safer."

"It's a hell of a lot quieter," she replied, her eyes focused on the barracks. "Back then, there was an almost constant backdrop of explosions as the ordinance guys worked on unexploded bombs and mines left by the Russians. Fun for all," she concluded. She glanced over at Prowler, back at the old barracks; frowned deeply. Something was definitely wrong.

"Would you two excuse me?" Prowler said, suddenly. "I think I see an old buddy of mine." Without waiting for acknowledgment, she ran off toward where a man in uniform was checking his weapon.

"How long have you been here, Perry?"

The small talk would put him more at ease and distract him while she reached out psychically to do a more thorough scan of the old two-story buildings clustered in the distance.

"Eight months. I'm a civil engineer, part of the army's efforts to train the locals. I teach welding. I understand you're an archeologist?"

She nodded, her gaze going back to the barracks. There was a buzzing sound coming from that direction, and under normal circumstances she would have asked if the man next to her heard it. However, she was picking up the vibration in the temporal bone, not her ear, which meant the sound was psychic in origin and therefore, she would be the only one who heard it.

"Is anything wrong, Dr. Ross?"

Without answering, she began running in the direction of the barracks. There was a barbed wire fence between the base and the Soviet era buildings, but she knew instinctively there would be a gate that would let her through. She didn't have to look over her shoulder to know that Prowler and several officers were right behind her. She halted at the fence. There was indeed a gate, though it was padlocked.

She studied the cinderblock buildings. The buzzing had increased in volume to the point it drowned out almost all other sound. She shifted her eyes to the left and down, defocused them, and tried to determine what was causing it.

"What is it?" Prowler asked, a bit short of breath from the sprint to the fence.

"Something's wrong." She pointed. "There."

"Can you be more specific?"

"Give me a minute."

She appreciated that the soldiers were quiet while she stared blankly into space, concentrating. It was coming at her as a thin line of energy, sound energy. Needing to get a better visual, she closed her eyes and shut out everything but the buzzing. It was a stream, yellow in color, and it was flowing straight at her. Pouring herself into that stream, she psychically swam against its current toward the source. It was difficult. The energy was viscous, almost like egg drop soup, and moving through it was taking time, something she suspected they didn't have. She took a deep breath and let it out, using the exhalation to add leverage as she swam energetically upstream. She arrived at the source, gasped.

"A bomb. There's a bomb in there. Get -."

"Here," one of soldiers snapped, pushing her aside and stepping up to the gate. He unlocked it, pushed it open and ran through. Behind her, another soldier was speaking rapidly into a phone. Prowler stepped up to her.

"Later, I'd like you to explain how you do that, okay?"

She nodded and stepped toward the opening.

"Ma'am, you need to remain here. The sergeant is prepared to handle this."

"No, he won't know where to look. I have to help him." She ran after the soldier, a sense of urgency driving her. Calm, she told herself; stay calm. Focus.

"Sergeant," she yelled, "don't touch anything. Wait for me."

Kaila thanked the angels who watched over soldiers that the man had decided to listen to her. After all, she was a civilian and had no authority over him. He was standing in front of a building on the outside of the cluster, furthest away from the camp. Later, she decided, she would ask just how it was he knew which one.

"It's hard to explain, but if you open the door you will detonate the device. It isn't hooked up with a motion trigger, but there is something -." She stopped, focused. "The device is large, white; it's a metal box. It was inserted through the floor. There are wires running out beneath the floor boards."

"Vibration trigger," he responded, his tone abrupt. "Motion, yes, but a different type, older technology from the way you describe it. Since there's no infrared beam to be disrupted, I doubt just opening the door would set it off. My guess is, if we were to throw the door open and it banged against the wall, the vibration energy would reverberate along the floors and set it off. We'll go ahead and wait for the ordinance guys."

Kaila described everything she *saw* in great detail, as quickly as possible. The men nodded several times, asked few questions, and prepared to enter.

"You can return to the base, Dr. Ross. We've got it from here. Thank you for all your help."

She didn't want to leave, but Prowler was dragging her back through the gate. "Come on," she said, gently, "we need to get as far away from here as possible. Besides, there's more than one general waiting to have a word with you."

"So much for being a blade of grass."

"Kaila? You never were, were you?"

"In my dreams," she replied, and followed the officer toward the central command. It was going to be a long day.

She smiled ruefully. We*ren't they all?*

They passed numerous officers on their way to the command center. Kaila found it hard not to salute them. It was instinctive to follow the major's actions and show them that kind of respect.

The command center was housed in another two-story cinderblock; very sterile, but heated, at least. They were escorted to a room that reminded her of a grade school cafeteria. Folding tables had been set up in rows along the sides, a handful of chairs arranged so that all eyes would be facing a white board that took up almost an entire wall.

About a half a dozen officers from multiple branches of the armed forces were waiting for them.

"Dr. Ross, Major Anderson, thank you for joining us. Please take a seat."

Kaila would have preferred to stand, but didn't want to start off on an adversarial note. She sat in a chair on the end in the front row. Nervous energy had her on edge, so she laid her hands flat on the table and let out a breath, forcing herself to relax. Beside her, Prowler seemed completely at ease.

"First of all, I've been notified that the bomb has been disposed of, safely. Dr. Ross, I can't tell you how grateful we are for your assistance."

She nodded, distinctly uncomfortable under the general's scrutiny.

"We're conducting an investigation of our own as to how and when the bomb was placed in that old bunker, but if you have any insight you believe would be helpful, let us know.

She nodded, again choosing to remain silent. One thing she knew about the military, redundancy was a tedium they didn't appreciate.

"Dr. Ross, everyone in this room has the highest clearance levels," he explained. "They have extensive experience in matters of national security and are responsible for affairs of strategic importance for Operation Enduring Freedom. As such, I can assure you, they have a need to know."

"I understand, General."

"Why don't we start by having you step up to the front and share with us whatever you believe is appropriate?"

"Wait a minute," another officer spoke up. "I understand Dr. Ross was very ill with influenza. If you would prefer to remain seated, we will certainly understand."

"Thank you, sir, I actually prefer to stand. If you don't mind, I may pace a bit." She let out a breath, stood. Prowler sent her an encouraging smile.

"First of all, I want to assure you that unlike some of my colleagues, I have never subscribed to the idea that information should be shared only if there is a need to know. That is too subjective. How can I fully understand just what it is you may need to know? Therefore, unless I am advised specifically not to share something, please be assured I will provide full disclosure. Honesty is important to me and is something I respect above all else in others."

Few smiles, but several nods let her know she had begun to gain their confidence.

CHAPTER TWENTY-SIX

"That was brutal," Kaila groaned, flopping on the bed, face down.

"Well, if it's any consolation, I think you handled yourself and that whole thing remarkably well. That was a tough crowd."

She pushed herself up on her elbows. "They have reason to be." She sighed. "They have a responsibility to the men and women living here, not to mention the ones back home." She paused. "They are intimidated by what I do."

"Don't you think that's kind of normal? It's something they don't understand, so fear is a normal reaction in many cases; especially if they feel threatened."

"Not to mention a good percentage of them were probably raised to believe stuff like that is evil." Kaila sighed. "I could do without the fear, though. It would certainly make working together a lot easier."

"Give it time. They just met you."

"Colonel Miller knows me."

"From before?"

"Not exactly. I've worked with him, with his unit, but not here; Iraq."

"He seemed to respect you."

"He's never had an issue with me. Not that I'm aware of, anyway." She pushed a hand through her hair, rolled onto her back, and stared at the ceiling. "Beats all that hostility constantly coming at me from Foster."

"From what I hear, it isn't all hostility."

Kaila glanced over, rolled her eyes. "He's a man, isn't he? He isn't going to hold my afflictions against me when it comes to enjoying my body, but that's a far way from a relationship of respect and honesty."

"I think you're being awfully hard on him. Dan's okay. You should give him a chance."

"You're preaching to the wrong person on that one, Prowler. It's the other way around."

She opened her mouth to answer, but someone knocked at the door. Without continuing the conversation, the lieutenant got up to answer it.

"Perry, hello."

"I was wondering if you ladies had had anything to eat. We have a group of folks who try to get together periodically for dinner. They're looking forward to meeting fresh faces."

"That's kind of you to invite us, we'd love to come."

"Dr. Ross," he said, a bit more formality in his voice than there was before.

Kaila smiled and followed them toward the retail area. A mix of military and civilians milled about. They joined a rather large group seated at a few tables set alongside each other.

Not surprisingly, dinner was far from relaxing. It wasn't just the awkwardness of meeting new people; it was everything everyone else felt about what had transpired that day, felt about her. More than one civilian studied her with an intensity that bordered on rudeness. She could sense all the usual suspects; fear, curiosity, distrust, and even hostility.

SSDD, isn't that what Kroeger used to say? She mentally started, glanced around, half expecting to see him standing in line for a meal.

It wasn't the sentiment that startled her so much as the fact that she actually remembered something positive. She had spent a great deal of effort over the years shutting out all feelings and memories related him in order to protect herself from his influence. It was disturbing to think he may be breaking through her mental defense, no matter how innocuous the frame of reference seemed to be.

"So, Dr. Ross, what exactly brings you back to the Stan?" Perry asked.

"If you can believe, they want my expertise in order to determine whether, with all the excavations going on, there's a chance that ancient artifacts may be uncovered." She rolled her eyes.

"Oh," another civilian engineer chimed in, "you mean like the Bactrian Horde that was recovered?"

She nodded. "It's extremely common, on a global scale, to start laying the foundation for a major construction effort, only to discover they were digging up an ancient city. Although it's more likely to happen in a place like this; places with an ancient and rich history, it really does occur on a regular basis, all over. For instance, in 2005, they were laying the foundations for condominiums in San Francisco and uncovered the remains of a ship that had been there since the gold rush."

"Is that what your psychic abilities are for?" asked another civilian, "to help find buried treasure? Kind of like dowsing uncovers hidden water sources?"

"Hunting for treasure?" Someone scoffed. "Have you ever seen the headline *Psychic Wins Lotto*?" The group chuckled good-naturedly and she smiled.

"Do you do tarot readings?" someone asked, suddenly.

Here it comes, she thought. In spite of her discomfort, she kept smiling.

"No, I don't. I don't do prognostications, I don't do parlor tricks. I actually spend a great deal of my time trying to block out my abilities," she said, truthfully.

"Why? Seems to me if God gave you a gift like that, you should use it."

She sighed. Why did everyone who wasn't a psychic assume it was a gift?

"Because," she said, working to keep her tone light, "I have no control over it," she lied. "I have occasional *episodes,* I guess you might say, where information or hunches come to me. I used to have dreams about the future when I was a kid but they stopped when I was a teenager." She needed to get the subject changed. "I never felt comfortable with the attention I got as a result of having sharp instincts, so I quit listening, shut it off. My life has been much more peaceful ever since. I guess you could say I chose to get by using good old-fashioned hard work and determination."

She prayed they would let it go.

"Well, if you get any premonitions that involve me or my family or our safety," someone said, "let me know."

"Of course," she replied. Of course she wouldn't, she thought. That was one lesson she had learned the hard way. Never tell anyone when you foresee something negative in their future unless you know you can do something to alter it.

"Perry," the major spoke up, "I want to thank you for inviting us to dinner, introducing us to everyone here. I think we'd better head back. You know, jet lag?"

"Of course. I'll see you ladies tomorrow. Dr. Ross? I'll be happy to lead you to where we are working with the locals so you can see where we are doing the construction and training."

"That would be terrific, Perry. It was nice meeting everyone. Good night."

Once they were back in their hut, Prowler sat on the bed and faced her.

"I'm sorry you had to go through that."

Kaila smiled, kicked off her shoes, and sat on her own cot. "Don't worry about it," she said, dismissively, "I get it all the time."

"That blows. It must be tiring."

"Well, it depends," she said, breathing out a sigh.

"On what?"

"The malice, or lack of, that is behind it. Any time someone tells me that what I have comes from the devil, I want to punch their lights out."

Prowler raised her eyebrows. "Does that happen often?"

She snorted. "More than you'd think. In spite of living in the twenty-first century, we are far from an enlightened culture. We are, in every way, a culture filled with superstitious religious fanatics. Hell, people were banning

Harry Potter, for chrissake. They forbade kids from seeing the movie. How crazy is that?"

"You gonna go to the showers tonight or tomorrow morning?"

She shrugged. "When I got on the plane, I resigned myself to the fact that I would be showering every other day at the most."

"I can wait. We can go together in the morning."

＊ ＊ ＊

Entering the subway, Dan glanced at his watch. There was quite a bit of time before the train he'd booked passage on, the *Red Arrow,* left Moscow. He let out a sigh, realizing he was about to do something completely out of the ordinary. He was going to do the tourist thing.

Hours later, as he made his way to his cabin, he frowned. For the second time that night he got the feeling he was being watched. He had taken every precaution to ensure his safety, given that Americans were often targets abroad, but he hadn't seen anything that gave him pause. Still, he couldn't shake the feeling that someone was following him. One of Porter's operatives sent to make sure he followed orders? It wouldn't be the first time.

Stuffing the SAT phone in his backpack, he frowned. Upon checking in, he'd been advised that no tail had been assigned. He set his meal box on the seat across from him and secured his passport out of sight. In spite of the fact that everything had gone smoothly, he couldn't shake the feeling that something was wrong. He'd spent the last twenty minutes mentally reviewing his movements after leaving the apartment. He slowly sifted through each location, replaying details as if watching a film. There was nothing obvious, such as seeing the same individual in multiple locations. Still, he decided, he would get off the train before his stop and double back. It wasn't uncommon for an operative to change course if he thought the situation warranted it.

Feeling better, he was about to stash the pack overhead when the door o his cabin opened and three men entered.

"This is a private cabin," he growled as they made themselves at home.

"Please, Major Foster, don't," the smallest of the three said, halting Dan as he started reaching into the pack. The man nodded to one of his companions, a large dangerous type Dan suspected had a rap sheet the size of Texas, and the thug reached over and took the pack while the man to his left, looking equally dangerous, held a Marikov semi-automatic aimed straight at his heart.

"Allow me to introduce myself," the smaller man said. "I am Chad Kroeger."

It wasn't the first time Dan had looked death in the face. He studied his adversary calmly. Somehow, he knew without a doubt, today was not the day he was going to die.

"Accompanying me to St. Petersburg?" he drawled, purposely ignoring the man with the gun.

"Actually, Major Foster, it is you who will be accompanying me. We'll be getting off at the next station, where we'll switch trains."

Dan sighed. "Just where is it we're going?"

❋ ❋ ❋

Kaila bolted upright. Across the room, Prowler rolled to the floor, weapon drawn. "What is it?" the officer hissed into the dark.

"I need to talk to Jack Porter. It's an emergency."

"What's up?"

"I know where the crystal is."

"We're not in danger?"

"No more than usual," she answered, swinging her legs over the cot. "You can go back to bed. I can find my way."

"You're kidding, right?" her roommate answered, pulling on her winter gear. "After a rude awakening like that?"

"I'm sorry," Kaila said.

"You live like this? Thank god I'm not a psychic."

You have no idea.

"Get General Garson, right away," Prowler told one of two young marines guarding the command headquarters. "Tell him to wake anyone with a need to know."

"Since I'm about to get my ass chewed out for bringing him out of a dead sleep," the young man replied in a southern accent, "mind telling me whose orders I'm acting on?"

"Dr. Ross," Kaila answered, wanting to save her friend any fallout. Being outside the military chain of command would come in handy here, she realized. "Tell him I need to speak to Jack Porter right away."

"If you need Porter, then why -?"

"Go," Prowler ordered. The young man's expression made it obvious he didn't appreciate taking orders from a couple of women. However, he disappeared toward officers' country.

"Can I get you a cup of coffee, Dr. Ross?" A young soldier approached, carrying a tray. Setting it down, he grabbed two paper cups, thrust one in her direction, and the other at the major. "It's awfully cold out."

"Thank you," she replied, cupping her hands around the cup, grateful for the small amount of warmth.

"Damned poor substitute for a warm bed," Prowler groused, "but thank you."

Behind them, a door opened and several bleary-eyed men filed in.

"Looks like coffee all around," the young man said, walking back to the kitchen area.

"This'd better be good," a lieutenant-colonel snapped. "I was dreaming of my wife and I haven't seen her in eight months."

Visions of being thrown into a medieval dungeon swam before Kaila's tired eyes.

"Glad I'm just here for the coffee," Prowler mumbled. "Girl, you might wanna get your pretty self to the front of the room before these men fall asleep in their chairs."

Realizing she was right, Kaila stood and made her way toward the front. She eyed the young officer loading a tray with cups. "I'm sorry, do you have clearance? If not, -."

"Get Strauss in here," someone barked.

Wait staff with clearance? She looked at the group, surprised by the number of men who'd been roused from their slumber. She cleared her throat.

"Thank you for coming, though I can't say I understand why anyone other than General Garson is here. Not," she added, holding up a hand when one of the men was clearly ready to reply, "that I need to know. You can speak to him personally about why he felt it necessary to drag you from your sleep." She turned to the commander. "I need to talk to Jack Porter."

"What's going on, Dr. Ross?"

"I know where the stolen technology is."

"May I suggest you start from the top?" someone suggested in the gravelly voice of someone rudely pulled from a comfortable sleep.

She resisted the urge to smile. The man who'd spoken looked like an angry teddy bear with bloodshot eyes, his white hair sticking out in all directions. She reached for the coffee, managing to scald her tongue in her effort to gain composure.

""When Jack Ross first contacted me about the stolen technology, my understanding was that Chad Kroeger was responsible for its theft, that his plan was to auction it to the highest bidder, and that the agency believed his motive was monetary gain. I was asked to help locate Kroeger before the auction took place, the idea being that if we found him, we would find the technology."

The men listened quietly, their expressions ranging from annoyance, to grim determination, to polite interest.

"I advised them it was unlikely Kroeger was after money, given that he is independently wealthy. That's how he perceives his power; waving the magic green wad. I suggested they look to his history when trying to determine his motive. He is like a child with the need for constant attention combined with a desire to be a hero. He is highly intelligent and had a good track record for success, so what bordered on a pathological need for praise and admiration was overlooked."

She let out a breath. This is where the rubber met the road, where she practiced what she preached. *The truth, no matter how painful.*

"Kroeger's motivation has never been about the US government or national security. Oh, I'm sure he is providing some cock and bull story about his intentions being altruistic, but the truth of the matter is that this is about me, and about the US military, and about what happened right here some seven years back."

"The Hindu Kush?" General Garson queried, frowning.

"It isn't the event, it's what the event came to mean; what happened before, during, and after. The event is merely a catalyst."

"People died in that catalyst," one of the officers, a marine colonel, snapped.

"No one knows that better than I, sir. I -."

"Dr. Ross," the general interrupted, "we've reviewed the file and while each of us here may have our own bias as to what and why, it is of no benefit to anyone if you are put on the defensive. Please, let's continue with what's relevant."

"Yes, sir." She blew out a breath. "The truth is; Chad Kroeger is not in possession of the technology. In fact, it never left the United States."

CHAPTER TWENTY-SEVEN

Dan's mind raced. Train stations were fairly public places. Surely, there would be an opportunity to create a diversion, a scene, to make a break for it.

"I've a pretty good idea what you're thinking, Major Foster," Kroeger said. "You will fail. More than that, you will be responsible for the death of an innocent."

Kaila? During the long stretch they'd been traveling, Dan had tried to get as much rest as possible. He needed his wits about him and he was confident he wouldn't be shot as long as he didn't try anything. Still, sleep had been interrupted by visions of green eyes and wavy blonde hair.

He realized he'd tried and convicted Kaila Ross without truly hearing her side of the story. He'd even sentenced her with his rejection of her psychic ability, holding it between them and making sure he had a clean getaway. What was worse, he'd led her in one direction and then turned tail and ran at the first opportunity they'd had to deepen their relationship. He'd thrown painful events, over which she'd had no control, in her face.

It wasn't easy to take a hard look in the mirror when the person staring back at you was wrong. And he was wrong, about many things; too many. For the last seven years he'd hidden behind grief so that he didn't have to see some rather unpleasant truths. Not that he was surprised. He was a man of action, not emotions. It had been one of the reasons he'd done so well in the military. In general, he didn't waste time arguing, simply acted in what he believed was the best interests of the military and the mission, and while he wasn't as gung-ho as some career men, he had shown himself to be a valuable asset on more than one occasion. He stared out at the night and steeled his resolve. This might be one of a long line of dangerous missions to complete, but his intention at the end of it was to make sure he did everything he could to repair things between himself and Kaila.

He'd been so lost in thought; he hadn't noticed that one of the thugs had left the berth. The door opened and he looked up. His jaw dropped as he took in one of two individuals stepping through the doorway.

"Major Dan Foster, may I present Miss Jessica Porter?"

Porter?!

"Sit there, if you please?"

The girl couldn't have graduated high school.

"Are you okay?" he asked, making an effort to keep the fury from his voice. No need to scare the poor kid anymore than necessary. He had a pretty good idea how he must look in his peasant clothing with several days' beard growth.

"Yeah," she answered, a little breathless.

"They haven't -?"

"No harm has come to Miss Porter, just yet. And we'd like to keep it that way, wouldn't we, Major?"

"You son of a bitch," he growled.

"Save me your heroic diatribe, Foster. I know you have a soft spot for the ladies. If you wish to see this young woman come out of this alive, you'll do exactly as I tell you. Is that clear?"

Ignoring Kroeger, he looked into the young woman's eyes. "We're going to be fine, don't worry. I *will* get you out of this."

"Enough."

She turned to stare out the window, but not before she'd flashed a brief smile. She believed him; more than that, she trusted him. "You might want to get some sleep," he suggested. With that, he leaned back, folded his arms, and closed his eyes.

* * *

"Dr. Ross, do you know for a fact that the technology is still on US soil?"

In spite of the outside temperature, she was sweating. The man who'd asked was another bleary-eyed, angry looking senior officer who didn't like making decisions without facts to back them up. Little did he know, there were times when hunches and psychic feelings were more reliable than what appeared black and white.

Now I remember why I left this gig.

"Let's just say that because of my unique insight, I will be able to provide Jack with a probable location."

"How probable?" the cranky man inquired.

"Within a two or three mile radius." She ignored the raised eyebrows and refused to *prove it*. Like psychometry, Remote Viewing was psychic 101; basic stuff. She wasn't going to waste valuable time explaining that. "I have a high degree of confidence that the crystal is in Southern California, very close to where it was developed."

"How can that be?"

A knock on the door prevented her from answering. Prowler took a note from a young soldier. She nodded, shut the door, and handed the note to General Garson.

"Jack Porter needs to speak with you; it's urgent."

The officer known as Strauss rolled a cart with an intricate looking communications setup over to where Kaila was standing next to the general. He pressed a button and adjusted a knob. "Mr. Porter? This is Bagram. I have General Garson."

"Where's Dr. Ross?"

"I'm right here, Jack. What's happened?"

"The bastard has my daughter."

"Jesse?" Kaila asked, incredulous. She'd met the girl years before at a political fundraiser. A typical teenager, rebellious and determined to distance herself from anything that suggested otherwise, she'd stood eye to eye with Kaila, with dark hair and eyes that were incredibly perceptive. If she recalled correctly, the young girl had a nose ring and a rather interesting tattoo, a testament to her parents' tolerance.

Kaila's musings were halted by the sound of a woman sobbing. *Helen?*

"As you can hear, my wife is beside herself."

"Jack, it's obvious there's a lot more going on here than you've let on. If we're going to untangle this mess, we're going to need full disclosure."

"Understood."

"You have the stolen technology," Kaila stated. "That's what I picked up, why I came out of a sound sleep. I knew it was in So Cal. I was briefing everyone here and we were about to call you to share the information."

"Porter, how do you figure into this? Why did Kroeger take your daughter and leave the technology?"

"I told you," Kaila replied, "this was never about the technology. It was always about Kroeger and his need for attention. It was always about his wounded ego." She paused, looked at the men who were now standing around the communications cart. "His, not mine."

"This isn't the time," Prowler hissed.

"No, she's right." Porter sounded resigned. "This is exactly the time. Kaila? You can add my wounded ego to that list. If I hadn't let it get in the way, who knows -? From here out, you take the lead. Tell us where to go next."

Although she felt relieved, his acquiescence brought her no satisfaction.

"First of all, I did a quick scan. Your daughter is alive. She's tense, but she's handling the situation. I don't detect any outright panic."

"Can you tell us where she is?" Helen asked.

"I'll work on that later. Right now, I'd like to know how it is your daughter became part of this. You're withholding information, Jack. That could be deadly."

The silence on the other end of the phone stretched to the point she was beginning to wonder if the connection had dropped.

"Helen, why don't you -."

"If this has to do with Jesse, I'm staying."

"What'd you do, Jack?" Kaila asked. She hoped that by keeping a business-like tone, she could steer the conversation into the realm of productivity, not hysteria.

"It has to do with how we were getting the technology to Berkeley. It was my idea."

"I'm listening."

"About eight months ago, Jesse got a job working at a psychic shop; the kind that sells crystals and candles, incense, that sort of thing."

"In So Cal?"

"Yeah, in a strip mall. They're a chain and there's one up in the Bay Area. The technology looks similar to the crystals that are sold as jewelry, so I had it fashioned into a necklace, the idea being it could be transferred with a shipment of other gems up to Northern California, where an operative would pick it up and deliver it to Livermore."

"You used your daughter in one of your games?" Helen shrieked.

"Mrs. Porter?" It was Prowler. "Can you please wait until we've hung up before taking a rolling pin to the man? We want to get your daughter back, which means Kaila needs all of her questions answered."

"What happened, Jack?"

"I told Jesse that the son of a friend needed work, and would she put in a good word for him at the shop. He would do heavy lifting; retrieve the inventory when it came into Long Beach. Everything was working out fine, just as planned."

"Kroeger got a job working at the shop up in Northern Cal," Kaila stated. "That's how he knew about the shipment."

"More than that," Prowler added, "it's how he knew about Porter's daughter. Did he even know about this technology? Kaila, you said he was out of the loop, out of the system. If that was true, how would he have learned about the technology? I'm assuming you didn't mention it to your daughter, Jack."

"Of course not. I don't know how Kroeger found out."

"I have an idea," Kaila replied. Every eye in the room was pinned to her. She took a deep breath and flashed a grateful smile at Prowler , who was handing over a cup of water.

"If he's nothing else, Kroeger is methodical. He's patient, which made him good at his job. My guess is that he was planning on seeking revenge on everyone he felt had wronged him back in 2003, who'd cost him his respect and his job."

"He did that to himself," one of the officers spat.

"He wouldn't see it that way," she answered, dismissing him. "He blamed me; that much was obvious. I guess he blames Jack, too. It was Jack who terminated his position. Chad would see Jack as being responsible for the loss of respect."

"So, you think he's been watching my family, waiting for the chance to take Jesse?"

"Exactly. He probably thought it the highest of ironies that she was working at a psychic shop. Honestly? He probably found out about the technology by accident. In fact, it wouldn't surprise me if he'd actually planned on striking sooner, but after learning about the technology, delayed so that he could work out how to involve me."

"What do we do now?" Prowler asked.

"Jack, Helen, you two stay at home," Kaila directed. "Kroeger's an egomaniac. He will find some way to rub this in your face, Jack. Keep track of everything, every nuance. Contact Jesse's employer, see what you can find out."

"What are you going to do?" Porter asked. The sound of someone sobbing softly carried through the line and Kaila quickly folded her arms to block her solar plexus. She had to keep Helen's emotions shut out if she wanted to get information quickly and cleanly.

"I'm going to locate Jesse and consult on a plan."

"Call me as soon as you have anything."

"Will do. Helen? We'll get her back; alive. I promise. Kroeger's an asshole, but he isn't planning on killing your daughter. I can feel it. He wants Jack to grovel. He wants the US government to grovel. And, ultimately? It's me he wants dead."

Kaila walked to the door.

"Where are you going?" one of the officers snapped.

"I need to locate Jesse, and I can't do that with a bunch of pissed off military officers throwing their anger into the mix."

"I'll go with her, sirs," Prowler replied, quietly, taking Kaila's elbow. "Kaila? What do you need?"

Perry Garfield opened the door to his contractor's hut and stood, rubbing his eyes, and trying to stifle a yawn.

"Perry, I need to use your room."

"Hello to you to," he answered.

"It's an emergency," Prowler said from where she stood next to the psychic.

"Sure. Yeah, okay," he replied. "I'm -."

"Later," the major snapped, crowding the door so that he'd step inside.

"I need you to leave," Kaila ordered, stepping through the door. "I need to be alone."

Prowler thrust a coat in the sleepy man's direction. "Get your winter clothes on, and while Marlene Dietrich here does her thing, I'll buy you a cup of coffee. And, I promise I'll explain as much of this as I can without having to kill you after."

"Oh, I can't wait," he replied, stopping just outside the door. "I knew there was more to your story." He pulled the door shut and followed the major into the frosty pre-dawn morning.

Once they were gone, Kaila wasted no time. Spotting a desk, she sat down and began opening drawers. "Excellent." She pulled a set of drafter's tools from the bottom drawer and set them on the desktop next to several sheets of paper. It made sense that the contractors used older technology when teaching a new craft. The locals didn't have computers or fancy CAD programs. Hell, many of them didn't even have electricity.

Grabbing a compass, she inserted a small pencil and set it on a sheet of paper. Then she closed her eyes and let her mind wander while she stretched out psychically.

CHAPTER TWENTY-EIGHT

"I have to go to the bathroom."

"Best idea I've heard in hours," Dan replied, his eyes still closed. In spite of his earlier advice to the teen, he hadn't slept. He'd merely rested with his eyes closed and tried to keep from overanalyzing things, lest the infamous Dr. Kroeger pick up his intentions with too much detail. Common sense dictated that he would make a break for it at the first opportunity. In reality, the fact that he had a teenager to look out for added only a small bit of complexity. He doubted Kroeger would try anything as long as they were in such a public place. Even though they had a private berth, there were other passengers on the train, and not all of them could be counted on to look the other way. Hell, for all he knew, a half dozen or so were operatives from various governments, and while they tended to keep to themselves, if they saw a way to get into the good graces of the United States, as bargaining power for their own governments, Dan felt they could be counted on to help.

"Edik will take her," their captor replied, referring to the smaller of the two henchmen. The larger thug, Anatoly, was sleeping. Dan noted with some amusement that the bigger Russian was drooling against the train window, giving him the appearance of the village idiot.

"What about me?" he groused.

"You can't be serious, Major?"

"I mean I have to go as well."

"Since Edik is well armed, and you are aware that he won't hesitate to plaster her brains on the walls of this train, you may go, provided you go first. Edik will have his weapon aimed at her the entire time."

"I know the drill, Kroeger."

"Very good. So long as we understand each other."

Dan stood and sucked in a sharp breath. His muscles had cramped; particularly his right quadriceps. He'd had to have reconstructive knee surgery, leaving one of the muscles a bit shorter. It wasn't always a problem; only when he sat still for too long. Across the berth, Edik had Jesse's arm in a tight grasp.

"You'll look a bit conspicuous manhandling the young girl." He pointed at his gun. "I don't think she's going to run, knowing you can put a bullet in her spine. Just let her walk in front of you and don't be an ass."

The man looked to Kroeger, who nodded once. Dan slid the door open and walked left, toward the bathroom, which was located at the end of the car. He could hear the girl's boots as they shuffled behind him, followed by the heavy footfalls of the thug. No one else was in the companionway. He stopped in front of the bathroom.

"I'll be right out."

"Uh-huh." She was staring down at her Doc Martins.

He wanted to offer reassurance, but didn't want to waste any time. Just as he was about to step into the small bathroom, Kroeger popped his head into the hallway and looked in their direction. Dan met his gaze briefly, keeping his expression neutral, before stepping inside. He mentally evaluated various scenarios. They had to get off the train. He was pretty confident he could overpower the thug who was pressing a gun into Jesse's back. He didn't even care that Kroeger had his backpack, which held his paperwork. It was the girl. How could she handle the jump from a moving train when he didn't have a lot of time to coach her? Someone pounded on the door.

"Too long," Edik groused.

"Right, right." He opened the door. The young girl stepped around him and slammed the door. She had her purse with her. Would the fates be with them? If her passport was in her purse, they would have a much easier time of things. Even though Kroeger had removed Dan's travel documents from the backpack, he only got his military ID. His passport was taped snugly to his body. Being in Special Ops meant planning for any contingency, including an ambush.

Edik reached around him, pressing the gun into his kidney, and pounded on the door. "Too long."

"Christ, man. You aren't married, are you? No sisters? Women never get out of the bathroom that fast."

Kroeger stuck his head into the hall and, satisfied everything was under control, slipped back into the berth. It looked like the winds of fortune were indeed blowing in their direction. Deciding it was time to make his move, Dan coughed.

"I need some water."

"Bathroom."

"Right." He knocked on the door. "Jesse? I need a drink of water." Knowing he had only seconds, Dan sent up a quick prayer and twisted, catching the thug momentarily off guard. Covering the man's mouth, and squeezing hard, he grabbed Edik's gun hand, twisting, then pushing, and managing to dislocate his elbow. The Russian's cry of agony was muffled by Dan's hand. Still, he needed to insure silence. He used the gun to knock the man unconscious.

The girl still hadn't opened the door, but if he pounded on it, he would alert Kroeger to trouble. If he could get the unconscious Russian into the bathroom and then get the girl into the other car and off the train, it would buy them time. Knowing Kroeger would be looking out any minute, Dan used the gun to break the handle of the bathroom door.

"Jesse, listen -."

He couldn't believe his eyes. The bathroom was empty. "You've gotta be kidding me," he gasped, dragging Edik's body inside and pulling the door shut. He had only seconds. Arranging the Russian so that he blocked the door, Dan stood on the toilet seat and looked out the opened window the girl had obviously gone through to escape. How far back?

Someone pounded on the door and yelled something in Russian.

"Probably what's taking you so long?" Dan muttered, examining the window opening. It would be tight but he could do it. He'd rather not make any noise by breaking the frame. Whoever was in the hall pounded again.

"Here goes nothing," he said, gritting his teeth and diving through the opening.

* * *

"We've lost contact with Dan Foster."

"What?" Bob Murphy all but roared into the phone. "How? When?" Next to him in bed, his wife swung her legs over the side and reached for her robe. Without saying a word, she left the room.

"He should have checked in once he reached St. Petersburg," Jack Porter replied, tiredly. "I've had my man there working on it, but it's as if he vanished."

"If anything's happened to him," Murphy growled.

"My daughter's missing."

"Jesse?" The general was pacing the floor of his bedroom. "What the hell's going on here, Jack? This is turning into a fucking nightmare."

"And that nightmare's name is Chad Kroeger. Look, I don't have time to tell you all of it. I need you on the next flight Los Angeles. One of my guys will pick you up at LAX and bring you out to me."

"Make it John Wayne; I can take military transport."

"Not this time. We don't want to alert Kroeger to the fact we have all the players scrambling in the middle of the night. The President is in the loop and several agencies are working together."

"Under you?" the general snapped.

"Under Dr. Ross. She has the lead."

"Where is she?"

"At Bagram. Garson is with her."

"Well, you're right about one thing. All the right people are involved. Okay, I'll be on the first flight I can get. Who do I notify?"

"Let me give you the number. Kid's name is Chesky."

The bedroom door opened and Kate walked in, carrying a glass of amber liquid. "How many days' clothing will you need?" she asked, opening a drawer.

"Make it five. If I need more, I'll make arrangements. You're the best," he said, kissing her nose and drinking deeply of the burning liquid. He closed his eyes as the whiskey reset his equilibrium. "The best." Across the room, Kate smiled and kept packing.

* * *

"Jesse!" For the last twenty minutes, Dan had been walking on the train tracks in the direction they'd come from. Every few minutes he would call out. He hoped to God the girl was okay. It wasn't as bitter as it could be, but he knew they couldn't remain in the elements much longer. He thought about what she'd been wearing. Black boots, some sort of leggings with leg warmers over her calves, and a woolen dress that had been worn over a turtleneck. Fairly warm, but what she didn't have, was a coat. "Come on, kid," he panted. "Be okay."

His face was going numb. He took his next step and froze. Had he heard something? The wind was blowing toward him, whipping snow and ice into his eyes, making it even more difficult to see. What had possessed her to jump out the window?

There it was again. *"Jesse!"* He turned his ear toward the direction he thought the sound had come from. He definitely picked up something, but was it a human voice?

Adrenaline surged at the possibility she was okay and close. He didn't want to waste precious energy by running, but he definitely picked up the pace, continuing to yell periodically.

"Foster!" Jesse yelled, literally slamming into him. "Are you okay?" She was breathless from running. He frowned. If she was sweating, she would soon start shivering. He grabbed her, held her away from him. "Jesse? I didn't see you. How did you find me?"

"I figured you'd come after me, but the train would have been further along by that time, so I walked in this direction."

"Remind me to tell your dad what a resourceful kid you are," he replied, raising his voice to be heard over the howling wind. "Where'd you get that?" he asked, indicating a pea coat. Relief began to thaw his terror. He'd been worried he would find her unconscious and dying of hypothermia, and he wouldn't know where to go for help since they were probably in the middle of nowhere.

"There are homes dotted all through these mountains. I knocked on someone's door and a nice old woman answered. She tried to get me to stay but I told her I had a friend out here still. She gave me the coat."

"She spoke English?"

"I don't know. I managed to make her understand, okay?"

For a brief moment, Dan actually pitied Jack Foster. Resourceful, intelligent, and independent; a terrifying combination in a teenager. "You -."

"Come on, you can't stay out in this much longer, you'll get frostbite."

He allowed her to lead him along the tracks, holding her hand as they went. Although it rattled his ego slightly, he couldn't help admiring the young woman for taking the lead in the escape. Thanks to her ingenuity, they were probably going to make it out of this alive. He shook his head in amazement. He'd never met a kid like her. She'd never lost her cool; not once. "How'd you -?"

"Later," she yelled up at him. "Conserve your strength."

He didn't need to be told twice.

"Here we are."

"How in the hell did you ever find this place?" he panted, climbing small wooden steps toward an open door. Heat flowed out from the small house in waves.

"I smelled the fire," the teen replied, pointing toward smoke rising into the sky. In spite of the late hour, an almost full moon had enabled them to see that they'd managed to get off the train near a small, mountainside village. She pulled him inside. "This is Genka."

"Does she speak any English?" he asked, coming to stand behind the teen. He brought his hands to his mouth so he could blow warm air on them. They were red from exposure.

"Why don't you ask her?"

"Do you speak any English?"

"Some."

"Thank you." He pointed toward the thick coat the teenager was wearing.

"Food?"

"I would love some," Jesse answered. "I haven't eaten in hours."

"Do you still have your purse?" he asked, following the two women into a small kitchen.

"Yes."

"Passport?"

"Yep. That idiot thought he could intimidate me with his gun."

The owner of the small home, a woman in her late sixties, turned at the word. Dan held his hands up.

"He's okay," Jesse said, jerking a thumb in his direction.

"Gee, thanks."

The woman ladled soup into bowls and pointed toward a loaf of bread on the counter. While Jesse was helping set the table, he got glasses and proceeded to fill them with water. Taking the last bowl from Genka, he used his free hand to pull a chair out for her.

"Why?" the woman asked, once they were all seated.

"Running," Dan answered. "This is delicious."

"Why?" she repeated, pointing first at the teen and then at him.

"I was kidnapped by a bad guy," Jesse answered. "This guy was kidnapped by the same bad guy."

The woman's expression made no secret of the fact she had a hard time believing anyone could kidnap him.

"They had big guns," the teen explained. "And three men."

"And you."

"Yes," Dan agreed, "they used her to get my cooperation."

"How?"

"I jumped off the train," Jesse answered, doing an admirable job understanding the meaning behind the woman's monosyllabic questions.

"How did you know you weren't jumping to your death?" Dan snapped. "It was pitch dark out."

"While you were sleeping, I was studying the landscape."

"I wasn't sleeping," he retorted. "I was resting. There's a difference."

She rolled her eyes. "Whatever. All through these mountains, there were impossibly high snow drifts dotted by tiny homes with smoke rising from the chimneys. It reminded me of a lot of the European countries, like Germany and Switzerland. Anyway, I figured we had a better chance of surviving if I could get us out of there."

"You?"

"It worked, didn't it? I was a handicap to you, so I had to take myself out of that equation."

CHAPTER TWENTY-NINE

"I think you've been watching too many movies," Dan suggested, mopping up a bit of soup with his bread.

Jesse sighed impatiently. "My dad's a spook. I'm in the way of knowing the business, I guess you could say."

"Your dad taught you to jump off of moving trains?"

"You don't have any daughters, do you?"

"I have sisters."

"So, you must have taught them how to take care of themselves, right?"

"I never taught them how to jump from moving trains, no."

"Dan, the bathroom was at the end of the train car."

"What does that have to do with anything?" he snapped.

"Food," the woman ordered, effectively silencing them.

"Thank you, it was delicious."

Jesse began clearing the dishes and waved the woman to stay seated while she cleaned up.

"What does being at the end of the car have to do with anything?" Dan asked, coming to stand next to her. He dried the dishes and put them away. In the small kitchen, it wasn't hard to figure out where everything belonged.

"There's a ladder to take you to the top of the train at the end."

"You jumped from the top of the train?"

"What kind of a moron do you take me for? I climbed onto the ladder and waited for a good place to jump. I didn't see any tunnels coming up, so I figured I was safe enough."

"That's why I was able to find you so quickly; you hadn't jumped too long before I did. When I saw the open window, I didn't know how far back you'd leapt."

"You probably would have found me sooner if I hadn't gone straight toward the mountains in an attempt to find help."

At that point, he noticed she wasn't wearing the leggings.

"They were wet from my walk through the snow," she explained, following his gaze. "The coat reached low enough but Genka wouldn't let me out until I put these on."

"Son," the woman added from where she was still seated.

"I'll have to thank him," Jesse replied, sticking her leg out and turning her ankle to show off the rolled up bottoms.

"Dead."

"Oh, I'm so sorry."

"Soldier."

Dan turned to look at the older woman. "I'm very sorry." He turned back to the girl. "You're lucky. If -."

"If ifs and ands were pots and pans, there'd be no need for tinkers." She smiled. "Saw that in a movie once."

They returned to the table. The kitchen was toasty and Dan had run his wrists under warm water. The pins and needles effect brought about by returning circulation was welcome. He'd had a heck of a time holding the soup spoon, his fingers were so stiff.

"Do you have a phone?" Dan asked the teen.

"No International coverage. Besides, you don't honestly think we'd get a signal out here?"

"Tomorrow," the Russian woman said.

"Genka -."

"Town."

"I think she means she doesn't have a phone, but can take us to one tomorrow."

The woman smiled. "Sleep."

"I don't -," Dan started.

"Sleep," the woman insisted.

"Foster? You look like the walking dead. I haven't slept since this whole episode started. I don't think we're in any danger. Even if that creep, Kroeger, manages to disembark at the next stop, I don't see how he can find us tonight. I honestly think we're safe, until tomorrow at least."

In the end, he acquiesced, but only after insisting that he spend the night in the living room, guarding the front door. The woman took Jesse to a small bedroom near the kitchen and tucked her in.

"Come."

Dan followed her back to the living room where a fire crackled in a small hearth. Jesse's leggings hung over the back of a chair in front of it. The home was small, but well kept. Between the fire in the living room and the one burning in a small Franklin stove in the kitchen, the entire house was a comfortable temperature. Still, he wondered if he'd ever thaw; after two hours he still felt like a popsicle. Obviously, his body hadn't adjusted from his lengthy stay in the tropics.

Genka pulled a book from a shelf and held it out to him.

"I appreciate the offer, ma'am, but I'm beat. Besides, I don't read Russian." That wasn't true, but he didn't need to have her thinking he was a spy. She shook the book at him.

"Okay." He took it and immediately smiled. With his eyes on her face, he opened the volume and withdrew a Glock.

"Thank you. I have to admit, I feel a lot better with this."

She left the room, returning in a few minutes with a pillow and an old woolen blanket.

"Thank you," he said again, "for everything."

"Tomorrow; phone."

"Good night." Feeling more secure than he had since being on the carrier, he quickly fell into a deep sleep.

* * *

"So, this is the thing that's caused so much trouble."

"I think you mean Kroeger, don't you? That," Porter told General Murphy, pointing to the small laser crystal, "was just a matter of convenience; an opportunity for the bastard."

Between the cars parked in the driveway and those lining the canyon road, it looked as if the Porters were having a party. Fortunately, nearby residents tended to be eccentric, and therefore, usually kept to themselves. Even if they thought the sudden intrusion into their quiet neighborhood strange, they wouldn't do anything about it. General Murphy had arrived after an uneventful flight to find Jack's wife alternating tears with curses over the situation. Knowing it was a wise man who kept out of other people's marital woes; he'd simply hugged her and assured her he would do everything in his power to make sure Jesse was returned safely. "We have something he wants, so we're in a good position."

"Another life. What good is it to trade a life for a life?" she'd asked.

"That other life is a highly trained agent working with and surrounded by highly trained soldiers, all of whom are coming up with a plan to get your daughter home safely. I have confidence."

"I asked you here for a reason," Jack said, drawing the general into the library, where several agents were either talking on phones or typing on laptops.

"I should hope so," the general replied, laconically. "I assumed you didn't drag my ass out of bed just to tell me Foster was missing."

"Of course not, but it woke you up, didn't it? I needed you firing on all cylinders."

"What do you want?"

"I want you to take this up to Livermore." He handed over the laser crystal which was embedded in a jeweler's setting and dangling from a stainless steel chain. "Your contact will meet you at Oakland Airport, but I don't want you releasing this until you're inside the labs in Berkeley. You're to give it to a Dr. Silus Meltrius. He's expecting you."

A young man walked up and handed the general an envelope. Jack nodded toward it.

"That's your ID; it'll get you past the security gate. Your photograph and fingerprints have been transmitted and are on file within their computer systems. You've been cross referenced to ensure there are no delays."

Murphy opened the envelope and spilled the contents on the sofa where he'd taken a seat. He looked up at the security liaison. "Jack, sit down before you fall down. You look ready to snap. God knows, it's understandable, but you won't do anyone any good by -."

"Why do you think I'm handing everything off? This is my daughter we're talking about. I can't trust my own objectivity. I have grabbed the best of the best and put them on it. I have to do what I've asked so many others to in the past; wait it out and let the professionals do their jobs. It's what they're trained for."

"Tell me about Foster."

"He made contact in Russia and picked up his travel package. We know he made it onto the train headed to St. Petersburg. However, he never reached his destination. He got off before, but we don't know which stop. We haven't heard from him since."

"Just because he didn't check in, doesn't mean he didn't make it. How do you know he got off the train before St. Petersbug?"

"We had an agent waiting at the station; to make contact. He never got off. The man spoke to the right people. Dan got off the train somewhere between Moscow and St. Pete, but no one saw where."

"Sir?"

"Yes," both men answered, looking up at a young agent.

"We have Dr. Ross on the phone. She needs to speak with Mr. Porter."

"Put it on speaker," Jack instructed the agent.

"Jack?"

"And a roomful of others. My name is General Murphy, Dr. Ross. What have you got?"

"Is Jack there?"

"I'm here," he answered.

"She's in Russia, not incredibly far from Moscow. The name I get is Saratov."

"Got it," another agent said, turning his laptop to display a map. He pointed. "That star, there." He hit a few keys and an enlarged photo of the city appeared.

"Are you certain, Dr. Ross?" General Murphy asked.

"Certain enough to instruct you to send agents. She isn't on the move any longer. I feel she managed to get away from Kroeger."

"How do you know this?" the general asked.

For several seconds, there was silence.

"Never mind," he said, finally. Standing, he took the phone from the agent and turned off the speaker. "Dr. Ross? Hold a moment." He looked at the security liaison. "Jack, go get someone on the Russian angle. There's a Russian Air Force Base nearby, so I'm sure we have someone in the area." He waited until the man was on the other side of the room before putting the phone to his ear.

"Dr. Ross? This is General Murphy. Dan Foster is missing. Is there any possibility you can locate him?"

"What a beautiful city," Jesse said as they drove into Saratov. "I love how Europe is so old; so much history. California has the Spanish settlements, but they're a poor comparison in terms of architecture or age."

Dan looked over his shoulder at the teen. She appeared well rested, in spite of the fact that Genka had woken them both before dawn to help out on her farm, something they were both more than happy to do.

"Food," the woman said, parking her truck, a vehicle that had definitely seen better days. Dan would arrange to have a tune-up and oil change as repayment for her help. Money or a new vehicle would only bring the woman attention she didn't need or want.

"We just ate," Jesse protested from the back seat.

"Food," the woman repeated, indicating they should follow her.

"Jesse, -."

"I wouldn't speak if I were you," the teen hissed. "Just follow. We don't need anyone knowing we're American if we can help it."

Dan smiled. Americans stood out the world over, and he more than most. The teen could pass for a Brit, with her nose ring and tattoo, but Dan would never blend. Even with his beard and peasant's clothing, his build and his gait would give him away. Still, he trusted the older Russian woman to keep them out of trouble.

"Food."

They walked into a bakery filled with a handful of patrons. Dan fought the urge to blow on his cold hands. The temperatures were slightly above freezing, but the wind made it icy. However, such a move would only have people staring. They stood patiently while Genka spoke rapidly to a young man behind the counter. It was obvious they were discussing the Americans. The guy looked at them, eyes wide, and then disappeared into a back room.

"Phone," Genka hissed.

Within seconds, a burly Russian with salt and pepper hair, and a thick, grey beard came around the counter, looking them up and down. Keeping his eyes on Dan, he spoke to Genka. The two conversed quietly for a few minutes, periodically gesticulating. Genka returned and pushed them toward where the older man had disappeared around the corner.

"I guess we should follow," Jesse said, her voice low. She took the officer's hand and pulled him forward. "You speak Russian, don't you?"

"Why do you say that?"

"I saw your eyes. You understood."

"Just as they understand and speak English."

"Why didn't you -?"

"Shush. It's always smart to say as little as possible until you know what you're dealing with."

"Good advice," the burly man said in English. He led them into a tiny, cluttered space behind a storage room. A fine white dust was over everything. The Russian smiled, waved a hand. "Flour. Baker's problem." He wiped down a chair and gestured for the teen to sit down. "Now. You tell

Boris why you need phone. We maybe in danger here, Genka and me."

"I realize that," Dan agreed. "I need to get this girl out of Russia and back to her parents in California. She was kidnapped."

"Genka say you, too."

"I had things under control until she was brought aboard the train."

The man nodded, but said nothing. For several seconds, he simply studied them. "Someone listen. You know? Not secure."

"I understand. It won't be a problem."

An unsecure line did present a problem. Dan wouldn't be able to go through any of the normal channels. For several seconds, he considered his options.

"I could try calling one of my friends?" Jesse suggested. "Anyone listening wouldn't expect that."

"It's a good idea, but you'd put us in danger by alerting them to our location."

"Could I at least say what country we're in?"

"No," Boris replied. "Listen to him."

"Okay," Dan said, "I have an idea. You can hand me the phone."

"Would you repeat that?" Kaila asked, incredulous. A young soldier was standing at the door to the hut she shared with Prowler. She'd been trying to get a quick nap as she'd barely slept in days.

"There's a Tim Brightman on the phone for you, Dr. Ross" the man repeated. "I was asked to escort you to the command center, so you can speak with him."

"Of course, thank you. Let me get my coat on." She followed the young officer through the command center to a small office. General Garson and two other men were waiting for her. The general handed her a phone.

"Hello?" she said, uncertainly.

"Kaila, I just got the strangest call from Dan Foster."

"Foster? He called you?" Everyone in the room froze.

"He said to call you and you'd explain everything."

"That's it? That's what he said?"

CHAPTER THIRTY

"That's it."

"Okay, Tim; let me think for a minute."

"Do you need privacy?" the general asked.

"No. Tim, this might take some time. Where can I phone you back?" She scribbled down a number and hung up. "General, is there a map of Russia in here?"

Three men scrambled to fulfill the request. Taking one of two maps being thrust in her direction, she sat down and ran her fingers over the cities of Moscow and St. Petersburg, and then, Saratov.

"I don't -." She frowned. Her inability to read Dan probably meant she wouldn't be able to get the information they needed. Maybe Tim or another member of the club would have better luck.

"Is there a problem, Dr. Ross?" the general asked. She was about to answer when she caught sight of the young marine who'd escorted her to the command center. She stared so intently, the officers all turned their heads. Sensing that he had become the center of attention, the young man looked up from where he sat at a nearby table, writing in a notebook.

"Ma'am? If my presence here is a problem, I can make myself scarce."

"No need for that," she replied, smiling and walking up to him. She gazed down at his notebook. "You're writing a letter?"

"Yes, ma'am; to my sweetheart. She's back in Iowa. I try to write her once a week."

"What's you're name?"

"Corporal Keanes, ma'am."

"Well, Corporal Keanes, I want to thank you. Because you were sitting here at this moment, writing to your sweetheart, you helped me solve a very tough problem."

"I did?" He looked at the officers in confusion.

"Yes." She turned to the officers. "I need to find Prowler. I think I know how to find Foster."

"How?"

She glanced at the young marine before answering.

"I can finish this in my quarters."

"No, that won't be necessary. This isn't classified." She looked over at the officers. "Psychometry is the ability to pick up information by holding or touching an object. I think I could locate Major Foster if I could touch something he'd written on; if I could touch the ink. Prowler has a notebook and I know for a fact that Dan wrote something in it before we left the carrier."

" Corporal Keanes, please go find Major Anderson and explain what you just heard. Ask her to bring the notebook here." The officer who spoke looked at Kaila. "I want to see you do this."

Oh, goody, a dog and pony show.

Twenty minutes later she called Tim back.

"Dan disappeared from a train somewhere between Moscow and St. Petersburg. Jack Porter's daughter, Jesse, was kidnapped by Kroeger. My read tells me she's in Saratov and so is Foster."

"So, they're together?"

"Seems logical, don't you think? Dan wouldn't phone you if he was alone. He'd be able to get himself out without any problems. If he's reaching out to you, I'd say he has Jesse with him and needs to arrange for an extraction."

"But why call me?" Tim asked, interrupting her musings. "I'm on the other side of the world, literally."

"My guess is that he's not in a secure location, which means no secure line. He can't call any of the regulars. Even if he'd called Sean in Palo Alto, it would have tipped Kroeger off."

"Do you think Kroeger's aware of this?"

"He's definitely working with someone. He has plenty of contacts of his own and if he is still involved with -."

"I got the picture," Tim interrupted. "Dan said he was calling back in an hour, so our clock is ticking. What's next?"

"Mr. Brightman? This is General Garson. I see you work for Jack Porter's organization."

"When I'm on vacation from my day job here at the U.S. Embassy."

"Right. Well, you're about to take another vacation."

"I gather I'll need a winter coat?"

"You might want to throw in a scarf. Dr. Ross will meet you in Moscow. From there, you'll take a train to Saratov."

"What do you want me to tell Foster when he calls?"

"To enjoy his vacation. He'll know what it means."

"Yeah, stay put. Will he -?"

"Dr. Ross will have the details. Book your flight."

"I hope he can sleep on planes," Kaila remarked. "I need to find Major Anderson, give her an update."

* * *

"What'd they say?" Jesse asked, quietly. For all her bravado, Dan knew she had to be nervous, if not scared.

"We need to avail ourselves of Genka's hospitality for a little longer." He looked at the baker. "I need to buy enough food so the woman can feed us for a couple of days."

"I'll be by with a delivery this afternoon," the man replied. Dan handed him a wad of cash. "I take it this won't be a problem? That it's American? I'd like to hold onto the Russian money I have."

"Will not be problem. Now, go. Leave out back and walk to church. Genka pick you up there."

"What's going on?" Jesse asked as they walked through the town. "How are we going to get out of here?"

"First of all, we're in no immediate danger. Worst case, we'll be turned into the US Embassy in Moscow. No one has any reason to suspect we don't belong here, and in spite of what some people think, Russians are just like everyone else."

"They love their children, too, right?"

"Sure. Okay, there's the church. How are you holding up?"

"Now that I'm away from that creep? Fine. What a dweeb."

When Boris drove up later that afternoon, Jesse was gathering eggs from a small henhouse. Dan went out to unload the delivery van.

"Come," Genka said, handing the baker a cup of clear liquid and taking a bag from the van.

"Vodka?" Dan asked, smiling.

"Good way to warm up on winter day, da? You have?"

"I've had. No more, thank you. You relax while I put these away."

"That one," the man said, pointing to a small box. "Special care."

"Right." Dan smiled, withdrawing a weapon and a phone.

"Not secure."

"Right." He reached for the last of his cash, but stopped when the baker held up his hand.

"You find other way, da?"

"No problem. One day, a couple of months from now, you'll receive a thank-you."

"Christmas present, da?"

"Ho ho ho."

"That's a lot of food," Jesse said, setting a basket of fresh eggs on the table.

"Good," Genka replied, pointing to the basket.

"I was going to haul some wood in."

"Jesse, I don't think she expects you to -."

"What else am I going to do? I don't speak or read Russian, so that leaves out my better options." Without another word, she walked toward where wood was piled under a tarp. A steady drizzle was falling, but the girl genuinely seemed happy to be busy.

"How long you be here?" Boris asked.

"Hopefully, only a day or two. I know the cavalry is on their way as we speak, but I'm not sure where they're coming from, so I don't know how long it will be before they're here."

"How they find?"

"I'll call my friend tomorrow morning and see what I can find out."

"Back to work," he said, standing. "You keep safe." The baker pointed to the older woman. "My family."

"Cousin," Genka explained.

"I'll guard her with my life, friend," Dan assured, shaking the man's hand. "Thank you, for everything."

Jesse was piling wood outside the kitchen door.

"You listen to him," Boris said, pointing to Dan. With a wave, he got in his van and drove toward town.

"Let me help you with that," Dan started, but Genka was patting his sleeve.

"Come."

He followed her to a larger bedroom in the back of the house. She was pointing at a window. "You fix."

"How've you been?" Tim asked, releasing Kaila from his embrace. He was a tall man so she came up to his chest.

"Tired. I slept a little on the flight here. I feel like I'm in a Tom Clancy novel. Spy work is never like what we see in the movies; except for the awful parts. At least, for me, which is why I got out of it."

"Too bad you didn't realize you'd signed up for life, eh?"

"We're staying at a hotel. We're supposed to be newlyweds, and you're trying to trace your Russian ancestors; or something like that. It's all in the packet."

"I was briefed on the way to the airport."

"The apartment Dan used would have been perfect, but it's got to remain vacant for three more months."

"Yeah, we don't want the Russians thinking we're back in the game to the level we were before the Wall came down."

"Right. What a hassle. How do we keep it all straight?"

"By not thinking too far outside our assignments," he said, kissing the top of her head. "I think I could get used to being married to you."

"Watch it."

"I'm on my best behavior, I promise. Besides, I've no interest in having Foster kick my ass."

She snorted. "Trust me, you have nothing to worry about from that quarter."

"Trust me," he countered, "I do."

Once they were checked into their hotel, they went in search of a restaurant.

"I'm looking forward to eating in a real restaurant," she said, linking her arm through his. It was easy to fall into the role. Tim was handsome, but more important; he was a friend. There was genuine affection, so anyone observing them would have no reason to doubt there was a real connection between them.

"Been rough?"

"Have you ever been to Bagram?" she hissed.

"Here, this looks like just what we want." He opened a door and escorted her into a small café.

"Thank God for vodka," he said a half hour later. Knowing they were being watched by just about everyone, they'd kept their conversation to the mundane. They didn't refer to any travel plans; though they did discuss some of the tourist activities they planned, going so far as to ask the waitress for her thoughts on which ones were worthy.

"Why don't we go back to the room," Kaila said, suggestively, leaning over to kiss Tim on the mouth.

"I'm going to have to be awfully careful with this," he told her as they stepped into the hotel room and removed their coats. He looked around. The contacts assured them the room, at least, was clean. They would be able to talk freely. "If I'm not, you'll break my heart."

"Off it, Tim. Besides, I'm sure you have someone back in Santiago."

"Talca, actually. I met her while helping out with Sean and Kian's rescue. She works at the hotel where they were staying. She's a student at the university and her family owns a winery. She's very sweet."

"But?"

"You know the drill."

"Yeah, I thought so. All your brave words to me about trusting someone outside the organization, yet you don't do it yourself."

"Yeah, but -."

"Don't worry. I'm not going to play the hypocrite by lecturing you about what I don't do myself." She sat down on the couch, facing him. If anyone was watching them through the window, they would simply see two people having a conversation. The electronic equipment in the coat closet would ensure their conversation would be safe, and she made sure she wasn't in direct line of sight, lest they were trying to read her lips.

"Here." She pulled out a pamphlet. "We're to get on the train to Saratov. Actually, our tickets read Tashkent, but we'll get off before. We'll be doing the tourist thing, so we're booked into a hotel."

"Based on my last contact with Foster, I've a pretty good idea where to meet."

"Good. We have a contact who'll be waiting for us. He'll take Jesse to St. Petersburg, where Jack and Helen will be waiting."

"That'll get the attention of the Russian authorities."

Kaila sighed. "I know, but it can't be helped. Helen about had apoplexy when I suggested they meet her in Paris. She said if the wife of a high ranking CIA operative couldn't be kept safe while touring in Russia, she had no faith in any of it; or any one."

"Ouch. Listen," he said, standing and stretching. "I'm beat. Do I have time to catch some z's before our train leaves?"

"'fraid not. You can sleep on the train."

"I can't sleep in moving vehicles."

On impulse, she leaned over and kissed his nose. "Poor Tim. You can lean on me. My energy should help."

* * *

"They're on their way?" the teen asked, eagerly.

"Yep. We'll meet up with the contact tomorrow. He'll take you to St. Petersburg."

"I'm not going with some stranger."

"Jesse, I can't go with you. I have orders to follow Kroeger's trail."

"He's Russian, right?"

"Who, the contact?"

"Yeah."

"Well, yes, but Jesse, I can assure you, you'll be perfectly safe."

"No." She stood near the living room fireplace, arms crossed, her mouth set. It didn't escape his notice that her lips trembled.

"If I get Dr. Ross to go with you, would that make you feel better?"

"You, Foster. I want you." She brushed away a stray tear. "Don't you understand? I trust you. You've kept me safe."

He walked over and pulled her into a hug. "Jesse? I know it may be hard for you to believe, but *you* kept us safe. You are amazing. I can't wait to tell your dad."

She sniffled. "He'll probably try to enlist me."

"And your mother would hand him his head. Listen," he said, turning her face up to him. "I'll go with you. You deserve to feel safe."

"Won't you get in trouble for disobeying orders?"

He laughed, a body shaking laugh; the kind that released endorphins. "Wouldn't be the first time. Why don't you go get some sleep? We have a big day tomorrow."

Genka had been standing in the doorway, listening to everything. She came forward and took the teen's arm, then led her toward the small bedroom. Once they'd gone, Dan fed a few pieces of wood into the hearth and sat in a chair facing the fire.

"You, sleep."

"I will. I need to prepare."

"Sleep is prepare," the older woman said, sagely.

"Yes, but there's a lot at stake here. Jesse's safety is paramount."

"Sleep. Boris help. Me, too."

"Right. I think I'll sleep here tonight," he said, pulling the Glock into his lap and settling the blanket on top. His back ached from nights spent sleeping on the hard floor. The chair would be a welcome change, even if it was a bit lumpy.

CHAPTER THIRTY-ONE

"I never realized Saratov was so beautiful," Kaila exclaimed.

"I'm glad Russia's more open," Tim replied. "It certainly makes our job a lot easier. Before the Wall came down, it was next to impossible to travel here."

"You've been here?"

"I've been to Moscow, but here? No. Engels, the Russian Air Force Base, isn't too far away, though and I've read the reports."

"It's cold down here by the river. Let's find a place to get a cup of coffee."

"What time are we supposed to meet at the church?"

"Not for two hours."

"Have you ever met Jessica Porter?"

"Yes, at a fundraiser a few years ago. She was going through puberty. It was fun; *not*."

"I love how adults conveniently forget that we've all been there."

"Not me," she replied, turning her nose up. "I was a perfect adolescent."

"Remind me to send your mom a Christmas card. I'll call her for New Years and follow up on that one myself."

"Here, this looks like a good place. We can watch the ships go by."

"What time you go?" Boris asked. He would be taking Jessica and Dan in his van, bringing them along on his deliveries before dropping them at the church.

"We meet in two hours," Dan replied. "How long do your deliveries take?"

"Half done. The rest? Maybe an hour, maybe less."

Using Boris had been a last minute idea. They were originally going to have Genka drive them in her old pickup, the intent being that she would take them on a small tour of the city with the church one of many stops. However, Jesse had pointed out that they'd already been to the church with Genka, so maybe they should meet the contact somewhere else. The girl was worried that the older woman would be punished for helping them.

"Jess," Dan assured, "she is in no real danger. The Russians aren't after us, Kroeger is. He won't go after a local. He's not stupid and it would take him away from his true goal."

"Kaila Ross."

Dan had shared enough information to put the girl at ease and convince her that Kroeger would not try to kidnap her again.

"Exactly." Still, Dan conceded, the girl had a point about the location and Genka. It was then that he decided to call on Boris. "That's brilliant," the teen had agreed. "There are no windows in his van, so we can sit in the back."

"I have a feeling people may know we're with him, but you're right. We will be safe enough. He can go back to the bakery, and we can walk to the church."

"No," Boris corrected. "I drop you on other end of street. Have delivery. You get out and walk. Not from shop."

"Fine." He looked at Genka. "I am indebted to you; we both are. I'll make sure the right people know."

The old woman smiled. "Keep safe." She was pointing at Jessica.

"I'll protect her with my life," he replied in serviceable Russian. Her eyes all but disappeared beneath the wrinkles of a smile. Jesse hugged the old woman, who ruffled her hair. They followed Boris out and climbed into the van.

"Did you ever play the game Candyland?" Kaila asked.

"Didn't most kids?" Tim replied.

'The colors of that church remind me of that game."

In spite of the weather, there was a sizable crowd visiting the historical landmark. While some of them were obviously tourists, others were likely students from one of the universities.

"It's a lot bigger than I realized; population wise," she continued as they took in the surrounding area.

"Almost a million people."

"Remind me to take you along on my next vacation," she joked. "You're a wealth of almost useless facts."

"Dr. Ross?" Kaila turned. A man standing behind her opened his coat just enough that she could see the gun's muzzle. "I trust you won't be making a scene? Now, if you and Mr. Brightman will follow me?"

Next to her, Tim stood stiffly enough to let her know he also had a weapon trained on him.

"It's okay," he murmured, "we knew it was possible he'd find us."

Tim was right. In reality, Kaila didn't mind. With his focus on her, Kroeger wasn't likely to go after Porter's daughter again.

"Get in."

She glanced at Tim. "I'll go, but he doesn't need to -."

"Both of you," the man snapped, "and quickly. Remember, no trouble."

Without another word, she slid next to Tim. The man who'd held a gun on her slid in, crowding her.

"Well, well, well. It's been a long time, wouldn't you say?"

"Chad." Kaila sighed. She also wasn't surprised she hadn't felt her former lover. With all the people in the area, she would have had to be psychically scanning for him and since she'd been focused on feeling Jessica Porter, she'd missed the negative tremors she'd learned to associate with Chad. Kroeger. Beside her, Tim set his hand on her knee and gave a reassuring squeeze. When she felt a bit of soothing energy flow into her body, she smiled. She'd forgotten he was a healer.

"Isn't that sweet," Kroeger spat from the passenger seat. The car was in motion and he was watching her in the mirror on the visor. "Tsk, tsk, tsk, Kaila. So many men willing to throw themselves on a grenade for you? It must have you absolutely throbbing."

Filled with revulsion, she refused to reply.

"Follow that car," Dan snapped. He hated dragging Jessica into the situation but he knew if he didn't act, Kaila was as good as dead. "How the hell did he find us?" he mumbled.

"Didn't you say he's a psychic?" Jesse asked.

"It has to be more. That man has to have connections, else he wouldn't have known how to find her, let alone force her and Tim into the car at gunpoint."

"Former KGB," Boris said from the driver's seat.

"Realistically, how many am I likely to be up against?" Dan asked.

"Six, maybe seven. I know man with gun. His brother killed, he mercenary now."

The idea of working against hired guns didn't disturb Dan. A man defending a cause of the heart beat out someone working for money every time. He looked at Jesse.

"You stay with Boris, no matter what. I will come back for you, but this is going down and I don't want you anywhere around when it does. You go with him; he'll keep you safe until I can get back to you."

"You listen to him," Boris said, nodding from the front of the van.

"I understand," she said, her voice trembling.

"Here. You hold onto this." He handed her the gun that Boris had given him days before. He'd managed to have a new firearm issued and delivered via the bakery. He would have preferred his own gun, but as that was lost along with everything else in the backpack, he decided to be happy with the preferred P226 over the older weapon the Russian had given him.

"There's the safety. Don't pull that trigger unless you intend to kill and wait until whoever it is is close enough. Go for the head or the heart if you can, but the stomach will do. I wouldn't bother with the kneecap thing because there's no guarantee the man will stay down."

"Right; I saw *Scar Face*."

Dan shook his head. "You're making me reconsider having kids."

She smiled, her lips trembling.

"It's going to be okay. I promise." He gave her hand a squeeze. "I really promise."

"You listen to him," Boris called from the front seat. "I keep you safe; you see."

They drove in silence as they followed the other car along the river. Dan was impressed by Boris' cool composure and his ability to follow at a discreet distance. "I know this place," he said from the front. "Lots of warehouses. Lots of space for trouble."

"They're slowing down. Let me out." He turned to the girl. "I'll see you soon. You stay with Boris." He looked at the Russian. "You call me, tell me where she is. Don't turn her over to anyone, not even another American. I'll be in touch as soon as I can."

"Good luck," the teen said, "and I'll be okay." She smiled. "Him, I trust."

Flashing a quick smile, Dan shut the rear door and headed toward where the car they'd been following was parked near the entrance to a warehouse. Walking slowly, he moved his eyes in every direction, absorbing. He was far from unnoticed, but the people working in the area went back to whatever it was they'd been doing after assuring themselves he was no threat.

"If you'd stand over there, Mr. Brightman?"

Dan plastered himself against the side of the building, and listened. Two men who had been in the process of loading crates onto a flatbed moved off after hearing the comment. They probably surmised what it meant. Dan wondered if they would go for the authorities, and if they did, would it make the situation worse or not?

"Kaila, you and I will be leaving. Get back into the car, if you please?"

Dan recognized Kroeger's voice. He wanted to know what was going on, how many hired thugs he'd be facing, but he couldn't risk giving himself away.

"Kaila, don't."

The tone of Tim's voice told Dan the man was worried. That meant Kaila was in real danger.

"It'll be alright, Tim," she assured the Embassy man, her voice steady.

She didn't plan on taking the man on herself, did she? He'd seen how she'd reacted to his photo on the carrier. Her emotions would definitely be a liability.

"Kaila, -."

"Mr. Brightman, I want your silence," Kroeger ordered. "Kaila, you get in the car or I will blow his brains out."

So, the man was armed. That meant at least three guns. As Dan reviewed his plan, a car started. He waited, crept closer to the entrance; drew his weapon. Thankfully, the contact had sent a Sig with a silencer. He only prayed no authorities or other innocents showed up at the wrong moment. The car drove forward. Dan aimed; fired.

"You safe here," Boris said, pulling into the farm yard. "Genka protect."

"Where are you going?"

"I have deliveries."

"You're leaving me here alone with an old woman?" Behind her, the Russian woman laughed, making her turn. Jesse's eyes widened. She was holding a lethal looking gun, and it was obvious to the teen that she was quite at ease with the weapon.

"You safe. See you later."

"Come," the old woman instructed. "Work."

Kaila didn't flinch when the back of the driver's head flew into the backseat. Next to her, Kroeger momentarily froze, so she took advantage. Even as blood splattered, she dove into the front seat and grabbed the wheel, simultaneously kicking the gun from the hand of the man in the passenger seat and then slamming the breaks so she could jam the car into park.

The thug who'd been riding shotgun was trying, in vain, to subdue her. She was holding her own, not because of her training, but because she was lashing out with every pent up emotion she'd held in check since her fight with Foster on the carrier. When the driver side door opened, she prepared to face another attacker.

"Dan, thank God."

Before she could say another word, Kroeger leaned over the seat, gun drawn.

"Good-bye, Kaila." He fired.

Certain she'd heard two shots; Kaila tried to keep her eyes open. The pain in her chest was horrific, however, and it was all she could do just to breathe. Every time she tried to draw a breath, a searing fire tore through her chest. She coughed and tried to tilt her head back, but couldn't move. Was she paralyzed? Before she could determine an answer, everything went black.

"In here," Dan ordered. "Set her down there."

Tim Brightman carried Kaila over to the bed in the room off the kitchen, and lay her down gently.

"Move." Genka was inserting herself between Tim and the bed.

"Do as she says," Boris said of his cousin. "She help."

"Tim, this is Genka. I have every reason to trust her."

"Here." Jessica handed the Embassy employee a cup with clear liquid. "Vodka." She handed one to Dan. "Is she going to be okay?"

"Yes," the Russian woman answered. "Out."

"But," the teen protested.

"Out."

"Go," Boris ordered.

"You," the woman said, pointing at Dan, "stay. Help."

"Why him?" Jesse protested. "I'm a woman. She's going to have no shirt on."

"I speak Russian," Dan replied, not meeting her eyes.

"You've seen her already, haven't you?" Jesse's eyes widened. She smiled. "She's your girlfriend. Why didn't you say something? You poor guy, all this time you must have been frantic."

"Come on, Jesse," Tim said, guiding the young woman out. "Have you tried this stuff? It's pretty good."

It worked. The prospect of being treated as an adult had the teen cooperating.

"What do you need me to do?" Dan asked, speaking Russian.

"Go boil some water and bring back what Boris gives you. He will know where I keep my supplies."

For the next two hours, Dan followed instructions while the Russian woman removed the bullet, which was actually lodged deeply; and cleaned and dressed the wound.

"Now, go," the woman said. She needs rest. I will stay with her. You go make call for help."

Dan sat on the floor in the living room, his back against a couch. Tim and Jesse were playing a game of chess, and Boris stood, staring out at the driveway, gun in hand.

"I don't think anyone will trouble us," Dan told him, coming to stand next to him. He looked out into the growing darkness. "Kroeger's dead and our contact has everything under control, including the local authorities. You won't be indicated in any way."

"Thank you," the man replied in Russian. "I love my cousin very much. She's a good woman." Because he knew Dan spoke their language, he continued in Russian. "She's been alone a long time."

"When was her husband killed?"

"In Afghanistan," he replied. "Long time ago. Sons gone, too."

"I'm sorry for her. She lives alone and works this farm by herself?"

"No. Dimitry, he works here when he is not at the bakery with me."

"He's your son?"

"Yes. He is good boy, but young. I hope he goes to university someday. Now? He says no more school."

"You have a good family, Boris. You can be proud."

CHAPTER THIRTY-TWO

"I need you," Tim said, tapping Dan.

"Go," Boris urged. "I watch." He walked over and sat across from the teen. "I play chess, though not good. Too aggressive, make mistakes."

"I'm not that good either," the teen replied, setting the pieces up.

Dan followed Tim into the room where Kaila lay unmoving on the bed. He hated that she was so pale. Genka started to protest, but stopped when Tim held his hand up.

"Tell her I need to climb in with her, in that bed."

"What?" Dan snapped.

"You, too. I'm going to initiate you into our little club," he said, "into her world."

"What are you talking about?"

"Yes, what you mean?" Genka inquired, coming to stand protectively over Kaila.

"Kaila's body will heal, but I'm worried about her mind, her psyche. Kroeger was causing her tremendous pain, subjecting her to the hate and anger he was pushing at her. Every negative and sick emotion he had was being picked up, intimately, by that woman right there." He pointed at where she lay sleeping.

"I don't understand," Dan asked, staring helplessly, his hands at his sides.

"Thoughts and emotions are simply another form of energy. Kaila is a receptor to that energy, which is why she is able to detect information most people can't. She is like a radio; she picks up signals. Unfortunately, not all the signals are harmonious."

"Remote Viewing," Genka said, nodding. "Russian spies do, too. She is spy?"

"No," Dan replied, "she's an archeologist. She used to be a spy, but she quit many years ago."

"They never quit," the old woman quietly replied.

"So, you're saying he did something to her mind?" Dan asked.

"More than her mind, her whole body. She needs all her energy to recover from this gunshot wound. I need to get the psychic toxins left by Kroeger out, to free her up so she can focus on physical healing. You're going to help me."

"Just how the hell am I going to do that? I'm no psychic."

"I know that," Tim snarled, "take off your shirt and get into that bed. Face the window."

"You are, aren't you? A psychic, I mean. Christ."

"Very good, Foster" he replied, pulling his sweater off. "Now get your shirt off and get into that bed." He leaned down and pulled the covers back. Once Dan was in bed and facing away from them, he crawled in on her other side and gently turned her so that her bare chest would rest against Dan's back. He moved so that his chest would press up against her back.

"I want you to hold still."

"What are you going to do?"

"That doesn't matter."

"I mean, what should I expect?"

"I'm going to slide her arms over and under you. I want you to hold her hands over your solar plexus and put your own hands on top of hers. I'm going to channel the toxins out of her and into you."

"How -? Ok."

"Dan? You're going to feel it. You're going to feel sick, very sick."

"Sick how? You mean like I have the flu, sick?"

"You'll know."

"You're enjoying this, aren't you?"

"I'm not. I'm worried about her. However, I think this is going to help you understand her in a way nothing else could and that," he finished, "is incredibly satisfying."

"You love her."

"Of course. So do you. Shut up and close your eyes and breathe regularly."

Tim placed his hands around her body, sliding them over her solar plexus. She was unconscious, but breathing steadily. Interlacing his fingers, he ignored the penetrating gaze of the old woman, closed his eyes, and went to work.

Tim continued to move his own energy through Kaila, into Dan, even when her body shuddered and he heard Dan's sharp intake of breath. For more than a half hour he worked, not stopping until he was as certain as he could be that Kroeger's mental and emotional poison was out. Finally, he opened his eyes, disengaged from her body, and crawled out of bed. Reaching for his sweater, he called over to Dan.

"You can get out and put your shirt on. How do you feel?"

"Like shit," the officer replied, his voice thick. "I feel hung over."

"Now imagine that times a thousand. That's what she was dealing with. Now you know why I wanted her free of that."

Across the room, Dan stared out the window. Tim knew he'd given the soldier plenty to think about when it came to the beautiful woman laying in that bed.

"Is she okay now?" Genka asked.

"She should sleep just fine. Dan? I didn't channel everything into you. I took plenty of it into my own system. I knew you wouldn't be able to handle a full onslaught."

"How does she handle it?"

"Every psychic is trained, to some degree, to shield themselves. There's a sense of self-preservation, I guess. However, when you're as strong a psychic medium as she is? You need more. You've seen the pendant she wears? That helps, but it can't do it all."

"The vinegar and the amethyst -?"

"Exactly. Each of us has our own bag of tricks."

"Like a Native American medicine bag," Dan replied.

"Yes."

"Here," Genka said, walking up to Tim. "Against evil eye."

"Tourmaline," he said, smiling. "Put it in her hand, it'll help. Thanks."

"How'd -?" Dan stared at the older woman. Tim laughed.

"It's only the western world with its semi-paranoid culture that isn't as familiar with this stuff. You'd be surprised how many cultures still understand the symbiotic balance between man and nature. Mud baths, volcanic scrubs, salt washes, all of it has its roots in folklore, yet you find it at most of the world's top spas. That ought to tell you something. Come on, we need to let her get her rest."

"How long am I going to feel this way?" Dan asked as they went toward the living room.

Tim suggested he have a drink.

"That's not an answer, Brightman."

That night, Genka had a full house. Jesse shared the larger bed with their hostess while Boris and Tim slept in the living room; Tim in front of the fireplace and Boris stretched out near the door. Both men kept a gun within easy reach. Dan lay on the floor, next to Kaila, but couldn't sleep. He kept listening for the periodic deeper breaths she took, assuring himself she was okay. When she shifted and groaned, he scrambled to his feet and leaned close.

"Kaila? It's Dan. How are you feeling?"

She opened one eye and looked at him; smiled weakly. "Like I've been shot." She licked her lips. "Can I have some water?"

"Sure, I'll be right back." He studied her for a moment before going to the kitchen. He sat on the bed and held the glass to her lips, taking care not to let the water get on the blanket.

"Jesse?" She cleared her throat. "Tim?"

"Sleeping. Everyone's okay. Everyone, that is, except you."

"Kroeger?"

"He won't be bothering you again; or anyone."

"Dead?"

"Shot him myself. It was quite satisfying, I have to admit."

"How you feel?" Genka asked from where she stood in the doorway.

"She's pretty groggy but I think she's on the mend," Dan answered. Kaila's eyes were closed, but she smiled.

"Good. Pain?"

"Not bad," Kaila replied.

"You," the Russian said, pointing at Dan. "You wake me if she in pain."

"I will."

He waited until the woman had closed her bedroom door before speaking again.

"She's gone. The truth. Are you in a lot of pain?"

"Foster, I don't like taking pain meds. I hate the way they make me feel."

"Is it because they interfere with your abilities?"

She opened her eyes, but didn't answer.

"When you're feeling stronger," he said, gently, brushing her hair out of her eyes, "we'll talk."

"How did you find me?"

"Honestly? Sheer luck. Boris was dropping us off a block away from the church. We were going to walk. We were half expecting trouble, so -."

"We?"

"The agent who was going to take Jesse to be with her parents. I called them, by the way, told them we'd be a little longer."

"So, you just happened to be looking in our direction when we were apprehended?"

It was on the tip of his tongue to insist she needed rest; that explanations could wait. However, part of him sensed her need for closure. He wanted to close the divide that had widened between them on the carrier but was afraid to touch her, lest he cause more pain.

"What's going on in that military mind of yours, Foster?"

"You can't tell?"

"Would you believe I can't read you?"

"Really?"

"Honest. It drove me crazy."

"I'm the only person on earth you can't -."

"I didn't say you were the only one I couldn't read," she interrupted.

"Okay. I was thinking how I would love to crawl in that bed with you but I don't want to cause any more pain by jostling your -," but he stopped. She'd scooted away from him, creating a space.

"No," he countered, standing and walking to the other side of the bed. He leaned forward and gently shifted her toward the other side of the bed. When she tried to turn her head, he reached out and gently restrained her. He crawled in behind her and slid forward so that his chest was against her back.

"What are you doing?" she whispered, placing her hands on top of his where they rested over her solar plexus.

"Spoons, I believe it's called?"

"Tim told you?"

He smiled into her hair, kissed her ear. "Tim told me. Let's get some sleep, okay?"

Three days later, they were ready to leave. Upon learning that Jessica refused to leave without Dan's escort, and that he wouldn't leave until Kaila was strong enough to travel, the Porters took a train from St. Petersburg to reunite with their daughter and thank the Russians who had protected her.

"Foster, if there is ever anything we can do," Helen Porter said, giving the Major a bear hug.

"I take back almost every nasty thing I've ever said or thought about you," Jack replied, shaking his hand.

"Your daughter deserves all the credit," he stated, and had the pleasure of seeing proud parents look at their child with a new level of respect.

While they were waiting for Kaila to gain strength, an army of men came and went. Every item on Genka's farm in a state of disrepair was fixed and her kitchen was restocked on a regular basis.

Boris' bakery gained a star on the proverbial spook map as a safe place to stop for coffee and a pastry. His son, intimidated by the sometimes fierce appearance of their visitors, began talking about attending university.

Finally, it was time to say good-bye.

"Thanks, Foster. From the moment you told me you'd get me out of there, I wasn't afraid anymore. Thanks for keeping your promise and thanks for telling my parents all those cool things about me."

"You're very welcome, Jesse. I have a feeling we'll run into each other from time to time. Your dad knows how to reach me if you need anything. Have a safe trip and good luck."

"Um, I do have one question? Why didn't you take Kaila to a hospital?"

He smiled. "Too many questions that couldn't be answered. I didn't want to put Boris and Genka in an awkward position. They're already associated with helping the Americans, which means they won't have a moment's peace from now on."

"What do you mean? Are they going to be thrown in jail?"

"Not at all. I just mean that every neighbor for miles will find a reason to stop by and hear the tale. It also means that the US agents will go out of their way to ensure their continued safety." He breathed a sigh. "And it *also* means they will be on the Russian radar for the rest of their days."

"Genka seems to like the attention," she whispered, conspiratorially. He smiled.

"Boris is trying to get her to remarry. She may consider it now."

"What about you?"

"*Me?*"

"What's your next mission?"

"I was on schedule for retirement. This hasn't changed my mind about that."

"Then what will you do when you leave here?"

"Go home, see my family. Maybe go visit Sean and Kian in Palo Alto. After that -?"

"He's going to come with me," Kaila said, walking up.

"Go with you where?" the teen wanted to know.

"I have an opportunity for a new dig," she replied, "but as usual, security might be an issue."

"This is the first I've heard about it," Dan grumbled, but he winked at the teen.

"Take her home with you," Jesse suggested. "Introduce your ladylove to your family."

"Ladylove?" Kaila and Dan said in unison.

"Gotta go," she said. "My parents are waiting." She hugged the Russians, promising to keep in touch, and ran out to where her parents were waiting.

EPILOGUE

Kaila's hair whipped into her mouth. It tasted salty.

"We won't go out too far," Dan assured, working the wheel, "since it can be rough this time of year."

"Not to mention, a little chilly," his mother added, spreading a blanket over Kaila's lap. "But don't worry about catching a chill," she assured, "this fresh sea air is just what you need to regain your strength."

"Thank you, Mrs. Foster. I'm not worried."

"How's your stomach?" Dan's father asked, elbowing his son aside. "I can take this. You go sit next to Kaila."

"The homeopathic stuff you gave me worked like a charm," she shouted over the wind. "I'm not the slightest bit queasy, thanks."

"Best stuff, that," he answered with a nod and a wink, "Mother Nature."

Kaila was glad Dan had persuaded her to go home with him. He'd argued that the sea air would be just the thing, and he'd been more right than he knew. The ocean was incredibly healing for psychics.

"How are you feeling?" he asked, sitting beside her, and tucking the blanket under her legs.

"I'm fine, really. Tim told me what you did," she said, her voice low. "Thank you."

"I didn't really know what he meant when he said I'd understand. I think I do now."

"It isn't like what most people think."

'No, I imagine it isn't. I'm sorry -."

"No," she said, placing her fingers over his lips. "No apologies. We both made a lot of mistakes. I think we can just move forward, don't you?"

"I like that. I have to tell you, I'm glad I did this."

"Did what?"

He nodded toward where his parents stood at the wheel. "They like you."

"Oh."

'They didn't like Staci. I mean, they liked her, just not for me. It's one of the things my father and I fought about the most, next to my joining the Air Force instead of the navy."

"Well, since this is true confessions, I'll tell you something I've never shared with another soul."

"Okay."

"Do you know why I went into archaeology?"

"I assumed you like history and knowing where we came from; learning about other cultures, that sort of thing?"

"I like working with the dead much better than the living."

"You could have been a mortician, if that's the case."

"I guess I should clarify. I like working with the long dead. The people who lived long ago communed with nature. They revered objects, believed in their magic, so the things I dig up are filled with positive energy, usually."

"What about when you dig up weapons?"

"You mean like spear heads and the like?"

He nodded.

"By the time they're dug up, they typically have begun to revert back to their basic materials. The psychic residue has evaporated, I guess you might say. It's much worse if I have to touch a murder weapon from a recent time. Which is why I quit the agency. I couldn't handle the constant pain and terror, not to mention the sadness."

She tried not to think how one of those she'd felt in 2003 could well have been Staci Foster.

For awhile, they sat in companionable silence and stared out to sea. The wind made it difficult to be heard.

"Will your family -?" she asked, close to his ear.

"Be afraid of you?" Dan prompted, gently. She nodded. "I don't have to tell them, if you don't want me to."

"If I'm around them long enough, they'll find out. Everyone does."

"My family comes from generations of fisherman; people who had to listen to their instincts and respect Mother Nature's predictions over those made by the weatherman's scientific instruments." He kissed her nose. "No, they won't be afraid."

"I still want to work as an archaeologist. I find such a peace. I don't want to lose that."

"I'm not asking you to. Between the two of us, I'm the one without prospects."

"Oh, I wouldn't say that. I think you have excellent prospects." She leaned her forehead against his.

Maybe I could get used to being around someone I can't read. She'd never noticed before, but being around Dan was similar to being in a cave on a dig. The idea of a new tool in her kit made her smile. It would be nice to have another way to get relief from the onslaught of emotions that came at her on a daily basis. When he suddenly pulled back, startling her, she looked up, searching his face.

"I loved Staci."

She nodded. "I know."

"But I realize now it was an immature love, like a kid, a friend I needed to protect." He looked over her head at the horizon, back into her eyes. "Not the kind of love it should have been,."

"Yeah?" She was at a loss for what to say.

He nodded.

Knowing he didn't expect an answer, she leaned on his shoulder, closed her eyes, and tuned out the world. Salty droplets occasionally sprinkled across her cheeks. She let out a sigh. At last.

Psychic Peace.

ABOUT THE AUTHOR

Elizabeth Maxim spent twenty years working as a consultant in the Information Technology industry. Her customer base included global Fortune 500 companies and she is a repeat speaker at industry conferences.

Elizabeth was raised with the belief that the best doctor is Mother Nature. She studied alternative medicine with an MD for several years before eventually earning a Doctor of Philosophy in this field. She also holds a bachelor's in holistic childcare.

Visit her website at elizabethmaxim.com.